TAKEN

Sheppard & Sons Investigations, Book 1

Eveline Rose

Sword & Rose

Dedication

This book is dedicated to all the women who are stronger than they think are, and the men who love them.

Also by

<u>Sheppard & Sons Investigations:</u>

TAKEN: Jack and Meg's story
BEATEN: Jamie and Emily's story
MISSING: Doug and Beth's story
BETRAYED: AJ and Blake's story
CAGED: Jaden and Catelyn's story
TRAPPED: Ashley & Nathan's story
The Storm Outside is Frightful: The Sheppards
BURNED: Madi & Matt's story
HUNTED: Nina & Austin's story
ABDUCTED: John & Mary's

WebPage

Chapter 1

Meg

I wiped away the tears from my yawn as I searched for a parking spot near the rental office. Severe rain storms caused me to arrive at the extended stay motel in Weatherford, Texas, three hours later than I expected. I looked around the parking lot before getting out of my old, beat-up SUV and walking into the hotel office where the manager nodded his balding head in greeting.

"Hi, I have a reservation for Megan Hayes."

He found my reservation, his southern drawl elongating his words. "Yes ma'am, extended stay for five weeks?"

"Yup." I feigned enthusiasm. "Can I pay cash? I lost my credit card." Before he could start asking questions, I yawned behind my hand. A big, loud one. Then apologized for my rudeness. I didn't want him asking questions. All I wanted, no needed, was to go to my room, take a shower, and get some sleep. Unfortunately, I needed to unload my car first.

His hand grazed mine as he handed me my key. "I'm Logan. Call the main number if you need me for anything."

I shivered. "Thanks." I wouldn't call him.

I set the last box down with a grunt, then plopped down on the couch and looked around. *It could be worse.* The room was decorated like most cheap motel rooms. The faded, stained light brown carpet was several shades lighter than the old couch, and a few pieces of southwestern landscape art hung on the cream-colored walls. At least the kitchen, ugly in its barren whiteness, was stocked with the essentials.

I was exhausted and needed a shower, but my stomach was growling. I double checked the deadbolt and door chain before eating a chocolate chip granola bar. It wasn't much, but it'd keep my stomach from rumbling. I unpacked my toiletries, pajamas, and door stop alarm from my beat-up suitcase. Before taking my shower, I wedged the alarm under the door.

The bathroom was almost as white as the kitchen, a small print of a desert sunset hung above the toilet, providing the only color in the room. The shower pressure was weak, but plenty hot enough that it felt good as I washed the road grime off and relaxed before going to bed.

I stared absentmindedly into the mirror as I combed my long strawberry blond hair. *My dark roots are peaking through, time to dye them again.* I thought about why I'd chosen Weatherford when I left Indiana. I'd always wanted to visit Texas, and it was far from Indiana, so I decided it'd be a good place to start over. After hours spent researching small towns in Texas, I'd settled on Weatherford. It had the off the beaten path feel I was looking for, yet it wasn't so small a new girl in town would cause a big stir. At least I hoped not; the goal was to blend in, not stand out.

"I'll be safe here."

Well, safer. I don't think I'll ever be truly safe.

As I brushed my teeth, I reminded myself no one knew where I was, so I should be safe, or at least feel safe for now. I looked in the mirror. *If I say it enough, I'll eventually believe it.* I hadn't told Agent Jones yet, but I would once I found a job. My parents didn't know my new name, so they wouldn't even know where to start, if they should suddenly decide they wanted to look for me. I very much doubted they would, since they hadn't bothered to do so since I'd left Boston six years ago. Still, I should probably look into getting a gun and some training, just in case. It probably wouldn't hurt to take another self defense class to brush up on my skills. I decided long ago, after surviving a childhood of drunken abuse, I never wanted to feel defenseless again.

I stared into my dull brown eyes before taking my contacts out and revealing their true emerald green color, then glanced away. My eyes were my most notable feature not only because of the color, but because my right eye had two blue spots. My grandma always said they were a blessing from God.

I checked the door locks one more time before crawling into bed. My baseball bat was within reach. I expected to fall asleep instantly after a long day of driving in the rain and lugging boxes, but I tossed and turned instead. I finally gave up trying to fall back asleep and picked up my favorite historical romance. After reading for a few minutes, I conjured up visions of a tall, dark, and handsome hero I could call my own. A hero who would love me, cherish me, protect me. *Who am I kidding? Real heroes don't exist. I have to protect myself.*

I must have fallen asleep because I scared myself awake with my screams again. I sat up and gasped for air as I looked around. It was still dark and a quick glance at my phone told me it was a little after two. *No point in staying in bed.* Falling back asleep after my nightmares was impossible. Needing to wash away the lingering memories crawling on my skin, I took another shower.

"They can't hurt you anymore." I almost believed me. Almost.

After four days of making calls and filling out what felt like hundreds of applications for receptionist, secretary, and admin assistant positions, I had scheduled three interviews. Two were today.

My shoulders slouched as I walked back to my car after the first interview. It hadn't gone well. I was mulling over all the things I thought had gone wrong when I saw him. *FUCK! I just got here. How'd he find me?* I needed to run or hide, but my feet froze to the ground. My breath caught in my throat. *I'm dead if he turns around and sees me.* I forced my right foot to step back, then my left. Before I could take another step, he turned around. My knees almost gave out as relief flooded my system. *It's not him.* I leaned against the building and forced air back into my lungs, waiting until my heart beat at its normal rhythm again before moving.

I'd only taken a few steps when movement in the shop window beside me caught my attention. A woman, wearing a long-sleeve, black t-shirt with a brown apron over it, was hanging a help wanted sign in the window. Grannie's Coffee Bar. *This could be my lucky break.* I'd worked as a barista to help pay my way through college, so I knew I was qualified. Barista jobs were usually part time, but at least I'd be earning a paycheck while I looked for something full time. I lifted my chin and walked in, hoping I'd be a good fit for the job.

I took a deep breath, inhaling the rich scent of freshly brewed coffee. *Mmmm, I love that smell.* I asked the woman at the counter for an application. Now that I was up close, I could see the embroidered logo on her apron, a big white coffee cup with the steam from the coffee forming a silhouette of a woman's head topped by a big bun, Grannie's Coffee Bar written under the cup.

"Here you go. My name is Beth. Let me know if you have any questions."

"Thanks, I'm Meg. Is this a full or part-time position?"

"It's 35-40 hours a week, mostly days," she answered. "Are you looking for full time?"

"I am." I took the application. "Thanks, Beth."

I tapped my feet in time with the country song playing softly on the speakers as I filled out the application. I could see most of the shop from my seat in a corner booth. It reminded me of an old western saloon with aged dark wood booths on the edges of the dining room, and high-top tables surrounded by brown leather bar stools in the middle. The coffee counter occupied most of the wall opposite my booth and bright ceiling lights provided plenty of light, while the soft hanging chandelier lamps provided a rustic candle glow over the booths and tables. Pictures of old saloons and black and white photos of employees decorated the walls while cowboy hats on racks, and old glass bottles arranged on shelves finished the look. It was kitschy but cute. I liked it.

There was no one in line, so Beth read my application when I handed it to her. "Looks good. Any chance you have a few minutes to talk to Mary, the owner?"

Thankfully, I did. I didn't want to appear too eager, so I glanced at my watch before answering. "I do. Thanks."

A few minutes later Mary introduced herself and offered me a cup of coffee. *Yes, please.* Free coffee is always hard to resist. I cradled the warm cup, hoping it might hide my shaking hands. *Hopefully, Mary can't see how nervous I am.* I hated talking about myself during interviews.

"As I'm sure you've noticed, Weatherford is a small town. Everyone here knows everyone else." She chuckled. "And here at Grannie's, we're one big, happy family. I know a lot of businesses say that, but here it's true. My grandmother bought this building when I was a little girl." Her eyes had that faraway look as she glanced around. "She renovated the beat up old bar and turned it into a coffee shop. My mom was the owner before passing the torch to me. And Beth," she tilted her head towards the counter where Beth was stocking cups, "isn't just my right-hand woman, she's also my best friend."

"Did your grandmother name it Grannie's?"

"No, she called it Rita's Coffee Saloon. She kept saloon in the name because she wanted to tie into the history of the building, plus she loved the cowboy saloon feel." She sipped her coffee. "I changed the name to honor her when I took over ownership."

"That's sweet."

"Thanks." A soft smile formed on her lips. "Gran wanted the shop to be warm and inviting, so she mixed the saloon decor with soft floral fabrics and pastels."

I wrinkled my nose as I tried to envision the two different styles together in the shop. I felt bad for making a face until she laughed.

"Exactly! My mom and I got rid of most of the 'granny' decorations after she passed. I've thought about redesigning it completely, but I can't bring myself to do it. The cheesy decor is part of the shop's charm."

I laughed. This wasn't quite what I'd expected when I sat down to interview with Mary. I felt a lot less nervous as we talked about the history. "It must have been nice working with your grandmother and mom." I would've loved working with my grandmother and listening to her tell me stories as we prepped the kitchen for the dishes we'd cook together. My favorite memories were of the times I spent with her in the kitchen. Sadly, I didn't have memories like that of my mother.

"It was, most of the time. Though I was glad to get away for a bit when I went to college." She laughed. "You'd think I'd be tired of the theme by now. But when I was away, I actually kind of missed it." She shrugged. "People seem to like it, so I'll probably never change it. We have a steady flow of locals, and tourists love taking pictures inside."

"That's good. Do you think you'll pass it on to one of your kids someday?"

"Nah, my two oldest sons, Jamie and Jack, work with their dad, John, as private investigators. My youngest son and only daughter are still on active duty in the military." She sighed. "Maybe I'll get lucky and one of them will give me a grandkid to pass the shop to."

I wasn't sure what to say, so I took a sip of coffee to buy a few seconds. Before I could figure it out, Mary spoke.

"Enough reminiscing." She picked up my application. "Your application looks good, but I noticed you have an extended stay motel listed as your current address." Mary sounded inquisitive rather than judgmental, but it didn't matter. I started fidgeting with my purse strap, hoping she didn't think I wasn't worth hiring. An extended stay address screamed, "I'm not sticking around."

"It's temporary. I moved to Weatherford last week, and unfortunately, I need a job before I can sign a lease for an apartment." My words ran together.

She nodded. "What made you decide to move to our small town?"

"I wanted a change of scenery and always thought a small town in Texas would be a great place to live." *Please don't ask for details.*

"Can't argue with that. How did you like being a barista on a college campus?"

"I liked it. It was always busy, so my shifts flew by and I got to meet lots of people." I lifted my coffee cup. "And free coffee for a college kid is always a nice perk."

She raised her own cup. "I bet. I missed the free coffee when I was in school." She asked me a few typical interview questions. What'd you like best, least? How'd you get along with your co-workers, managers?

I asked about pay, benefits, and hours. The job paid better than I'd expected and had typical benefits for a small business, and the hours were mostly weekdays, which was a bonus.

"Beth used to be my only full-time employee, but I realized having a second full-time person during the weekdays was good for business. Our morning regulars like the consistency. Unfortunately for me, my other full-time barista is moving."

Unfortunate for Mary, but good for me.

Mary stood up and shook my hand. "Thanks for taking the time to talk to me. I'll check your references and run a background check. I think you'll be a good fit, so if everything checks out, you'll hear from me."

I had a good feeling I'd be getting the call. Not wanting to jinx myself by getting too excited, I prayed. *Please, please, let me get this job.*

After leaving Grannie's, I went to my next scheduled interview. It was a part-time receptionist position at a motel in Fort Worth. Not only was the place dirty and run down, but the manager gave me the creeps. The motel I was staying at wasn't great, but it was better than this one. I cut the interview short and practically ran out the door after saying goodbye. On the drive home, I said another quick prayer, begging to get the job offer from Mary.

Mary called later that evening and offered me the job. *Thank God!* I accepted and told her I could start right away. The sooner I started earning a paycheck, the better.

Grateful I didn't have to keep job hunting, I did a little happy dance after hanging up.

Chapter 2

Meg

I'd only been working at Grannie's for a week and wanted to make a good impression, so I kept myself busy wiping down the tables after the morning rush. So far I liked it; everyone was nice, and the shop was usually busy, so I was making good tips. I hurried behind the counter when I heard the bell above the door ring. Three men walked in wearing matching navy blue polo shirts with a white shield logo embroidered on the upper left corner. I watched them as they approached the counter, their heads turning left and right.

The oldest of the three reached his hand over the counter and introduced himself. "Hi, you must be the new barista, Megan. I'm John, Mary's husband. It's nice to meet you." His unblinking stare drilled into me, like he was trying to read my mind and didn't like what he could see.

Mary's husband.

"Hi, I, um, I'm Meg," I stuttered as I reached out to shake his hand. *Oh My God, he's going to think I'm an idiot.*

John gave me a quick, firm handshake before turning to the two guys with him. "I'll get your mom."

I felt like a deer caught in the headlights as I watched John walk around the corner towards Mary's office. *Holy shit! He's intimidating.* He was the complete opposite of Mary…

"Don't worry. He's not –"

I jumped and spun my head around. "Shit." *Fuck, I said shit.* "Sorry." *Crap, I'm making a complete fool of myself.*

"No worries." The shorter of the two laughed and held his hand out. He had short, dark brown hair and a friendly smile. "I'm Jamie, this is my little brother, Jack."

I shook his hand and looked from Jamie to Jack, my eyes landing on his chest. *Little brother?* My eyes moved up his chest to his face. He was at least four inches talle-*Damn!* I'd seen good-looking guys before, but never one who looked like he'd just walked off a Hollywood movie set. Tall, dark, and ruggedly handsome fit him to a tee. The tanned skin around his amber eyes crinkled as he smiled, and his lopsided grin held a hint of mischief. A small cut on the left side of his mouth held my attention. *I wonder what happened?*

"Hi." He reached out to shake my hand.

"Hi." I felt the heat rise in my cheeks. *Great.* "I, um, what can I get you guys?" I asked as I reached out to shake his hand. *Please tell me I don't look or sound as flustered as I feel.* My small hand disappeared in his strong one. He didn't pull his hand back right away.

Neither did I.

"We'll wait," Jamie answered. Then said to Jack, "Let's grab a table so Meg can help her customers."

Neither of us moved. I could feel Jack's stare boring into me, but I didn't feel like he was judging. Not like I had with his dad. He seemed… curious.

Oh no, can he see my roots? Sometimes they're more obvious when my hair is in a ponytail. I ran my hand over my head, smoothing out my tightly pulled back hair.

When Jamie snapped his fingers in front of Jack's face, he turned and pulled his hand away. Not wanting them to see how flustered I felt, I looked down, suddenly fascinated by the black pen on the counter.

He gave me a quick wave with one hand while nudging Jack with the other. "Come on, let's go."

"Jamie! Jack!" Mary's voice carried across the room as she walked into the dining room.

I watched the exchange out of the corner of my eye as I helped the five high school girls, the ones I hadn't noticed because I was too busy embarrassing myself in front of Mary's sons.

"Hi, Ma," they answered in unison, smiling.

After giving them both a hug, Mary came behind the counter, washed her hands, and started making drinks.

Beth came back from break. "I got this Mary, go see your boys."

"Thanks," she said as she finished the drink she was making. John came over to help her carry the coffees she'd poured for all of them. His smile radiated love. *He looks less intimidating when he smiles.*

I couldn't stop thinking about what had happened as I made the rest of the drinks. My brain switched between thoughts faster than a hummingbird in a garden as I worked. *What the fuck was that?* Grind the beans. *I don't get all flustered because a gorgeous guy smiled at me.* Tamp, press start. *He's just being polite.* Steam the milk. *Did I put the chocolate sauce in the cup? Crap.* Pour chocolate sauce in espresso and add steamed milk. *Focus.* Extra whip on the Mocha. *Don't think about it, just do your job.*

I called out the names as I set each drink on the counter. *Don't look over at Mary.*

I looked. Not because I wanted to look at Jack. No, I looked because I could hear the girls whispering near the counter, talking about Jack and Jamie, so it was perfectly normal for me to look at them. At least that's what I told myself.

Beth rolled her eyes in mock exasperation when she heard one girl say, "He's hot."

"I know, right?" Another girl said, "Wait, which one? I think they're both hot."

The others nodded and mumbled in agreement. They were right; both of Mary's sons were good looking, but Jack was the one I couldn't stop staring at.

I admired the bald eagle, with its wings spread in flight holding an American flag in its beak, tattoo on his right forearm. I told myself I wasn't staring, as I noted the faded reds and blues of the flag. Nope, not staring. Just appreciating his artwork.

I wiped down the counter and watched as Jack smiled and lifted one hand in a friendly salute to the girls. Then choked back a laugh when he rolled his eyes. The two inches of counter I'd been wiping over and over, as I stared at Jack, were spotless. *Look away.* The bells above the door barely registered when the girls left. Jack turned towards me, shrugged and raised his eyebrows. *Oh my God, he totally knows I was watching.* I stepped back and cleaned the espresso machine as if the fate of the world depended on it. *It's okay, it'll be fine, pretend nothing happened. Focus on cleaning and restocking. And for the love of God, don't do anything else to embarrass yourself.*

"It was nice meeting you, Megan." John called out as they left. It unnerved me when he used my full name—no one ever called me Megan. *I don't think I like it.*

I looked up to say goodbye and saw Jack watching me. Heat spread across my cheeks. Again. I knew they were a bright shade of red, advertising my embarrassment to anyone with eyes. Shaking his head, Jamie pushed Jack towards the door and laughed. I was certain he was laughing at me.

"Nice meeting you." I barely got the words out before the door closed behind them. *I really hope Mary didn't notice me making a fool of myself.*

I couldn't stop thinking about Jack as I finished my shift. He was taller than his father and brother, and he obviously worked out, a lot. Not that I noticed the way his blue polo fit snug over his chest and arms or his well-groomed stubble or how it matched his wavy, dirty blonde hair. His gorgeous amber eyes, speckled with gold, reminded me of pendants I'd seen sparkling in jewelry shop windows, were impossible not to notice, as was his flirty smile.

He was just being nice. Guys like him don't like girls like you.

"Does that happen a lot?" I asked Beth. We'd only worked together for a week, but I liked her. She was always nice, and didn't pry too much.

"What? Girls noticing Mary's sons?" She handed me some scones for the pastry display. "Sometimes." She laughed. "They were a little over the top. Most girls just stare and smile. The braver ones might flirt." She gave me some cookies. "Mary thinks it's a hoot how much attention her boys get."

"Do they flirt back?"

"Nah, they mostly smile and wave, like Jack did earlier."

"They seem like nice guys." Not that I knew them well enough to form an opinion, but it felt like the right thing to say. Besides, they were Mary's sons. How bad could they be?

"They are. Chase adores them. He wants to be just like them, like his dad, when he grows up." Chase was Beth Wyatt's four-year-old son. She hadn't told me the details, but she referred to Chase's dad as her late husband once, so I assumed he had passed. Not wanting to pry, I hadn't asked.

The rest of my shift was uneventful, except for the thoughts racing through my head. Sometimes I felt like I had no control over them, and I hated it.

Mary walked over as I clocked out. "Meg, before you go. John and the boys are teaching a women's self-defense class next Wednesday and I've arranged the schedule so Lisa can attend. You can go too, if you're interested."

"Thanks, how much is the class?" I hated to ask, but I'd only been working for a week and had a tight budget. I wanted to take another self-defense class, so hopefully I could afford it.

Although, I had just made a complete fool of myself in front of them and wasn't exactly in a rush to see them again.

"It's free. I have an in with the lead instructor." She whispered behind her hand like she was telling me a secret, "I think he likes me." She laughed at her own joke.

I laughed with her. It was cute how she talked about John. Her love for him was obvious from the way her eyes lit up when she talked about him. *I don't think my parents ever loved each other.*

"Thanks, that's really nice. Can I check and let you know tomorrow?" I answered while twisting my hands in my purse straps. This was a great opportunity and I shouldn't pass it up. *I'm sure I can get through the class without embarrassing myself.*

Driving home, I couldn't help but replay the day's events over and over, each time trying to think of ways I could've been less awkward. I wouldn't be able to avoid seeing Jack, or his dad and brother, Beth said they come in all the time, but I could minimize my interactions with them at work. But there was no way I could avoid them if I took the class. I didn't want a repeat of the train wreck I was today. *I can always hide in the back of the class and hope they don't notice me.*

After I parked, I double clicked my remote, making sure I heard the *beep beep* confirming my doors had locked before walking away. I barely remembered driving home because I was obsessing over the class.

I started thinking about the day again as I made dinner. Replaying it in my mind, I built a mountain of shame out of a molehill of embarrassment. I talked to the pan of boiling water, "I could quit." I shook my head back and forth and laughed. "Don't be stupid. No one notices half the stuff you drive yourself crazy worrying about and they don't give two shits about the stuff they do notice." *I should probably stop talking to myself.*

I reasoned with myself as I mixed butter, milk, and powdered cheese mix in the pot with the macaroni. *You're over-reacting, again.* It'd be stupid to turn down a free self-defense class because I embarrassed myself. *I'll tell Mary in the morning.*

I convinced myself of two things while I ate:

1. No one would remember me making a fool of myself. They had more important things to think about.

2. I would not make a fool of myself in the class.

I figured I could avoid being noticed if I hung out in the back of the classroom. Feeling better about the situation, I picked up my book and read as I finished eating.

Chapter 3

Jack

"You missed it AJ. Jack was drooling over mom's new barista yesterday." Jamie leaned against the wall in the office AJ and I shared at Sheppard & Sons Investigations, frequently shortened to SSI. I was one of the "and sons" but wouldn't be fully vested until after the new year.

My dad and Jamie started SSI three years ago, after a stalker murdered Jamie's wife, Isabelle. They couldn't do anything to save her, despite being good cops and doing everything by the book, so they retired and started the family business providing personal security and investigation services, so others didn't have to suffer the same fate. I remember the determination in dad's eyes when he said, "We can't go back and save Isabelle, but together we can save others from suffering her fate." He had paused and made eye contact with each of us. "And I can make sure no son of mine loses the woman he loves ever again." I shook my head to clear the memory.

Our desks were along the back wall of the small, neutral colored room. We each had a chair on the opposite side for clients, with two extras against the wall. Despite all the empty chairs, Jamie stood and hovered near me.

"I was not." I leaned back in my chair and swatted at him. Sometimes working with my big brother and my best friend was a real pain in my ass.

AJ lifted his left eyebrow as he turned his head towards me. "Dude, is she hot? Did you ask her out?"

Jamie easily blocked my hand. "You totally were."

"I totally wasn't." *I totally was.* Staring, not drooling. I couldn't help myself. "There's something about her…" Shit, I hadn't meant to say that out loud. *Now I'll never hear the end of it.*

"Ha, told you." Jamie pushed off the wall and strutted away.

AJ rolled his chair towards me. "Spill it Sheppard."

AJ was an inch shorter than me but broader, and he rarely called me Jack, preferring to use my last name, an old habit from our time serving together in the Army. We'd met when we were stationed in Germany and immediately hit it off. We'd stay up late, talking about anything and everything over beers, often closing the bars. Our Army buddies started teasing us, calling our friendship a "Bromance" but we always shrugged it off, knowing if we let the teasing get to us, it'd only get worse.

When dad mentioned wanting to hire another full-time person at SSI, I didn't hesitate to recommend AJ. I trusted him with my life and respected his work ethic, so it was a no-brainer to give AJ a glowing recommendation.

"I don't know." I shrugged as I stared out the window. "She-" I shook my head to clear it. "There was just… I don't know, man, there's something about her." I couldn't help it. I felt drawn to her—something about her eyes pulled me in. My phone rang, saving me from having to explain what I didn't understand myself.

"I gotta take this." I waved my phone at him.

AJ chuckled. "Saved by the bell." He slid his chair back over to his desk and started typing. I knew he had reports to finish for the papers he had served earlier today. Serving papers was one of our easier jobs, as long as the person being served didn't get violent. AJ said his job today was a breeze, which meant typing the report would be a breeze, which meant he wouldn't have to focus too hard and could easily eavesdrop if he wanted to. I'd put money on him wanting to.

"Hey Ma, what's up?" I leaned back, shaking my head, as my mother asked me what the girls should wear to the self-defense class.

"Ma, you know what they need to wear, so why are you really calling?" I rolled my eyes when she made it a point to stress Meg would be going.

"Jamie told me you might want to know."

"Uh huh, and what exactly did he say? Why'd he think I'd care if she goes?" I sounded more defensive than I would've liked, and of course, she picked up on it. I did care, well, care might be too strong, but I was glad Meg was going. Not that I'd tell my mom. I didn't want her playing match-maker.

Never one to beat around the bush, she came right out and asked me if I was interested.

"No, Ma, it's not that." If I showed even the slightest inkling, she'd start playing cupid. Had I noticed Meg? Yes, how could I not? She was beautiful. And when I shook her hand, it was like an electric shock shooting up my arm. But I wouldn't say I liked her. I wouldn't mind getting to know her, though.

Mom wasn't ready to let it go, and started telling me how nice Meg was. Not wanting to have this conversation, I cut her off mid sentence. I wasn't usually rude to my mom, but I really didn't want her setting us up. If I asked Meg out, it'd be on my terms.

"Sorry ma gotta run love you." I didn't pause between my words, pulling the phone away from my ear as I spoke. I punched the End button harder than I intended.

AJ coughed to cover his laugh. When he opened his mouth, I pointed at him, phone still in hand. "Shut it."

"I didn't say anything." He held his hands up in surrender and tried to look innocent, but the huge grin on his stupid face gave him away.

"Bullshit."

"Hey, did I tell you I got a message from Ana yesterday?" I asked AJ later that night, after we ordered our food.

"No, what'd that psycho want?" Harsh, but not unwarranted.

"She said she's sorry, and she misses me. She hopes I can forgive her so we can be friends." I tried mimicking her German accent and failed spectacularly.

AJ scoffed. "Tell me you told her to take a hike."

AJ didn't have a high opinion of Ana, and for good reason. She'd tried to fuck me over and broke my heart. We had dated briefly while I was stationed in Germany. What started as a fun fling grew into something more. She'd done and said all the right things and before long, I thought she might be the one, but then things had changed.

Thankfully, AJ had seen through her bullshit and pounded some sense into me. I still remember the conversation.

"Dude, you need to wake the fuck up and see it—she's using you."

I argued back. "I can't leave her, Janerek. She's having my baby." I had used protection, so her pregnancy was a shock, even though condoms weren't guaranteed to work one hundred percent of the time. The whole situation was a fucking nightmare. I hadn't wanted to marry her, but I couldn't abandon my responsibilities to her or our child.

"Don't you think the timing's a bit suspect? You break up with her and suddenly she's pregnant. Take her to the doctor, verify she's pregnant, and that it's yours before you marry her." He was right; I needed proof.

When I told her I wanted her to take a pregnancy test, she went bat shit crazy. "If you love me, you'd trust me!" She thought she could bully me into marrying her, but my eyes were finally open and I'd insisted on proof of paternity. When she'd realized I wouldn't back down, she admitted she wasn't pregnant. AJ had been right. Ana wanted to marry an Army guy and had picked me. I was an easy target because I liked to help people, especially women in trouble, and hadn't hesitated to help her. Ana wasn't the first woman to take advantage of my protective, supportive nature, but I'd sworn she'd be the last.

"I told her I wasn't interested in reconnecting and blocked her number."

"Good. You deserve better." He held his glass up. "To the single life."

"Amen brother." I tapped my glass on his.

Chapter 4

Meg

It'd only been five days since I'd made a total and complete fool of myself. *I'm sure they've forgotten all about me by now.* If I said it enough, I might believe it. I braided my hair and checked my reflection to make sure I was good to go. *Contacts! Can't forget those.*

Thirty minutes later, I arrived at the gun store hosting the class. I walked in and looked around. It wasn't quite what I'd expected. Not that I knew what to expect, but it definitely wasn't a clean retail space with clothes, and lots of things I couldn't identify, lined up on racks and shelves. The one thing I expected to see but didn't was guns. The store was quiet except for the sounds of muffled booms coming from the back. *That must be where the guns are.* I asked the salesman where the self-defense class was being held. He pointed over my shoulder to a tall floor mounted sign with the SSI logo at the top.

"Behind you, it's the door in front of the sign." He gave me a friendly smile. "Have fun."

"Thanks."

I walked to the door and peeked in. They'd set up chairs in a semi-circle along the edges of the room, with open floor space in the middle. John and his sons were talking while they unpacked black and red square pads. *Maybe I can sneak in unnoticed.* Keeping my eyes on the floor in front of me, I snuck to the back, choosing a chair that allowed me to see the door. Keeping my head down, I lifted my eyes to look at the only other women in the room. They appeared to be mother and daughter, the younger looked like she was about my age. They both had long, wavy, dark hair and wore black yoga pants and tank tops in slightly different shades of pink. I couldn't help but think, *I wish I had a relationship like that with my mother.* Three more women walked in and talked to John before choosing seats.

I inspected the floor to avoid accidentally making eye contact with one of the Sheppards. I couldn't avoid them completely, but I wanted to minimize the risk of embarrassing myself.

I was studying a stain on the floor to distract myself when I heard someone clear their throat. I looked up. Jamie was standing in front of me with a clipboard and pen in his hand. "Hey Meg. You snuck by us before we could ask you to sign in."

Heat flooded my cheeks. I reached out and took the extended clipboard. "Sorry." *Why am I whispering?*

"No need to apologize for snagging the best seat in the house." Jamie's tone was light and friendly, like he could sense my nervousness and wanted to put me at ease.

"Thanks." I handed the clipboard back to him and forced myself to smile, hoping it'd help me seem less nervous.

"We're glad you could make it," he said before walking back to the front of the classroom.

"Thanks." So far, so good.

John introduced himself and his sons after everyone signed in and sat down. They were wearing matching navy SSI t-shirts and tan cargo pants. Jack was a taller, younger version of his father. It surprised me I hadn't noticed when they visited Mary last week, but then again, I'd been too busy embarrassing myself to notice.

Determined to stay focused and learn as much as I could, I started taking notes as soon as he began talking, but put my pen down when I heard John say, "We'll hand out worksheets at the end of class."

"The most important thing anyone, especially women, can do to protect themselves is to Pay Attention To Your Surroundings." John emphasized the last five words as he made eye contact with every woman in the room, pausing and clearing his throat loudly to get the attention of two teens who were on their phones and clearly not paying attention. "The second," he continued after they put their phones down, blushing, "is to trust your gut."

He talked for a few more minutes, giving us examples of actively paying attention and what trusting our instincts might feel like.

"Alright, let's get your blood flowing. Stand up and give yourselves some room." He paused while we all shuffled into the middle of the room. I stayed in the back near my chair. "Jamie and Jack are going to lead the warm-up while I go over some tips and tricks to maintain your awareness."

Jack was on my side of the room. I tried to focus on warming up. Instead, I stared as the corded muscles in his arms rippled while he demonstrated the moves. My brain drifted to the sexy hero in the romance novel I was reading, who the author had described using words like "corded muscles". I never would have used those words if I hadn't recently read them. It wasn't like me to think about a guy that way. I tried not to think about them at all.

You need to pay attention! I shook my head to clear it and focused on copying his movements as he raised his right arm up and circled it back. My breath caught in my throat when our eyes met. *Fuck, he's watching me.* I saw Jack's grin a split second before I looked away. It'd be safer to watch Jamie. He was good-looking too, but didn't interfere with my ability to think clearly the way Jack did. *What's wrong with me?* It wasn't like I'd never seen a hot guy before. And I sure as hell didn't sit around staring at them like an awkward teenager. Must be the stress of moving, or maybe it's the influence of the book I'm reading.

John had everyone partner up. Most students partnered with their friends, but I didn't have any friends. The only person I knew was my co-worker Lisa, so I asked her if she wanted to pair up. I was grateful she said yes. We didn't know each other well, but had worked a few shifts together, so she wasn't a total stranger.

Over the next ninety minutes, we learned how to strike at noses and ears, and how to poke eyes – which brought a round of squeals and 'ew gross' from everyone. Every so often, John would encourage us to yell when we hit the pads, reminding us, "If you can scream, you can breathe." They walked around the room while we practiced, correcting our forms and answering questions.

"Not bad." I heard Jack say from behind me.

I turned around and brought my hands up in a defensive position. My reaction was over the top, but I'd been so focused I hadn't heard him walk up and he'd startled me.

He put his hands up. "Sorry, didn't mean to sneak up on you."

I put my hands down and laughed to cover my embarrassment. "Sorry."

"No worries." He smiled and offered us some advice. "You can add power to your hits if you use your whole body, not only your arm." He waved Jamie over and asked him to hold the pad. "Here, like this."

I watched Jack demonstrate the hit, but still flinched a little when he made contact. THWACK!

"I wasn't expecting it to be so loud," I said, wondering if Lisa had flinched too.

Jack stared at me as if he was searching for something. Lisa's giggle was followed a few seconds later by the sound of Jamie's hand hitting the pad.

"That sound is the difference between using your body, instead of only your arm, to throw a strike. Here," Jamie held up the pad for me, "you try."

I lined up in front of Jamie. As I was adjusting my feet, I felt a light touch on my shoulder. I stiffened. *I hate being so jumpy.* They weren't a threat.

"Like this," Jack said.

I tried not to think about Jack touching me as he moved me into position to get the most power from my strikes. *I should be thinking about one thing—hitting the pad.*

After Jack helped Lisa with her stance, he moved on to help another group. Jamie stayed and worked with us for a few more minutes.

It frustrated me, how easily I startled, and I was eager to take my frustrations out on the pad. I hit it with all my strength, and must have done it right this time, because it made a much louder thwack, and my hand stung.

"Good job." Jamie smiled and turned to Lisa. "Your turn."

Towards the end of class, John taught us how to break free if our wrists were ever bound with duct tape. We all chuckled when Jack joked about pink being Jamie's favorite color as he wrapped his brother's wrists with bright pink duct tape. Jamie showed us how to break free. He wasn't successful the first time, and some of the girls snickered. John took advantage of the situation and explained that it might take more than one try. "The key is to keep trying."

The three of them went from group to group, loosely wrapping everyone's wrists and talking them through the process of breaking free.

"Pink or Silver?" Jack asked when it was our turn. Lisa picked pink and before I knew it, she'd broken free and it was my turn. Jack was standing in front of me, moving his hands up and down like he was comparing the weight of the two rolls. Wrinkling my nose at the hideous neon pink roll, I pointed at the silver. I held my breath and thrust my arms out, willing my hands not to tremble as Jack wrapped my wrists in a single layer of tape. The image of a short, fat, bald man flashed before my eyes. I almost gagged as the all-to-real memory of alcohol on his breath invaded my senses.

I closed my eyes and reminded myself I was safe. I don't know how long I stood like that before two large, warm hands gently wrapped around mine.

"Meg?" Jack asked softly.

I met his eyes and inhaled sharply. The depths of compassion I saw there surprised me. Holding my hands, Jack gently turned me towards the wall, so no one else could see my face. *It must look bad, me freaking out like this.* I blinked back my tears.

"I can unwrap-"

Shaking my head, I barked. "No." *Crap.* I hadn't meant to sound harsh, but I needed to do this. To conquer my fear. I whispered, "Sorry."

He nodded. "It's okay. Take a deep breath and let me know when you're ready." His voice was confident, reassuring. His eyes were understanding, comforting.

I nodded, closed my eyes, and took a deep breath. Then another. "Ready." I whispered as I exhaled. Then I lifted my arms above my head and swung them down towards my legs as fast as I could, pulling them apart as I did. The zip when the tape ripped was music to my ears.

"I did it." Did I sound as shocked as I felt? I smiled, then quickly looked at the floor as tears filled my eyes. It pissed me off how easily I teared up, especially when I was happy. I blinked a few times and looked up at Jack.

He smiled and held up his hand for a high five. "Good job." After I clapped my hand to his, he asked, "You okay?" So only I could hear him.

I smiled. "I am, thanks."

He nodded and moved on to the next student.

I rushed out as soon as class was over, too embarrassed by my earlier anxiety attack to stick around. In my haste to leave, I forgot to grab the handouts John had mentioned at the beginning of class.

Chapter 5

Jack

I slid my sunglasses on top of my head as I walked into Grannie's the morning after the class. "Hey Beth, is Meg around?" I asked as I approached the counter.

"Hey Jack, yeah, she's in the break room." Beth tilted her head in response. "You know the way."

"Thanks." On the short walk to the back, I thought about what I wanted to say. I didn't think she'd appreciate me bringing up what happened in class. Her fear hadn't gone unnoticed. After class my dad asked if she was okay, saying, "I noticed her reaction when you taped her wrists. Her fear was palpable, even across the room. And she practically ran out once class was over."

After we'd answered questions and packed up, I stopped by the counter to chat with the range manager, Grant, an old friend from high school. I held back when I saw Meg looking at pistols; the desire to protect her coursed like hot lead through my veins. After taking a second to collect myself, I turned and walked away. I didn't think she'd appreciate the interruption.

"Morning, mind if I join you?" I asked as I walked into the break room. She was sitting at the table, facing the door, reading. Her head snapped up. I watched as the pink spread up her neck and across her cheeks.

She bit her lower lip. "No." Then lowered her eyes back to her book, her shoulders rounding in like she was trying to curl up and hide.

Damn, I hadn't expected that reaction. I mean, I wasn't expecting her to jump for joy, but she looked like she wanted to be invisible. I told myself it was because she was still embarrassed about last night and ignored it.

"Thanks." I pulled out the chair across from her and turned it around. Putting the handouts on the table in front of her as I sat down. "You left before we handed out the class material."

Meg looked from her book to me, to the papers, then back at me. "I'm sorry. I–"

I cut her off. "No need to apologize. Self-defense classes can be triggering." Fuck. I realized my mistake before I finished as I watched her whole body tensed up.

She straightened her back and squared her shoulders. She tried to exude confidence, but I could see the fear in her eyes. Was she trying to convince me, or herself?

It was my turn to be embarrassed. "I'm sorry. I didn't mean to assume."

I shouldn't have been thinking about how gorgeous she was, but I couldn't help it. Owning her power looked good on her, even if it was a mask to hide her fear or shame. I'd noticed it last night too. She had a fierce expression on her face when she was hitting the pads, and I had a feeling she was seeing a face she wanted to smash.

I could see the pain in her eyes, mixing with the angry denial. "But I think someone has hurt you, and I'm sorry."

I watched as her eyes glazed over for a second, lost in what must have been an unpleasant memory. I swear I could hear the second hand of my digital watch ticking in the silence as I waited for her to come back to the present. Finally, she blinked a few times and brought her attention back to me.

"Thank you. And thanks for…" She paused, as if she was thinking about what to thank me for. Picking up the papers, she said, "For dropping these off."

I watched quietly as she put them in her book, closed it, and stood up. "I, uh, have to get back to work. Thanks again."

"Yeah, of course." I stood up and watched as she put her book in her locker. "Hey, I almost forgot. I wanted to talk to you about something. Can I meet you here when your shift is over?" One of my goals in coming here today was to offer her more training.

She hesitated, confusion written all over her face. She glanced at the clock and said, "Yeah, um, sure, I'm done at two."

There was zero enthusiasm in her voice. I had a feeling she only agreed because she didn't have enough time to come up with excuses for why she couldn't. That feeling sucked. I wasn't arrogant, but I also wasn't used to women acting like they didn't want to talk to me. I shook it off. What mattered was that she had agreed. I'd have the chance to talk to her later, and hopefully convince her I was a good guy.

I smiled. "See you then."

Afraid Meg might try to sneak out before I got there, I arrived fifteen minutes early. The rich, robust smell of the coffee shop always felt like coming home. I'd practically grown up here. The sounds of beans grinding and milk steaming were part of the soundtrack of my childhood.

At the sound of the bell, Meg looked up from the pink, yellow, and blue packets of sweeteners she was re-stocking, cheerfully calling out. "Hel-" she saw me and her cheerful tone fell flat. "Oh. Hi, Jack."

Was she disappointed I showed up? I didn't want to think about it, but I did. And it hurt. I wasn't used to getting such a cool reception from women and I didn't like how it felt.

The door opened behind me and a group of teens walked in. The sound of their high-pitched giggling filled the shop. Meg cheerfully called out, "Hello, I'll be right with you."

As she walked back to the cash register, I tried not to think about how much I would've liked it if she'd greeted me with the same enthusiasm she greeted the new guests. They got cheerful; I got guarded, or maybe disappointed. *I'm overthinking it.* She seemed nervous, or embarrassed, when I stopped by earlier. Maybe it wasn't about me.

I'd never thought this much about any of mom's baristas before, but there was something about her. Sure she was pretty, but ma had hired pretty women before so that wasn't it. There was more to Meg than met the eye. She was a mystery I wanted to solve. Not wanting a repeat of what had happened with Ana, I reminded myself to be careful.

I waited, lost in my thoughts, as I watched her.

I snapped out of it about the time she took the fourth drink order. *Dumbass, why are you still sitting here?* I walked behind the counter and washed my hands.

Maybe she'd stop being so nervous around me if she sees I'm a nice, helpful guy. I could sense her watching me as I stepped up to the espresso machine and grabbed the first drink sticker.

"What are you doing? Should you be back here?"

She'd clearly forgotten my mom owns the place. I raised one eyebrow. "I'm helping you, and for your information, I was making Frou Frou coffee drinks before I could walk."

"Frou Frou?" She snort-laughed before turning to the next customer.

"Yup." Her laugh made me feel all warm inside, like the first sip of hot, freshly brewed coffee on a chilly day. I hadn't expected her laugh to affect me so much.

I heard her call out thanks over the sound of the steamer as I got to work.

We worked together quietly, getting the eight drinks to their thirsty owners. I ran the espresso machine while Meg mixed frappes at the back counter.

Lisa came in as we finished. "Hey Jack, been a while since I've seen you back here," she said, as she walked to the back.

"Hey Lisa. Just helping with a large order." In case my grin wasn't smug enough, I said, "Told you." I finished wiping down the counter, poured myself a large black coffee, and went back to the booth. I picked a seat with a full view of the dining room.

When Meg finally joined me, she scooted into the booth and leaned her back against the wall. *Does she always sit where she can see the door?* She glanced towards it often.

"Thanks again for helping." Meg hesitated before asking, "Why didn't you go get Mary?" She corrected herself, "I mean your mom."

"It's fun to whip up Frou Frou drinks once in a while."

"Even if you don't drink them." She nodded towards my cup before glancing at the door. "So, why do you want to talk to me?"

Interesting choice of words. The slight emphasis she placed on the word *me* didn't go unnoticed. Did she think she wasn't worth talking to? Man, someone really did a number on her.

I considered the best way to answer. Something told me I needed to tread carefully, because she'd be sensitive to my words and tone. I opened my mouth and realized I had no idea how to tell her I saw her looking at guns last night and wanted to offer my help without sounding like a creep.

"Listen, there's no great way to say this, so I'll just say it. I saw you looking at the guns last night after class and I asked Grant about it." Nope, not creepy at all Sheppard.

Her pupils dilated. "You what?" Her voice cracked. "You followed me?"

I shook my head. "Grant's a friend. I saw you when I stopped by to say hi after class." I paused. "He said you asked about taking shooting lessons."

"You asked about me?" Meg was trying to sound angry, but her shaky voice gave away her fear. "Why do you care if I want lessons?"

"I don't, I mean, I do, but not… Please, just hear me out." How did I lose control of this conversation so quickly? *And why am I so tongue-tied?* Where was my confidence? "It's not a big deal and I'm not judging you, I swear." I wish I knew how to put her at ease. "I'd like to help you." Grant said she'd left disappointed when she saw the cost of shooting lessons. "I've taught lots people how to shoot guns. I could teach you." Not only did I want to help, I wanted to know more about her.

"No." Meg's quick, harsh, almost rude response felt like a door slamming in my face.

She apologized and reframed her reply. "Thank you for offering. It's really very nice of you."

I could sense the 'but' she hadn't said. "But?"

"But I'm not even sure I want a gun. Or if I want to learn how to shoot one. I was curious. That's all. So thanks, but I'm okay." She stared at her fidgeting hands while she explained. I was pretty sure she didn't know she was giving herself away, but to me, it was as if she had a neon sign flashing above her head, "I'm lying."

I wasn't willing to give up yet, so I tried a different tactic. "How about this? I take you to the range so you can appease your curiosity. I have everything you need; you only need to bring you. Then you can decide if you want a lesson or not."

I sat quietly and watched the emotions flashing across her face, grateful she hadn't refused me instantly. I did my best to appear patient despite feeling quite the opposite. Why was I so worried she'd still say no? I barely knew her and shouldn't care this much. But I did.

I wanted to help her. I've always been the guy who wanted to help others. Especially women. I reminded myself to be careful, so I didn't get taken advantage of again.

"Can I ask you a question?" Meg lifted her gaze to meet mine. I nodded, so she continued. "Why?"

"Why what?"

"Why do you want to help me?"

The quiet sadness in her voice tore my heart in half. Did she really believe she wasn't worth helping? Had no one ever helped her before? A visceral need to find the fucking asshole who'd hurt her and beat him to death ripped through me.

She was waiting for me to answer, so I needed to say something, anything, except what I was really thinking. I answered, "I'm a sucker for a pretty face." *Fucking idiot, that was so far across the line it wasn't even in Texas anymore.*

I was about to apologize when I noticed her lips quiver. A sad smile formed as she shook her head in disbelief.

I didn't give her time to say anything. "Here's the thing. I'd offer to teach any of Ma's girls if they wanted to learn." It was true, but I didn't mention I'd never felt inclined to offer.

She released an exasperated sigh. "If I say no, will you keep trying?"

"Yes, yes, I will." I wiggled my eyebrows to lighten the mood. "You'll give in to my charm, eventually." Good God, I hope that sounded charming, not pathetic.

"Okay, fine. You win." Her small smile didn't quite reach her eyes. "Thank you."

"I expected you to make me work harder." I laughed.

When she tried to leave before setting a date and time, I stopped her. I had a feeling if she didn't commit to a date now, she'd always be busy when I reached out to schedule. I also knew I'd be the one reaching out, because if given the chance, Meg would pretend this conversation hadn't happened. Of course, I knew setting a date today didn't mean she wouldn't cancel.

We agreed to meet at the range the following Sunday at ten am. When I offered to pick her up, she politely declined. I gave her my business card and had her text me, so I had her number, just in case.

Chapter 6

Meg

I contemplated texting Jack several times over the next few days to cancel our appointment. I refused to call it a 'range date' like Jack did. In the end, I decided against it because I really wanted to try shooting a gun. Besides, I told myself, it'd be rude to bail on him after he'd been so generous. I also didn't want to have to explain why I'd cancelled. Because, of course, Jack told his mom he was taking me to the range. The last thing I wanted to do was seem ungrateful.

When I got to the range, Jack was already there, relaxing against the counter, talking to the range manager. He stood up, stretching to his full six foot two height, as I approached. I tried not to think about how gorgeous he was. The plaid shirt he wore hung open, showing off the muscles under his snug navy blue t-shirt.

"Hey, glad you made it." His tone was friendly. "You remember Grant? If you have any questions, he's your guy."

Grant waved. "Hi, Meg, good to see you again."

"Hi." I waved back.

Jack shook hands with Grant and thanked him before leading me into a classroom.

I dropped my purse on a chair. It made a loud thud thanks to the book inside.

Jack chuckled. "What do you have in there, bricks?"

"No." I said shyly, "A book." Most people thought it was weird that I read so much, I was sure he would too.

"Do you read a lot?"

"Yeah, I never leave home without a book." I didn't tell him that, unlike most people, I didn't have any social media accounts or streaming services to occupy my time.

Jack was standing next to a table that had a bright red gun, some clips, and a black gun.

I nodded when Jack asked, "Ready?"

Jack pointed to the red gun. "This is a laser training gun." He picked it up and aimed it at the target positioned a few feet in front of the table. A red dot appeared on the X when he pulled the trigger. "We use it for practicing and training."

"Training?" I asked. "I thought this wasn't a lesson?" Lessons didn't fit in my budget, and I didn't want a pity one.

"It's not. I'm going to show you a few things, so your first time shooting is more fun." He grinned. "It's easier for me to show you in the classroom where we can hear each other."

I couldn't help but notice his lopsided grin. The left side rising a tad higher than the right. *Stop thinking about his grin.*

"Meg?"

Shit! I was staring, and didn't hear him ask me a question. I needed to pay attention. "Sorry, trying to imagine shooting being fun, not scary." I said to cover my embarrassment, hoping the heat I felt in my cheeks wasn't showing.

"A little fear isn't a bad thing when handling a gun." Jack faced me. "It can be dangerous if not done properly."

Jack started our non-lesson by going over the safety and range rules.

He showed me how to stand. "You need to be balanced and comfortable."

"This feels weird."

Jack snickered. "We rarely stand in a shooting stance, so it'll take some getting used to."

Next, he taught me how to hold the gun.

He had me pick up the red laser gun a few times to practice getting the proper grip. Not a lesson, my ass. *Oh well, too late to back out now. I might as well learn something.* Once he was confident I had it down, he taught me how to aim. It was a lot harder than I imagined it would be. It always seems so easy on TV–they just point and shoot.

"The only way for me to know if you're aiming properly is for you to press the trigger so I can see the laser on the target." Jack pointed at the target. "If you think you're lined up, slowly press the trigger. The red dot will tell me where the bullet would hit."

I aimed and slowly pressed the trigger.

"Good initial alignment, but the gun moved when you pressed the trigger."

He told me the goal was to press the trigger in a smooth, controlled motion so the sights didn't move. "Here, let me show you." Jack stepped up close to my side. "Aim at the target, then put your finger on the trigger, but don't press. Relax your hand. I'm going to put my finger over yours and press the trigger for you so you can see how it feels."

Jack placed one hand behind my right shoulder and placed the other one over mine on the gun. His warm hand felt firm on mine. It was hard to ignore the tingling sensations as he helped me adjust my grip. I'd never felt anything like that before. I passed it off as a nervous reaction and forced myself to breathe while relaxing my hand. Luckily, Jack was in full teacher mode, and probably hadn't noticed me tensing up or blushing. *Again.*

"You okay?" He stepped back.

Of course, he noticed. I nodded. "Yeah." I didn't trust myself to say more.

My body's reaction to him mortified me. I hadn't expected it, nor was I mentally prepared for it. So rather than think about it, I focused on the gun. I stiffened my spine and arms. Jack must have felt it, too.

"Relax, let me do the work." He pressed the trigger and the laser hit exactly where I was aiming.

"Now you try."

He made it seem so easy. I took a few more practice shots, trying my hardest not to let the laser move on the paper. I wasn't very successful. Jack reminded me I was doing this for the first time and it would take practice to get the trigger press down.

After a few mostly successful shots, Jack taught me how to load the magazine, gently correcting me when I called it a clip, "It's a magazine," using fake bullets he called dummy rounds. Then he showed me how to load the magazine into the gun. After I practiced a few times, he said I was ready to shoot on the range.

He told me a real lesson would have been much longer than twenty minutes. "There's so much more I could teach you, if you're interested."

I nodded, but didn't say anything. I wasn't ready to agree to another lesson.

Before going out on the range, Jack had me put on the eye and ear protection he was letting me borrow. It was weird not being able to hear anything. Jack put on a camo baseball cap with ARMY embroidered on the front, before putting on his own eye and ear protection.

He tilted his head and asked me a question. At least I think he did because I could see his lips moving, but couldn't hear him.

"What?" I yelled, unable to judge the volume of my voice.

Jack chuckled and pointed at his ears before taking them off. He repeated the question after I took mine off, too. "You don't happen to have a hat, do you? I forgot to tell you to bring one."

"I don't. I'm sorry. You said to wear a t-shirt and closed toed shoes, you didn't say anything about a hat." The excuse tumbled from my lips, sounding defensive, but I couldn't help it. I hated feeling unprepared, and I didn't want him to be upset with me.

"No need to apologize. I'm the one who messed up. Wait here. I'm sure I have one in my truck." Jack said before jogging towards the door. He returned a few minutes later holding a navy blue cap with the SSI logo embroidered on the front.

"Here." He grinned as he handed it to me. "Don't worry, it's new."

That grin. *I bet he's broken a lot of hearts.*

"You'll have to adjust it." He reached out for the hat. "Here, let me help." He fixed the size and curled the bill a few times so it wasn't so straight. He handed it back to me, then picked up my ear protection and turned a dial. "You can change the volume so you can hear me. The sound will cut out when the gun fires."

"Thanks."

I was dragging my feet as I followed Jack to the far end of the range, where he'd reserved a private training lane. Jack put a hand on the small of my back to nudge me along when I stopped to watch the people shooting.

When we got to our lane, Jack pulled a gun and some ammunition out of his bag and set them on the bench, then he unrolled a target and hung it up. After setting up, he waved me over to the bench.

I listened carefully as Jack gave me instructions. Now that I was actually on the range, I was way more nervous. *Am I really doing this?* I felt my breaths coming quicker and could hear my heart pounding in my chest. I had no idea how long I'd been standing there, panicking, before Jack gently touched my shoulder to get my attention.

"Are you okay? We can try again later if you'd like."

"Yeah. It's, I don't know, it's a lot. And I'm nervous." Scared was more like it, but I didn't want to sound like a wimp.

"That's normal. It's okay if you want to stop or take a break."

"Thanks. I think I'm good now." I wiped my sweaty palms on my jeans.

Jack nodded, then reminded me of the safety rules. He patiently guided me as I loaded one bullet into a magazine and then the magazine in the gun.

"The gun is loaded. Are you ready?"

I nodded, never taking my eyes off the gun as I picked it up. I didn't want to risk pointing it in the wrong direction.

He had me build my grip like I had in the classroom. I was extra careful to keep my finger off the trigger.

"When you're ready, aim at the center of the target."

I extended my arms and aimed at the big black X.

"This gun doesn't have a safety, so all you need to do, when you're ready, is press the trigger."

I pressed the trigger. Jack had warned me about recoil, and the loud bang, and the bright flash that would happen when the gun went off. Knowing it would happen wasn't enough to stop me from yelping and jumping back. Jack quickly grabbed the top of the pistol.

"Wow!" I could hear the shock in my voice and feel the smile on my face.

Jack put the gun down and asked, "How'd that feel?"

"Powerful," I turned to him, "and loud."

He grinned. "Was it as scary as you thought it would be?"

"Yes, no, well, sort of." I couldn't decide if it had been scary or not. I mean, I yelped and jumped, but was it fear or surprise? It was probably a little of both.

"Want to try again?" he asked. "You'll get used to the bang and the flash, if you practice enough. You can also adjust the volume on the ear pro if it's too loud."

"Okay, thanks." I was staring at my target, searching for a hole. "I think I missed."

"Nope, you hit low left. See?" Jack pointed out the hole in the silhouette shaped target. "Not bad for your first try." Jack held up his hand for a high-five.

I clapped my hand to his when I finally saw the hole, surprised I'd actually hit the target. "Can I try again?" My initial fear melted away in the excitement.

"Of course." Jack smiled.

I shot a few more times, one bullet at a time, happy I didn't jump as much as I did the first time. After a few more rounds, Jack had me load two at a time. I didn't do great, but at least I was hitting the target. After I finished shooting, I watched Jack pack up his gear. Adrenaline still coursed through my veins. *I did it; I shot a gun!* It was scary at first, but Jack's calm presence helped me get past my fear.

He rolled up my targets and asked me if I wanted to keep them.

"Do people usually keep them?"

"Some do. It might be nice to keep it as a souvenir of your first time shooting. You can always throw it away later if you change your mind."

"Okay." I took them, thinking it'd be kind of neat to have them.

We could finally talk normally once we were off the range. "Thank you. That was fun," I said, handing him his hat.

"Keep it. Maybe you'll need it again?" It sounded like a question.

"Thanks. I don't know, maybe? It wasn't quite what I expected. But then again, I didn't really know what to expect. It always looks so easy in the movies and sounds so scary in the news. But it wasn't easy or scary, you know?" I was rambling; the adrenaline hadn't worn off yet.

He nodded. "I do." He packed up the rest of his gear. "Want to grab some lunch? I can answer your questions, and maybe we can plan another range date."

I checked the time. "Thanks, but I can't. I told Beth I'd watch Chase."

"When do you have to be there?"

"Three." I turned toward the door, ready to leave. I was hoping he would let it drop.

"It's only eleven-thirty. There's a café down the road. We can grab a coffee to celebrate while I answer your questions. You'll have plenty of time to go home and shower before heading to Beth's." He was persistent.

I should probably say no, but I didn't want to. "Yeah, Okay." I felt good, and having coffee with Jack sounded better than being home alone with my book.

Chapter 7

Jack

Meg insisted on paying for our coffees, saying it was the least she could do to show her gratitude. I conceded, in the brief time I'd known her, I recognized her sense of pride and independence. If buying me a cup of coffee made her feel better about getting a free lesson, then I was happy to oblige. After she paid, we moved to the end of the counter to wait for our drinks, my black coffee, and Meg's peppermint tea.

"Ma'll skin me alive if she ever finds out I let a girl buy me a coffee." I added a little extra southern drawl to my voice, making it obvious I was joking.

Meg's eyes opened wide. Her expression had me wondering if she was going to laugh or apologize. I gave her the world's most fake woe-is-me expression, complete with my hands over my heart.

My heart skipped a beat when she coughed to cover her laugh. She lifted her eyes, glossy from laughter, to meet mine, and smiled. It was the first time her smile reached her eyes, and it took my breath away.

"That look…" She sucked in a breath. "Was pathetic." She choked out, still laughing.

I smiled and bowed.

We thanked the barista as she handed us our drinks and walked to an open table.

I intentionally chose one so we could both see the door comfortably. Meg wouldn't relax if she couldn't see the door. *I wonder if she realizes how often she looks over her shoulder.* Most people, outside the military or law enforcement, never think about where they sit in a restaurant, but for those of us who've served, it's second nature to sit where we can see most, if not all, exits. I hated that something from her past forced her to live in fear.

She seemed nervous at first, but slowly relaxed as I answered her questions. When I reminded her she did great for a first timer, she blushed as she smiled. Her face glowed. Happy looked good on her. *I want to be the reason she smiles like that.* I fought back the sudden urge to reach across the table and brush a wayward hair off her face.

As we sat and talked, seeing Meg frequently check the door bruised my ego. *I'm a trained bodyguard, for Christ's sake. She should feel safe with me.* It might be egotistical, but I couldn't help it. *It's not about me.* My jaw clenched as I thought about the person who hurt her, my desire to punch said person growing stronger by the second. I wanted to ask her about it, but it didn't feel like the right time. She was relaxed and having fun, and I didn't want to ruin it.

We didn't stay long because she needed to go home and clean up before heading to Beth's. I had to resist the urge to touch her as I walked her to her car. I put my hands in my pockets to prevent myself from reaching out and pulling her into a hug when I said goodbye.

Maybe next time, because there was no way in hell I wouldn't find a way to see Meg again. She hadn't said no when I asked her about a second range date, and she clearly had fun. It shouldn't be too hard to convince her to come back for more.

Chapter 8

Meg

His weight crushes me when he passes out. I scramble out from under him and off the bed. I quickly tug on my clothes. Clothes I hate. Clothes I didn't choose myself but am forced to wear. Clothes that advertise I was paid to do a job. A job I'm forced to do. I pick up the client's phone and dial 9-1-1. Between sobs, I tell them I was kidnapped and raped. I tell them where I am. The lady on the phone tells me the police will arrive soon and asks me to stay on the phone. She asks my name just as I hear "You Bitch!" from behind me and feel two fat sweaty hands squeeze my throat.

My screams woke me up. I sat up in bed and clutched at my neck. The memory of his hands lingered. My lungs gasped for air as I looked around. "You're in Texas and you're okay. It was only a bad dream." I hoped saying it out loud would help me calm down.

A few hours later, I was working at the register when Jack strolled into Grannie's. It was Wednesday, and this was the first time I'd seen or talked to him since we'd gone to the range on Sunday. Which was probably a good thing. Nightmares had kept me up the last few nights, and I wasn't up to being social.

I watched as he put his hands on the bar and lifted himself up so he could lean over and give his mom a peck on the cheek. Mary's indulgent smile gave me the feeling this was a regular occurrence.

"Hi, Ma." Still leaning over the counter, he turned his head toward me. "Hey Meg. You want one too?"

Did he just wink? I felt the heat rising in my cheeks. Knowing my embarrassment was visible made me blush even more. Luckily, Mary saved me before I could stutter a reply and make a total fool of myself.

"Jackson! Behave yourself." Mary swatted him with the stack of cardboard cup sleeves she was holding. I giggled. *His full name is Jackson?* Who knew?

"Yes, ma'am." Jack stood up to his full height and gave me his order. "Can I get five large black coffees to go?"

Mary must have made a face behind me because Jack said, "Don't worry, they're not all for me."

"I figured, but five?" Mary asked.

"One is for Doug. The guy dad's interviewing today."

I rang up Jack's order while Mary poured the coffees, then panicked. Am I supposed to charge him or give him a discount? This was my first time serving someone from Mary's family. She had served them the last time they came in, and Jack didn't pay the day he helped me out, but that didn't mean he wasn't supposed to.

"Is there a, uh, family discount," I asked Mary, "or is it free?"

Jack answered, "Discount." He winked. "Ma's afraid we'll drink her out of business if she gives us free coffee."

"You would." Mary laughed as she turned to me. "SSI gets a twenty percent discount for office orders. My boys get the employee discount." That explained why he didn't pay the day he helped me. Employees drank for free during their shifts.

I processed his payment without embarrassing myself anymore.

Jack waited for his coffees at the end of the counter, watching me as I carefully carried over his order. The fifth coffee balanced precariously in the center of the other four.

"Careful, the center one is a little wobbly," I said as I handed him the tray.

Jack chuckled. "Of course, it's a crime to spill coffee this good."

"Damn straight it is!" Mary called out over her shoulder as she walked toward her office. "Give your dad and brother a kiss for me."

"Not gonna happen, but I'll tell them you wanted me to." He rolled his eyes. Something in his expression hinted they'd had this conversation before.

I wish I had that; I thought as I watched the comfortable ease between Mary and Jack. My relationship with my mother was barely existent, let alone good. She was always too drunk or high to build a healthy relationship when I'd lived with her, and I hadn't talked to her since moving out.

I started thinking about the last time I saw her. She was being arrested, charged with contempt of court for being drunk and shouting out in the courtroom. After ignoring my father's abuse for years, she'd chosen that moment to stand up for me. I think she was more interested in avoiding abuse charges herself than standing up for me. Not only had it been too little too late, but it had caused pandemonium in the courtroom.

Jack looked like he was about to say something, but the bells above the door interrupted him.

He glanced at the group as they walked towards the counter, then asked, "Can I text you later?"

"Yeah, sure." I nodded as I turned towards my customers and greeted them. "Hello. What can I get started for you?"

"Have a good one," Jack said to me before shouting towards the back, "Bye, Ma!"

Later, during some down time, Beth opened up a little about her late husband, Phil.

"Chase looks so much like his dad." She picked up her coffee and fiddled with the lid. "I wish Phil could have known him." She exhaled slowly. "He died before Chase was born."

I could see the depths of her loss in her eyes. "I'm so sorry." Poor Beth. Losing your husband was hard, but losing your husband while pregnant must have been devastating.

"Sometimes it's hard, raising him alone." Unshed tears pooled in her eyes.

"Does Chase ask about him?"

"Sometimes, but he's still too young to understand. I know I'll have to explain it to him when he's older."

Beth told me Phil had died in a car accident while on duty. He was a cop and had worked with John. She smiled when she talked about meeting Mary for the first time and how they bonded instantly.

"Mary's support after he died was invaluable. I don't know what I would have done without her. Without them. John's like a surrogate dad to Chase." She blinked away a tear. "Chase recently started calling him Uncle John, and he just beams every time he hears it." She radiated love as she talked about Chase's new obsession with dinosaurs and how annoying it was that all he wanted to eat was dinosaur shaped macaroni and cheese. *I wish my mom had loved me half as much as Beth loves Chase.*

"It's great you had them to help you." I didn't know what else to say because I couldn't relate. I didn't know what it was like to have someone be there for me.

Later that night, my phone's text alert beeped, shocking me. I rarely got texts, so I wasn't used to the sound. I closed my book, using Jack's business card to mark my spot.

Hey. You busy?

Not really, I'm reading.

Please tell me you're not one of those people who gets violent when someone interrupts you when you're reading...

Is he flirting with me? Nah, he wouldn't, would he?

LOL, no.

No you aren't or No you won't tell me?

No, I'm not one of those people. *eye-roll*

OMG How do I take that back? *I don't want him to think I'm flirting.*

Phew. Dodged a bullet there.

How was your day?

Good. Yours?

Good. Speaking of bullets, want to go shooting again this weekend?

Smooth.

wink I like to think so.

I typed "I shouldn't," then paused and deleted it. My fingers hovered over the screen. I didn't know what to say. I wanted to go, but didn't want to take advantage of him. And I couldn't afford to pay him for a real lesson, not yet anyway.

Meg?

Shit, I have to answer.

Don't leave me hanging.

I quickly typed, "I'm not sure," then hit send before I could overthink it.

I tried to convince myself the only reason I was even considering it was because I wanted to learn more, not because I wanted to see Jack. As usual, I didn't believe me. It was a little of both. I rolled my eyes, grateful Jack couldn't see me or read my mind.

> Please. I'll be lonely if you don't come with me.

He's definitely flirting, at least I think he is. But why? Never mind, it doesn't matter. I should say no. Spending too much time with him could be dangerous.

> What time?

My fingers betrayed me.

> I'll take that as a yes. What time works for you?

> I didn't actually say yes.

> But you will. What time should I pick you up?

I chuckled. He was awfully sure of himself.

> How about I meet you there. Is ten okay?

> It's a date.

I laughed and typed: Not a date.

Crap, he's not responding. *Did I offend him?*

And Thanks. How much will I owe you for the lesson?

I saw the dots appear, disappear, and reappear. What was he trying to say?

Not a lesson.

Good night. See you Sunday, unless I need a caffeine fix before then.

Good night Jack. Thank you.

I picked up my book but couldn't concentrate. My thoughts kept drifting back to the texts. After re-reading the same paragraph three times, I gave up and put the book down. I reached for my phone, hesitated, then picked it up. *It's ridiculous to read his texts again, right?* Right. I agreed and read them anyway. I wanted to make sure I wasn't reading too much into them. Was he really flirting with all those winking emojis? No, no way, I told myself, he's just being friendly. Successful, good-looking guys like Jack don't flirt with girls like me. Which is probably good, because I can't get involved. It'd never work out. I can't risk him finding out about my past, besides I was sure he'd run for the hills if he ever found out how damaged I was.

Chapter 9

Jack

I was grinning like a teenager after his first kiss. I never would have known if AJ hadn't called me out on it with a smug smile on his face.

"What's her name?"

"Who?" I put my phone down, feigning ignorance.

"The woman who's got you grinning like the Cheshire Cat?"

"No one."

"Right." Jamie said as he reached for a slice of the house specialty Meats Pizza, from our favorite pizza joint.

Not realizing Jamie and AJ had been watching me, I hadn't controlled my facial expressions, and they were making me regret it.

"Beer?" AJ got up and walked to the fridge, making himself at home in Jamie's house, where I was currently living. "So… who is she?" He asked again as he handed us each a cold beer.

AJ was an inch shorter but a lot broader, and solid muscle. People often misjudged him as being all brawn, but I knew better. Sure, he could kick your ass without breaking a sweat, but he was also perceptive and clever.

"No one." I shrugged, trying to play it off. "It's no big deal."

AJ and Jamie both coughed bullshit into their hands. They wouldn't let it go.

"A friend. Meg. I'm giving her shooting lessons. It's not a big deal."

"Meg? As in Grannie's Meg?" Jamie asked as he grabbed a breadstick. The heavy garlic scent made my mouth water, so I grabbed two.

"Yes, I'm giving her shooting lessons. Like I said, no biggie." I shoved half a breadstick in my mouth.

"And you're grinning like the Cheshire Cat, because…?" AJ teased.

I was pretty sure they knew I had a thing for Meg, but no way in hell would I admit it. I was still getting to know her, and I didn't need the hassle.

"You heard him. He's giving her shooting lessons." Jamie said to AJ, "I know I always get a goofy grin when I schedule a lesson, don't you?"

"Only if I think she's cute," AJ confessed. AJ and Jamie clinked their beer bottles in solidarity. *Fucking brothers.* AJ might not be blood, but the bond we formed while serving was just as thick.

I shrugged and was about to deny it, but AJ shut me down. "Don't even try to deny it dude, you're into her."

I took a bite of pizza, a string of hot greasy cheese got stuck in the stubble on my chin. I wiped it away before saying, "Fuck you, Janerek." Not the best comeback, but I couldn't think of anything better.

"Tread carefully, little brother. Ma likes her a lot, and you know how protective she can be," Jamie warned me.

I knew. We all knew dating someone from Grannie's was a bad idea. We couldn't risk the potential shit show if something went wrong with one of mom's employees. She'd kill us if she lost a good worker because of a nasty breakup.

Meg's worth the risk.

Meg's beauty had grabbed my attention, but it was her demeanor that had sparked my curiosity. I wanted to get to know her better, figure out her story.

"I know. I know. There's nothing for Ma to worry about." I sounded more defensive than I'd intended. Their raised eyebrows broadcast their skepticism. It was hard convincing them when I couldn't convince myself.

I watched her over the rim of my coffee cup, after we finished our most recent range date that wasn't a date or a lesson, debating whether to say something as she picked up her peppermint tea and sniffed. She didn't feel safe around me, and I wanted to know why. I must have looked like I wanted to ask her something because she glanced around nervously before asking, "What?"

"Can I ask you a question?" I lowered my cup to the table, still cradling it in both hands, doing my best to appear relaxed and non-threatening.

"Yeah, I guess so." Her voice wavered.

I hated hearing the fear in her voice. I didn't want her to shut down, so I opted for a less direct question than I'd originally planned.

"You know I protect people for a living, right?" I kept my tone light.

"Yeah."

"Do you believe if a threat came through the door, I'd stop it?" I lifted my coffee, hiding most of my face as I observed her reaction. I could see the slight tremor in her hands despite the death grip she had on her cup.

After a brief pause, and a glance at the door, Meg answered, "Yeah, I guess, it's just..." She paused, opened her mouth, then closed it again. She stared at her tea, as if it held the answers she was seeking.

"It's just what?" I asked gently.

"I'm used to having to watch out for myself." She didn't look up.

Seeing her shrink down, like she wanted to disappear, felt like a dagger to my heart.

"I got your back Meg." I said, then changed the subject. I didn't think she'd open up any more today.

"Next question." I nodded my head towards the plate. "You gonna eat both those chocolate croissants?"

Meg's soft smile didn't reach her eyes. She was clearly relieved I'd changed the subject, but wasn't ready to relax yet.

"No, one is for you. I got the blueberry muffin in case you don't like chocolate."

"Who doesn't like chocolate?" I said, before biting into a croissant. "Mmm. Delicious. Thank you."

Meg asked me about SSI while we ate, and was happy to listen while I talked about how my dad and Jamie started the business after the local police couldn't save Jamie's wife, Isabelle, from a stalker who killed her before killing himself. She blinked away unshed tears. I could feel the empathy radiating off her.

My dad and Jamie wanted to help people, and knew law enforcement couldn't do anything to prevent attacks, only investigate them afterwards. A harsh reality driven home by Isabelle's death. SSI gave them the opportunity to do things they couldn't as police officers, like offering protection services and investigating situations before things got out of hand.

"I always wanted to be a cop, like my dad. I was planning to apply to the police academy when I left the Army, but when he asked me if I wanted to work in the private sector with them, I didn't hesitate to accept."

"You're lucky."

"I am." I took a sip of my coffee. "What about you? Are you close to your family?"

Her energy deflated faster than a popped balloon as she curled in on herself. She put her hands in her lap. I was sure she was trying to hide the fact that she was wringing them. It didn't work. I could see the muscles working in her arms.

"I don't really have any family." She answered softly.

Something about her answer felt off. She sounded sad, but not like she was grieving them. There was some unpleasant history there, I was sure of it. My curiosity peaked, I wanted to know more about her family and her relationship with them. I also wanted to reach out and comfort her, to make everything alright, but all I could do was offer sympathy. "I'm sorry, Meg. If you ever want to talk, I'm a phone call away."

"Thank you."

We sat in silence for a few minutes. The desire to wrap her in a protective hug was overwhelming, but I didn't think she'd be receptive. I couldn't imagine what it'd be like not having my family around, even if we got on each other's nerves occasionally. I knew how lucky I was to have a big, loving family.

"I should go." Meg stood up and glanced towards the door before clearing the table.

"Yeah, okay." I helped her because I didn't know what else to say or do. I'd clearly hit a sore spot.

"I'm sorry if I brought up sad memories." I apologized as we walked towards the door.

"Thanks. It's okay, really it is. I don't like to think about it, that's all." She sounded sad, but looked tense. Making me wonder what had happened. I didn't think they were dead because of her phrasing, but she clearly didn't have contact with them.

I nodded as I opened the door. Instinctively, I placed a protective hand on her lower back as she walked past me. I expected her to move away, but she didn't, so I kept it there for a few steps before letting my hand drop to my side.

"Can I give you a hug?" I asked when we got to her SUV. It was for my sake as much as hers; I wanted nothing more in that moment than to erase her pain.

"Um," she hesitated, debating. After a few awkward seconds that felt like minutes, she nodded and said, "Yeah, yes."

I opened my arms and let her step in; she was in control. I wrapped my arms around her, one hand guiding her head to my chest. Meg felt good in my arms. My insides did some weird gymnastics when she released a soft sigh and her shoulders relaxed. *Too good.*

She pulled back and tilted her head up, making eye contact with me. Her eyes were glossy from tears threatening to spill over. "Thank you. You're always so nice to me."

The way she said it, made is sound like people being nice to her wasn't normal, and I hated it. *I need to change that.*

"You're welcome." I said, my voice gritty with emotion. I quickly changed the subject to something more comfortable. "So, are we on for next Sunday? I can bring different guns for you to try."

"I don't know. I feel like I should pay you for the less-"

"Not a lesson." I cut her off.

"Please." Meg stepped back, one eyebrow raised. "You're teaching me how to shoot. Admit it."

"Nope, " I popped the p, "just two friends hanging out at the gun range."

"Right." Meg extended the word. "Just two friends hanging out. And one of those friends happens to be teaching the other friend how to shoot."

"Exactly!" I crossed my arms and flashed a triumphant smile.

"So… what do you call it when you teach someone how to do something?"

I grinned, but refused to answer. She answered for me, "A lesson."

"Not a lesson." I said, oozing confidence as I stepped past her to open her door. "See you on Sunday."

"Unless you need a caffeine fix," Meg teased.

"Unless I need a caffeine fix." I grinned.

She hadn't actually answered me yet, so I asked, "Can I take that as a yes for next Sunday?"

"Maybe." She said as she got in her car.

I watched as she struggled with the idea, assuming I wanted something in return, but I didn't. Well, I did, but probably not what she thought. I wanted to get to know her better, but had a feeling it wouldn't be easy. I shut her door and watched her pull away. There was a lot more to her than met the eye. Megan Hayes was a mystery I desperately wanted to solve.

Chapter 10

Jack

Meg and I met at the range the following Sunday. After we finished shooting, I suggested we go to the coffee shop. I was hoping to get to know her a little better. We texted a little during the week, but I didn't ask too many questions. Since most communication is non-verbal, I wanted to talk to her face-to-face and put my PI skills to good use. I tried to pay for our coffees but gave up when she insisted she on paying. As Meg walked over, I could see she'd ordered snacks too. I didn't enjoy letting her pay, carry our order, or serve me, but she insisted. It seemed important to her, so I swallowed my pride. I appreciated her independent streak, but not the bruised ego.

We made small talk as we sipped our coffee and ate the cookies. "Oatmeal raisin cookies are the reason I have trust issues." I wrinkled my nose at the cookies on the plate.

She covered her mouth when she laughed then swallowed her tea before saying, "I don't like them either."

"Is it the oatmeal or the raisins you don't like?"

"The raisins. I love oatmeal cookies. Especially oatmeal chocolate chip." She sipped of her tea. The scent of peppermint hung in the air. I bet it tasted great with the chocolate chip cookie she was eating. "What about you? Why don't you like them?"

"It's the combo. I like oatmeal and I like raisins, but not together in a cookie." I ate the sugar cookie, it wasn't my favorite, but I knew she liked chocolate, so I left the chocolate chip cookies for her.

Meg rubbed her eye, causing her contact to shift. I saw a hint of bright green before her contact shifted back into place. It happened so quick I wondered if I'd even seen it. I knew I was staring, but couldn't help myself. Why on earth would anyone cover up gorgeous green eyes with plain brown contacts? Not that I thought Meg had plain or boring eyes. Quite the opposite. Her expressive eyes were the main reason I was so intrigued by her; they gave away her feelings, even when she was trying to hide them, and held her secrets.

I looked away before she finished blinking and could catch me staring. *Just ask her about it.* I leaned forward and rested my forearms on the table. I stared deep into her eyes. And chickened out. "You should carry eye drops. The range can be a bitch for people with contacts." Her hands clenched her tea cup as fear flashed across her eyes. I'd hit a nerve.

"Good idea, thanks." She looked down, hiding her eyes.

Damn it. I leaned back and crossed my arms. Should I push for more, or let it go? She closed herself off any time I got too inquisitive and it only made me more curious. "You're welcome." I let it go for now. It wasn't like me to wimp out, but with Meg, I felt like I had to take it slow and walk on eggshells. Like a timid kitten, she'd spook and run if I moved too fast.

Making a mental note, I added colored contacts to the growing list of reasons I thought she might be on the run, but not from the law. We ran background checks on all applicants at Grannie's and nothing had popped up, but I had a feeling she was running from someone and if I was going to help her, I needed to know more. She might not share, but I had other ways of finding out. I could do a little digging around, knowing I could learn a lot from a person's social media presence.

I changed the subject back to the cookies, hoping to lessen her anxiety. Picking up the last cookie, the dreaded oatmeal raisin, and holding it between two fingers, I winced. "I'll take one for the team." I scrunched up my nose in disgust as I chewed. Her laugh was hollow. I could already tell the difference between her genuine laugh and her fake one. And I had just suffered through eating an oatmeal raisin cookie for the fake one. *It might have been worth it for a real one.* Before we left, I convinced her to join me for another range date the following Sunday. I enjoyed our Sunday mornings together and wanted them to continue. Plus, I learned a little more about her each time we got together.

When I walked her to her car, she told me I didn't have to, and I replied the same way I always did, "Ma'd kill me if I didn't." It wasn't a lie, so much as an exaggeration. She wouldn't literally kill me, but I'd get a tongue lashing about failing to be a decent southern gentleman, and the dreaded speech about how disappointed she was. A fate much worse than death. I'd suffered through that speech more often than I cared to admit when I was a semi-rebellious teenager and planned on being the kind of son, the kind of southern gentleman, who never had to hear that speech again.

"I'll be out-of-town most of the week on assignment, but you can call or text me if you have any questions," I paused, "Or if you want to chat." Meg hadn't once reached out to me. She seemed content to let me take the lead. I was happy to take it, but I hoped someday she'd want to reach out to me too.

During some downtime on Monday, I did what everyone does these days. I searched Meg's social media accounts. My gut was telling me something bad had happened to her. I instinctively made a mental list of the most likely scenarios while I searched. Hiding from a stalker or an abusive ex? Witnessed a crime and is in witness protection? I doubted she was on the run from the law. *She might be a criminal mastermind, hiding in plain sight, but I doubt it.* She didn't give off that vibe, but being on the run or in protection would explain why she dyed her hair, I'd noticed her roots last week, and wore colored contacts, her reluctance to talk about herself, her family, or her past, and her constant anxiety.

My first search through the normal social media sites yielded nothing, so I dug a little deeper and found a recently deleted Facebook account. I scrolled through her page. There weren't a lot of posts, and there were no pictures of her. Weird, most kids in college over-shared on social media, but Megan Hayes was the exact opposite. Most of her vague posts were about her classes at the Community College she'd attended in Indiana. From what I could tell, she had been working her way through school, but didn't graduate, at least not before deleting the account. I pieced together a few things: she attended part time, didn't go out much or didn't post about it if she did, she didn't belong to any clubs, and she walked away from it all without notice shortly after her semester started. A few weeks later, she was in Texas interviewing for a job at Grannie's.

"What happened to you Meg?" I asked the empty room.

The account she'd created with her college email was only active for three years. I knew not everyone wanted a major social media presence, hell I was one of those people. I'd had a Facebook account forever, but since graduating high school, I rarely used it. It was mostly for professional contacts and opportunities, and keeping up with Army buddies. Still, the fact she opened her account when she started college and closed it days before moving to Texas raised a red flag for me. Especially when I added it to the growing list of mysteries.

I searched the other common sites and apps but couldn't find any other accounts. Typical college students broadcast their entire lives for all the world to see on multiple social media platforms. Meg only had the one, and she had barely used it. I found very little online about Megan Hayes prior to her first semester at college. Which was odd. It was almost as if she didn't exist before college. *Did you change your name?*

I couldn't ignore my gut instinct: Meg was hiding. But from who and why? *I need to talk to dad and Jamie.* I didn't feel guilty about using social media to learn more about Meg since it was a common practice, but I wanted to dig deeper. And digging into someone's past, especially someone you wanted to date, raised some serious ethical questions.

I rapped my knuckles on the doorjamb. "Hey dad, got a minute?"

"Yeah, son, what's up?"

"I, uh-" I realized I might sound like a stalker myself when I told him what I'd been doing, and wanted to do.

"I wanted to ask your professional opinion about something?"

"Do you need the room?" Jamie offered to leave the office he shared with our dad.

"No, I could use your input too, if you've got a minute."

Dad nodded towards a chair.

"Give me a second to save this." Jamie hit a key, got up and sat next to me. They waited patiently for me to begin as I thought about how best to approach the subject.

"You know I've been taking Meg to the range and teaching her how to shoot." They nodded but didn't say anything.

"Things aren't adding up. We all noticed her nervousness, and intensity, in the self-defense class. She showed signs of distress during the duct tape exercise, but we've seen that before with students, so I didn't think too much about it. She dyes her hair, and yesterday when we went out for coffee, she rubbed her eyes and her contact shifted. They're colored."

I could tell from their faces I needed to do a better job at explaining myself. "It's not weird that she wears colored contacts, but she's covering gorgeous emerald green eyes with plain brown contacts."

Jamie raised an eyebrow. "Go on." My father said as he waited patiently for me to make my point. *Thank God he trusts my instincts.*

"I've noticed a few other things, too." I counted on my fingers. "She doesn't talk about herself, or her family, and when I ask personal questions, she either changes the subject or shuts down." I looked at Jamie. "What I'm getting at is I think she's hiding from someone. I did a quick search into her social media. She had one account, briefly while attending college, and she only posted non-personal stuff, and no pictures. She closed the account just before moving here."

"Her background check came back clean." Dad said at the same time Jamie said, "Congruent with someone trying not to be found."

"I don't think she's a criminal, though based on the lack of hits when I ran a search, she's probably changed her name. My gut is telling me there's something here." Taking a deep breath, I voiced my fear for the first time. "I have a feeling Meg is in some kind of trouble."

Dad leaned back and steepled his hands before saying, "We need to know more about her, her past. If she is hiding from someone, who are they? And how much of a threat are they?"

I didn't have to spell out the potential danger to mom. Because Meg worked at Grannie's, they'd consider any threat to her to be a potential threat to everyone there. I might not convince them to help me for Meg's sake, but they'd help for mom, and everyone else.

After a brief pause, Jamie asked, "Are you two dating?" He knew I had a thing for her, hell he'd been teasing me about it for weeks, so it wasn't an unreasonable question, but it still pissed me off. My attraction to her had nothing to do with this, and I shouldn't have to defend myself.

"No." I shot him a dirty look. "We're friends, if you can even call it that."

"But you're interested in more." It wasn't a question.

"Honestly, I'm not sure. I'm intrigued by her and yes, I've shown interest, but for now, I'm not planning on pursuing a relationship with her." Unfortunately, I wasn't sure I was being honest with myself, so Jamie's reaction didn't surprise me. His expression said it all; he didn't believe me. To the random observer, my dad might appear bored, but he was listening, collecting information from what I said, and what I didn't.

"This has nothing to do with what I may or may not feel for her. She's be in trouble, and I want to help." I ran my hand through my hair. *Damn it.* No wonder Jamie thinks I'm lying. How could I convince them if I couldn't convince myself? Cops were great at reading body language, and I was the idiot trying to hide my feelings from two cops who'd known me my entire life. I didn't stand a snowball's chance in hell of convincing either of them I wasn't interested in dating Meg.

If I was lucky, they'd ignore it for the moment and focus on the bigger picture.

"I'm with you. I don't think she's a fugitive. Your mom's an excellent judge of character and she likes Meg. And Beth trusts her with Chase." Dad valued their opinions. "Your mother said Meg doesn't seem shy, per se, but she doesn't talk about herself or her life before Texas. Which alone isn't a red flag, but add it to what you've seen…" He tapped his fingers on his desk.

"Jack, write up what you've learned so far. We'll review it and then figure out what, if anything, we need to do next." Dad said, "Jamie, can you review Grannie's security videos for the last few weeks, see if anything stands out? I'll talk to your mother tonight at dinner, see if she's picked up on anything else."

"On it." Jamie went back to his desk and pulled up the video feed from Grannie's security cameras. "We'll figure this out, Jack, and if she needs our help, she'll get it." He might give me shit, but when push came to shove, I could always count on him.

I considered myself lucky to have a large, close-knit family, and to be working with my father and brother. We might not always see eye-to-eye, and we teased each other relentlessly, but we always had each other's backs. "Thanks." I got up to go to my office so I could write up a detailed list of what I knew and what I suspected based on my observations.

"Hey Jack," Jamie called out as I reached the door. "Have you talked to AJ about this?"

"Not yet. I'm going to talk to him when he gets back."
I didn't plan on telling him anything other than I thought
she might have a stalker. My personal protection job started
early Wednesday morning, so I was leaving Tuesday night
and coming home Saturday afternoon. I didn't think she'd
call me, even if she needed help, so I wanted AJ to keep an
eye on her. I'd be back in plenty of time for our range date,
and if I was lucky, she'd be more relaxed, and maybe open up
a little more.

Dad finally addressed the elephant in the room. "You need
to keep it professional, so hold off on asking her out."

I nodded. He was right, even if I didn't like it.

I stopped by Grannie's on Tuesday, timing it so I'd be there
at the end of Meg's shift. I wanted to see her before leaving.
It was strictly business, not because I couldn't stop thinking
about her. I'd spent the last few days convincing myself my
infatuation with Meg was nothing more than professional
curiosity. I'd always been inquisitive and I couldn't stop
thinking about the riddle that was Megan Hayes.

I reached for the door and stopped dead in my tracks.
My jeans felt a little tighter as my body reacted to seeing
her swing her hips in time to the music as she wiped down
tables. She was oblivious to the fact I was standing outside,
mesmerized. I took a moment to adjust myself, and to remind
myself to keep it professional.

Meg turned when she heard the bells alerting her to an arriving customer. Her smile lit up her face when she saw me. "Hi Jack."

Her smile was gorgeous, genuine, and it reached her eyes. It stole my breath away. This was the greeting I'd hoped for the first I came to see her and it was the only one I ever wanted to get. I gave her a big grin to buy some time while I sucked air into my lungs. My heart pounded against my ribcage. All because she seemed genuinely happy to see me. She wasn't making it easy to stay professional.

"Don't stop on my account." I would have been happy to watch her all day. I told my dad I'd keep my distance. Be professional. I'd meant it when I'd said it, but the way my body and heart reacted to her made me think it might not be possible. It was probably a good thing I had to leave for a few days; it'd give me time and distance so I could get my head on straight.

"Ha, give me a sec. I'll get your coffee."

"I need two, but no rush," I said as I watched Meg walk behind the counter and pour my coffees. When she handed me the steaming cups, I blurted out, "I like your hair like that." Fuck. I sounded like an idiot, and I was supposed to be keeping my distance. Double fail on my part.

Meg paused, holding my steaming coffees halfway between us. I held my breath while I waited for her to say something. She raised her left eyebrow. "Thanks." Her hair was in a ponytail, like it had been every time I'd seen her, so she probably thought I'd lost my mind.

I had to recover. "FYI, I'm going out of town for work this week, but I'll be back in plenty of time for our range date."

"Not a date." Her tone was flat, but her eyes were smiling.

I knew she'd say that, but before I could say anything else, I heard the bell ring and turned to see AJ walking in. I'd asked him to meet me here so I could introduce them even though I was fairly sure they'd met since it was his job, as the new guy, to pick up coffee for the office, but I wanted them to get to know each other.

"Hey AJ."

"Sheppard." He nodded towards the cups. "One of those for me?"

I handed him one. "AJ, have you and Meg been properly introduced?"

"Yeah, Beth introduced us on one of the many coffee runs you guys sent me on. Hey Meg, how's it going?"

"Good. You?"

"Living the dream." He raised his to-go cup.

"Grab us a table. I'll be there in a sec."

"Sure thing." He said over his shoulder as he walked away.

I turned when I heard the door open and lifted my coffee in greeting. "Hey Lisa. How's it going?"

"Heya Jack. Good. You?" she answered as she headed to the back.

"Good." Before I joined AJ, I asked Meg. "Want to join us for a coffee? You can tell AJ what a great instructor I am." *That sounded way better in my head.*

"I don't know. I don't want to interrupt your plans."

"No plans, just having coffee."

She paused. "Okay, if you don't think AJ will mind."

"He won't." I answered confidently, knowing it was the reason he was here.

Meg joined us after she clocked out. We made small talk while we sipped coffees. AJ and I talked about our time serving together and AJ joining Sheppard & Sons and Meg talked about her job at Grannie's and learning how to shoot, but quickly changed the subject any time we asked about anything else. After about thirty minutes, AJ raised his eyebrows. I nodded to answer his unspoken question, yes I wanted time alone with Meg.

AJ excused himself. "Duty calls. It was nice getting to know you, Meg. If you need anything," He handed her a business card, "Call me. Later Sheppard."

"Thanks AJ." She put his business card in her purse. I didn't think she'd use AJ's number, but I was glad she had it. Just in case.

"Where are you going for work?" Meg asked.

"Austin. Personal security gig." I couldn't share much else.

"Is that the same thing as a bodyguard?"

"It is, but some clients don't like the term." I shrugged.

We talked for a few more minutes before Meg said, "I should go."

As I walked Meg to her car, I reminded her. "I'll be back in plenty of time for our range date on Sunday."

"Not a date." Humor danced in her eyes. I loved our running joke. "Bye Jack. Good Luck. Wait, is that something you say to someone whose job is dangerous, or is it bad luck like saying MacBeth in a theatre?"

"No, it's not bad luck." I said around a barely contained laugh. She could be so cute when she got nervous. "Be safe is what my mom always says." It was sweet, her wanting to wish me luck. I wanted to believe it was because she liked me. "Luck isn't much of a factor in my job."

"Oh, okay. Be Safe. See you Sunday." Meg opened her door and climbed in, then paused. "Hey, what's your favorite cookie?"

"Peanut butter chocolate chip, why?"

"I'm going to bake you some. It's my way of saying thanks." She grinned. "For the lessons."

"Not a lesson, but since no sane man would turn down homemade cookies, I accept." I patted my belly.

"Good." She got in her SUV, closed her door and waved goodbye.

My phone buzzed, alerting me to a text from AJ.

I see what you mean. She really doesn't like to talk about herself.

Glad I'm not the only one who sees it.

I'll keep an eye on her while you're gone.

Thanks brother, appreciate it.

Chapter 11

Meg

After talking to Jack and AJ, I grabbed a late lunch before driving to the Fort Worth Public Library. I'd put off checking my old email account too long.

I used the public library computers for the same reason I turned off location services on my phone and paid cash for my motel – I wanted to be hard to find. I wasn't stupid; if someone tried hard enough, they could find me. But I wouldn't make it easy. I logged into my email account. There were seven new messages. My breath moved a few stray strands of hair as I exhaled the breath I hadn't realized I was holding. There were no new messages from the FBI, or Special Agent Jones, the agent who had handled my name change and initial relocation, which meant Sullivan was still in Boston. Agent Jones was the one who made sure I got to the women's shelter in Indiana safely, made sure I had everything I needed, and checked up on me regularly that first year. Now we only talked a few times a year.

The feeling of relief faded as I opened the most recent email from my mother, dated three days ago:

> margaret, why won't you answer my emails. i miss you. dads home now. he misses you too wants you to know he forgives you. call us. we can be a family again

I stared at the screen, too stunned to blink. My brain tried to process everything I'd read in her poorly written email and failed. It was too much.

I took a few deep breaths and reread the email. One part caught my attention: "he forgives you." *He forgives me? He, Forgives Me! What the fuck? He raped me, and then sold me to Sullivan to pay off his gambling debts! HE DOESN'T GET TO FORGIVE ME!* I sat there shaking, nostrils flaring, fists clenched tight enough for my nails to draw blood.

I needed to calm down before I drew attention to myself.

I forced myself to unclench my hands and wiped my palms on my thighs. I counted to ten to calm myself down and reread the email. She called me Margaret, so she still doesn't know I changed my name. She said he's home. Does that mean they're back together? Whatever, it doesn't matter; they deserve each other. I can't believe she said they want us to be a family again. She has got to be kidding me. We'll never be a family.

We never were. I felt tears well up for what never was.

I contemplated deleting the email, so I'd never have to see it again, but something in the back of my mind said I should keep it. I created a new folder with my mom's name, Debbie, and saved it there. Out of sight, but not gone.

There were four more emails from her. I hated how every once in a while she'd get a bug up her ass and start emailing me. It was always the same; she'd say she missed me and wanted me to come home. Usually, she'd give up after sending two or three emails, then forget about me again. And I'd be left with sleepless nights and the memories of a past I wanted to forget.

The oldest was three weeks old and didn't mention my father. Neither did the next two. The second most recent email, sent six days ago, was the first to mention him and it was only a couple of short, badly written sentences. Basically, he knocked on her door and begged her to take him back, and she did. At least now I know why she didn't give up as quickly this time. I shivered as an icy chill swept over my body. I didn't want to think about why he wanted me to go back.

I moved all her messages to the Debbie folder without replying. I had no desire to reconnect with my parents. The thought made me want to vomit. *If I never see them again, it'll be too soon.*

There was nothing in any of the emails to make me think they were actively looking for me. My mother's declarations were hollow words. After logging out of my email, I searched for news on Patrick Sullivan in Boston. I'd been checking the news more frequently since learning he'd been granted parole. I was terrified he'd come seeking revenge when he got out of jail. My search yielded a few new articles covering his release, but nothing else. My stomach turned, and I swallowed down bile as I stared at the old picture of him. He was waving to the news reporters, a smug smile on his fat face, as he walked into the courthouse. Sullivan had been confident he wouldn't get convicted. He hadn't planned on the key witness sealing his fate.

I puffed out a long sigh of relief. Sullivan was required to wear an ankle monitor as a condition of his parole, which meant he couldn't leave Massachusetts. Or come to Texas.

I closed the browser and restarted the computer. I always restarted the computers I used, so I didn't accidentally leave an account open.

My hand shook and my heart raced as my nerves got the best of me on the drive home. *An ankle monitor is all that stands between me and Sullivan. A vicious crime boss who wouldn't think twice about making me suffer until I begged for death.* I couldn't let my guard down, not for one single second.

Chapter 12

Jack

I went to the hotel bar Friday night after seeing my client safely in her room. My assignment would be complete once she boarded her plane home tomorrow morning. I couldn't wait to get home so I could talk to my dad and Jamie and hear what they'd learned about Meg while I was gone.

Jamie had done another traditional search into her history after I talked to them, but he couldn't find anything either. Not without investigating. Despite not having any concrete evidence, we all agreed there was something bad in Meg's past. Our guts told us she was running or hiding, and we needed to find out why, and from who. I wanted to help, but they said no. They were treating this like a formal case to protect the company, and I was too close. It might have started, informally, as my 'case' but I wouldn't be doing anymore research. It was the right decision, but I didn't have to like it. *I hate feeling useless.*

I called Jamie during a break yesterday, unfortunately he had nothing new to share. He assured me they were working on it, and reminded me to stay focused on my job.

"Yes, sir." I replied. I hadn't meant to sound so snarky. "Sorry Jamie, I feel so useless."

"I understand, but you're on assignment and that has to be your priority right now. I'll let you know if I find anything you need to know."

"Thanks."

He was right. Losing focus on an assignment could get me or my charge hurt or killed. I needed to be one hundred percent focused on the job at hand, not thinking about Meg.

I sat at the bar thinking about Meg while I waited for my food. I didn't feel like eating another meal alone at the bar, so I asked the bartender if they could deliver it to my room. When I got there, I turned on a baseball game. I preferred football, having played in high school, but there weren't any football games on. It didn't matter; the game was background noise while I ate.

I texted Meg while I waited for my chicken sandwich to be delivered.

Hey Meg. How's your evening?

Good. I've got a hot date…

I ground my back teeth. I had no right to feel jealous, but my jaw didn't get the memo.

With a good book. LOL.

My jaw relaxed.

Sounds exciting.

You still working?

Yes & no. Client is in her room so unless she calls, I'm done for the night.

You don't have to guard her door?

LOL, no, it's not that kind of job.

Shows you what I know.

I'd be happy to teach you. *wink*

Someone knocked on my door and called out, "Room service."

Gotta run, dinner's here.

Enjoy. Stay safe.

Will do. See you Sun.

I was pretty sure I had a goofy grin on my face as I answered my door. *Thanks AJ!*

I called my dad the next morning, after seeing my charge safely on her plane, to let him know the assignment was complete. I couldn't wait to get home. A home-cooked meal sounded heavenly after eating take out and pub grub all week.

On my way home, I stopped to fill the tank and pick up a coffee. While I was pumping gas, I noticed a dirty, strung out guy approaching, his hands in the pockets of his baggy jeans. Recognizing a potential threat, I adjusted my position, so I was between him and the only other customer at the pumps, a woman with a child in the back seat. I stepped behind my black sedan to address him. I would have preferred to stay behind the bullet proof company car but then I wouldn't be between him and the woman.

"Hey man, you okay?" I held my arms out in front of me in a non-threatening manner. I heard a door close. A quick glance back told me the woman was safely in her car.

"Got any smokes?" The guy scratched his neck. He had dilated pupils, and his lip kept twitching.

Fuck, he's tweaking.

"I don't, sorry." I stepped back as he continued approaching. It was too late to get away. He'd be on me before I could remove the gas hose and get in the car. Besides, I was confident I could take him. I wanted to avoid using my gun if I could, but that depended on his next actions.

He pulled a hand out of his pocket and pointed a kitchen knife at me. "Then give me your wallet!" The morning sun glinted off the chipped blade.

I reached for my gun, but a pink compact car pulled into the pump behind him. A young brunette got out and put her credit card in the pump. She was singing along with a song, completely oblivious to what was happening a few feet away.

I couldn't risk hitting an innocent bystander, so my gun stayed in the holster. I'd have to do this the hard way, hand vs knife. The hard way always sucked. I adjusted my stance as I answered in a calm, even tone. "Sure man. Just let me grab it for you." I wanted to move him as far from the girl pumping gas as I could.

I held one hand up and reached around slowly with the other as I spoke, intentionally drawing attention to my gun as I swept my jacket back. I hoped seeing it would discourage him from attacking, and he'd run away.

It had the exact opposite effect.

"Fucking pig!" He lunged at me, swinging the knife up and down wildly.

Instinctively, I brought my left arm up to block it. My only thought was stopping the attack. The dull, jagged blade sliced across my forearm, ripping it open. I ignored the pain and dripping blood, and stepped in close. His nose crushed under my fist. The sound of crunching bones told me I probably broke it. He dropped the knife and reeled back in shock and pain, bringing both hands up to his blood-covered face. A mix of blood and spit flew from his mouth as he hurled expletives at me. I stepped to the side, grabbed a wrist, and forced his arm behind his back. I kicked him behind his knee and shoved him to the ground. He continued screaming. I'm sure he wanted one of the gawkers to take pity on him and help. They didn't.

I was about to tell one of them to call 9-1-1 but heard sirens approaching. At least someone had the good sense to call the police instead of streaming the attack on Facebook.

The police arrived and my bad guy, who'd been sobbing into his blood-soaked hand as I held him in place, started screaming again. He wriggled and squirmed to get away from the officer who was trying to handcuff him.

An officer handed me a gauze bandage. I thanked him and identified myself as I wrapped it tightly around the long, deep, bloody cut. That was going to leave one ugly scar. The only thing worse than a knife cut was a dirty, chipped blade knife cut. I looked around for the brunette and saw her talking to a police officer. I was relieved she was okay. She'd have a hell of a story to tell her friends later.

"I'll give my statement after I get my arm patched up." I told Sgt. Newman, the senior officer on site.

"Not a problem, Mr. Sheppard. Mind if I call your supervisor to verify your credentials before you go?"

"No, sir." I handed him my business card and told him to call the main number. "If no one answers, I'm happy to give you John Sheppard's cell number."

He read the card. "Family business?"

I nodded. "I work with my dad and brother."

He stepped away to make the call. He released me a few minutes later. "I expect to see you at the station tomorrow morning to give your statement, oh nine hundred."

"Yes sir. I'll be there."

I checked my phone while I waited to be discharged from the ER a few hours later. Four missed calls, three voicemails, and over a dozen texts. I checked the voicemail first. Dad called me immediately after hanging up with Sgt. Newman.

Apparently, the good sergeant told him I got stabbed. *Great, ma's probably freaking out.*

The second voicemail confirmed my suspicion.

"Jack, please call us. Let us know you're okay." I could feel her concern through the speaker. I ignored the texts and called her, not wanting her to worry any more than she already had. She put me on speaker, so Dad could hear too.

"Hi Ma. I'm fine, I swear. Hi Dad."

"Your father said you got stabbed."

Panic lingered in her voice. "I didn't get stabbed. I got cut. Nothing a few stitches can't fix." Thankfully, it was the truth. When a person hears about a stabbing, it brings up images of a victim lying in a pool of his own blood. Hearing a person got cut isn't nearly as bad. People cut themselves all the time, so it rarely invoked fatalistic images.

To reassure her it wasn't a big deal, I sent a picture of my bandaged arm. There was no need to tell her I had sixteen stitches hidden underneath it.

"I'm good, Ma, I promise. I'll be home tomorrow after I give my statement to APD."

"Let us know if you need anything." I could hear the relief in his voice.

"I'm good. Thanks Dad." I was about to say goodbye when I realized he could help me. "Actually, can you get me a room for the night?"

"Sure thing. I'll text the details."

"Thanks."

"We love you."

"Love you too."

I didn't bother reading the text messages from Jamie or AJ before sending a group message.

> The news of my stabbing has been grossly exaggerated. Nasty gash on arm - gonna leave one hell of a scar & fuck up my tat -but I'm good. Statement at APD at 09, then home.

AJ: Cool. Chicks dig scars.

Jamie: Glad you're good. You call Ma? She's freaking out.

> Yup, talked to her and dad.

Jamie: Good.

AJ: Beers when you get back, give us the details?

> Sounds good.

> Shit, I'm supposed to meet Meg at the range at 10. Either of you free?

AJ: Yup.

Jamie: Yes.

Okay, I'll get in touch with her and let you know. Thanks.

I ordered room service after checking in. Breakfast was a long time ago and my stomach wouldn't stop grumbling. I texted Meg to tell her I wouldn't be back in time for our range date.

Chapter 13

Meg

Mary's face blanched after she answered her cell phone;
so I knew something bad had happened, but I didn't
know what, or to whom. She didn't tell me anything, but
I overheard her talking to Beth. My breath hitched when
I heard her say Jack got stabbed. My breath caught in my
throat. *Jack got stabbed? Oh God. Is he going to die? I may never
see him again.*

Jack and I were barely friends, so my intense reaction made
little sense.

Beth volunteered to stay late so Mary could meet John and
get more details.

"Beth, is everyone okay? Mary looked worried." I didn't
want to admit I overheard them. Beth and I were becoming
friends, and I didn't want her to think I was eavesdropping.

"She got some bad news about Jack. He got hurt at work."

"I hope he's okay." I really did, for Mary's sake, as much as Jack's.

She patted my arm. "Me too."

It surprised me when I got a text from him a few hours later. Surely, he had more important people to talk to.

> Hey Meg, I hate to do this but I have to miss tomorrow's range date. Jamie and AJ both volunteered to meet you there, if you'd like.

> That's okay, I can wait. Are you still at the hospital?

> LOL News travels fast. How'd you hear?

> I overheard Mary tell Beth you got stabbed.

> Cut not stabbed. I'm fine.

> Can I call you? It'd be easier.

> Of course.

My phone rang a few seconds later. Jack told me again he was fine. I had to admit it felt good to hear his voice. I asked again if he was still at the hospital, since he hadn't answered me. He told me he was relaxing in his hotel room, waiting for his dinner to be delivered. I laughed when he joked about how getting attacked makes a person ravenous. Hearing him joke was music to my ears. My shoulders relaxed for the first time since I'd overheard Mary. I'd been trying to pretend I didn't have feelings for Jack, but I couldn't deny my reaction, or what it meant.

When he re-iterated the offer for Jamie or AJ to meet me at the range, I told him I'd rather wait until he could go with me. *I only want to go with Jack.* I asked him what time he'd be back and if he wanted to meet for coffee. *So stupid. He'll want to see his family.*

"Can we do a late lunch instead? It's a long drive and it'll give me something to look forward to."

"Yeah." I was glad he couldn't see me blushing.

"It's a date. Text me where you want to meet. I'll call with an ETA after I finish up with Austin PD."

"Okay, good night."

"Good night." I was glad he couldn't see me, because I was sure I was grinning from ear to ear.

Chapter 14

Jack

I disconnected the call and stretched out on the bed, grinning from ear to ear despite my exhaustion from the day's events.

Meg hadn't replied with her usual "not a date". I convinced myself she was okay going on a lunch date with me, not just being nice because I got hurt.

I was flirting with disaster. I hadn't been in a relationship for years and the last thing I needed was to get involved with someone shrouded in mystery.

I wrapped my bandage in plastic before taking a hot shower to help my body relax. I collapsed into bed shortly after and slept like the dead.

I met with Sgt. Newman the next morning to give him my statement. It was a formality at this point, there had been several other eye witnesses on site, plus the gas station video surveillance footage, so it was quick and easy. I was on the road by ten.

I made good time driving back and arrived ten minutes before I had to meet Meg at a local pizza place. I scanned the parking lot for her car, spotting it as she opened her door. She waved when she noticed me. I didn't realize how tense I felt until it drained from my body at the sight of the big smile plastered on her face.

Meg closed the distance between us at a brisk walk and knocked me off balance, in more ways than one, when she wrapped her arms around my neck and squeezed. I adjusted my legs so we didn't fall over and hugged her back, my arms wrapped tightly around her waist. The unexpected surge of emotions had my head spinning. I tried to ignore how good it felt to hold her in my arms. And failed.

"I'm so glad you're okay." Meg said as she stepped back.

I released her. Reluctantly.

I crossed my hands in front of my pants to cover up the evidence of how much I enjoyed holding her. It was a perfectly natural response to being hugged by a gorgeous woman.

"Sorry for the ambush. I don-"

I cut her off. "Don't apologize. I needed a friendly hug." I put a hand on her lower back and guided her towards the door. "Let's go eat. I'm famished."

After we ordered, she asked if she could see my arm. Gauze covered it so there wasn't much to see, but I couldn't say no to her.

"Does it hurt?" She asked as I rolled up my sleeve.

"Not too bad. Just a big scratch, no biggie. See?" I held out my bandaged arm. She held my wrist and turned my arm left and right, her face scrunched up, something I now recognized as her thinking expression.

"That's a big bandage for a scratch."

"Well, I did say it's a big scratch."

I tried to pay for lunch when our server brought the bill, but Meg argued with me. I had half hoped this might be a date because she hadn't corrected me, but I should've known better. *It's probably better this way.* Our first date wouldn't be a last-minute lunch date. She deserved better. Meg wasn't like most women I'd dated; they'd rarely offered to pay, and they certainly didn't argue if I offered. *Especially Ana.* I appreciated Meg's independence, and knew this wasn't a date, but I could only take so much damage to my ego. I finally convinced her to let me pay by offering to let her leave the tip.

Before we left, we agreed to meet at the range on Wednesday to make up for the non-lesson we'd missed today.

My parents, and Jamie, were waiting for me when I got home. Mom ran over and wrapped me in a great big mama bear hug. *I'll never be too old for her hugs.* She poured all her love and worry into it, and I'm pretty sure I heard her sniffle. "I'm so glad you're okay."

"I'm fine, Ma. I promise." She wouldn't have been half as worried if Newman hadn't used the word stabbed.

She kissed me on the cheek, then swatted me on the back of my head. "You scared me half to death."

I pretended I didn't see her wipe a tear off her cheek.

"Ow." I rubbed my head, feigning pain. "In my defense, it was Sgt. Newman who scared you, not me."

Dad and Jamie gave me typical man hugs, patting me on the back and not saying anything. Ma glared at Dad when he ushered me and Jamie into his home office.

"Don't worry, I'll have them back to you in half an hour."

"You better." She put her hands on her hips to make sure he knew she meant it. *I want a love like theirs someday.*

Jamie sat in front of Dad's desk and opened his laptop. I sat next to him.

Something in their demeanor made me worry. "Is this about Meg?"

"Yes. We got a hit using facial recognition." He paused and rubbed his chin. "Some of this will be hard to hear, so I'm just going to rip the bandaid off. Until six years ago, Meg's name was Margaret Graham." He paused, giving me a moment to let it sink in.

"It was easier to find more information once we had her birth name."

I balled my fists in my lap in anticipation of what he was about to tell me.

"Both her parents got arrested shortly before the FBI changed her name."

Parents arrested? FBI? I opened my mouth to reply, but nothing came out. I thought she might be in trouble, but I wasn't expecting something of this magnitude. This was bad.

"Your intuition was right. She's hiding, but not from a stalker."

I looked from my father to my brother and back again. "Jesus."

"Her father, Gary, was involved with some bad people. He got a reduced sentence for turning state's witness against one of them."

"Why'd he get arrested?"

"Possession of child pornography, trafficking, and intent to solicit a minor." My father's voice was calm, matter of fact. Like he hadn't just dropped the mother of all bombshells on me.

"What the fuck!" The chair tipped over when I jumped to my feet.

"Sit down." His tone left no room for disobedience, so I picked up my chair and sat back down. I clenched my back teeth and put my fisted hands on my thighs. The desire to punch someone overwhelmed me.

They waited a few seconds while I calmed myself down. I used the breathing technique I learned in the Army. Breath in for four, hold for four, breath out for four, hold for four. After a few cycles, my heart rate was back to normal.

"Where was her mother during all this?" Jesus, no wonder she never talked about her family. "You said they both got arrested."

"Her mother was, and still may be, an addict. When the FBI questioned her, she claimed she didn't know anything about Gary's illegal habits. They arrested her at Gary's trial on drunk and disorderly charges and released her into court ordered rehab soon after."

"Christ." I ran my hand through my hair. "And the FBI?" I choked out, fear caused my voice to rise an octave.

"They changed her name after she testified against Patrick Sullivan, a Boston crime boss on their most wanted list. Meg was one of four underaged victims who testified. One of them called 9-1-1 from a client's phone, which led to Sullivan's arrest. They redacted the names in the court documents to protect the identities of the minors, so we don't know if Meg made that call." I stared, unblinking, at my father as he told me all this in a calm, steady voice.

"Christ." My brain was struggling to put it all together. Meg's history was so much worse than I'd expected.

"We've reached out to the FBI agent who handled the case to find out more. He may not tell us anything, but it's worth a try."

Jamie added, "Sullivan's a sick son of a bitch who won't lose sleep over exacting revenge against anyone who testified against him. If Meg's the one who called 9-1-1, she'll be his first target."

They waited as I leaned forward and ran my hand through my hair, processing everything they'd told me. Meg was on the run, and hiding from the mob. *This is bad.* My heart pounded against my ribs as I stood up and started pacing back and forth, clenching and unclenching my fists with each step.

"Wait, who'd her father testify against?" I had a sinking feeling in my gut.

Jamie looked at my dad, who gave him a subtle nod. "Sullivan."

"Sullivan?" I spit out the familiar name.

"The same. He was wanted for a laundry list of crimes, including trafficking minors." Jamie turned his monitor so I could see it. I stared at the image of a short fat man smiling and waving to the press as he left court, my blood pressure rising the longer I stared. I wanted to wipe the smug smile off his fat face forever.

"Please tell me he's still in prison." If Sullivan was out of prison, he'd want to find Meg.

"They released him on parole. The timing lines up with Megan's move to Texas. I think it's safe to assume she knows Sullivan is out of jail."

I couldn't speak. Anger and fear raged through me. I wanted to hunt down Sullivan and beat him to death with my bare hands. His death was the only thing that would guarantee Meg's safety. "Do you think…" I was barely holding it together, thinking about the things Meg might have suffered. Neither of them tried to finish my question.

I didn't think either of them had ever seen me look so shaken or pissed off. *Pull yourself together.* They waited as I took a few deep breaths and sat back down.

"How do I help her?" My voice cracked.

"First off, you don't." He pointed to himself and Jamie. "We do. You can't work–"

"The hell I can't!" I cut him off as I stood up and leaned over his desk. *So much for staying calm.*

He raised his eyebrows and waited as I struggled to control my emotions. "You're too close. And we can't have you digging into her past if you want to date her. It blurs the line of ethics and could appear like an abuse of your position. I won't risk the company's reputation." He paused. "Trust that we'll do everything we can to help her."

"I can't sit around and do nothing, Dad." This was so much worse than I'd expected.

"I know, Son. You can help her by being her friend and continuing to train her," he paused, "but keep it professional."

I nodded. I'd try, but it might already be too late. My reaction to her hug at lunch earlier was an unexpected emotional high, but I couldn't tell them that. It was bad enough they knew I was interested in her. Interested enough that I'd had lunch with her before I came here. And, of course, they witnessed my outburst, which was just as damning.

"You can't work the case, but we won't leave you in the dark, either." Jamie said. "Our plan is to learn more about Sullivan and how Meg was involved. He's on parole with an ankle monitor, so if he leaves Boston, there'll be a BOLO. We'll monitor her parents as well, but we don't consider them a threat. Doug agreed to move up his start date so we'll have an extra set of eyes and ears. His first priority will be to update the security cameras at Grannie's." Doug was a tech and surveillance guy who had served in the Air Force, and his skill set would come in handy.

It was a hard pill to swallow, but they were right. I was too close. "Thank you." I said around a mouthful of humble pie. They'd done so much to help me, to help Meg, and didn't deserve my attitude.

"We're contemplating putting a camera in the extended stay parking lot to monitor for suspicious activity." Dad leaned forward and put his forearms on his desk.

"Can we do that, monitor her apartment?"

"Not her apartment, the parking lot. We're walking a fine line, and wouldn't be considering it if the threat to Megan wasn't a potential threat to your mom."

"I'd still want to help her, even if there wasn't a threat to Ma." I made my position clear.

"I know, and you know we would too." Dad paused and Jamie picked up where he left off. "Listen, we know what she means to you, so we'll do what we can."

I opened my mouth to deny it, but Dad cut me off. "Don't deny it. Hell, Jack, you had lunch with her before coming to see me and your mom." He held up his hand when I opened my mouth to defend myself. "We're not upset. I'm just pointing out the obvious."

I didn't want them keeping me in the dark because of my feelings when I wasn't even sure what they were yet. *Keep telling yourself that.*

"We know you like her but, at least for now, you need to take it slow." Dad was right.

I nodded. Dating wasn't an option yet. Best to keep it professional.

Jamie asked, "Are you taking her to the range again anytime soon?"

"Wednesday." At least now I understood why she wanted to get a gun. Though I didn't understand why she was reluctant to let me help her. "So far, it's been fun. I'll subtly increase her training, so she's proficient faster." I wouldn't tell Meg, but we were no longer two friends having fun. She was training to defend herself.

"Good," Dad said. "Does she have a gun, or any other weapons?"

"No gun, not yet, but she's thinking about buying one. I've got one she can borrow until she buys her own. I don't know if she has anything else."

"Do you think she'll agree?" Jamie asked. "You've said she's reluctant to accept help."

"She is, but I'll figure something out." I was thinking of ways I could convince Meg to borrow one of my guns when I remembered the Wyatt Foundation fundraiser at Grannie's Halloween weekend. "Didn't Ma say someone donated guns for the raffle table?"

"Yeah, two last I heard." Dad asked, "Why?"

"I have an idea." I felt a little calmer knowing I had their support. "But I'll need Ma's help."

"Care to share?" Jamie asked. His grin hinting he knew the answer.

"Not yet."

I was getting ready to leave, after a few hours of letting my mom fuss over me, when dad reminded me they wouldn't tell me anything they wouldn't tell AJ or Doug. "To protect Meg's privacy, you're all on a need to know basis." It was frustrating, but I didn't have a choice.

I was halfway to the door when Dad said, "Be careful with Meg, you-"

"I know." I barked at him. *Shit*. Being rude to my father, personally or professionally, wasn't something I was in the habit of doing, but my head was still spinning from what they'd told me and I was tired of being told something I didn't want to hear.

"Watch your tone. It's my responsibility as your boss to make sure you don't lose focus and my job as your father to watch out for you."

"I know." I turned to face him and apologized. "There's a lot going on in my head right now."

"Accepted." He patted me on the shoulder.

Mom brought us a bag of leftovers from the kitchen. Food was her love language, so she was always trying to feed us. We never complained. "Thanks." I gave her a hug. "Bye mom."

"Let me know if you need anything." She couldn't help me with what I needed, but I appreciated her support none the less.

"Thanks."

Jamie said his goodbyes, and we walked out together.

"You know this could backfire, right? If she finds out, she'll likely think you betrayed her."

"I know." They were right, even if I didn't want to hear it. "I know." I had a lot to process before I saw Meg again.

Chapter 15

Meg

I went to the range thirty minutes before I was supposed to meet Jack and treated myself to an early birthday gift. Grant helped me find good eye and ear protection so I wouldn't have to keep borrowing Jack's. I liked our range dates and figured if I was going to get my own gun, I should have my own gear too.

Jack came rushing in at our scheduled time and apologized for being late.

"You're not late, you're exactly on time." I shook my head, trying not to laugh at how flushed he was.

"Looks like you went shopping while you were waiting." Jack nodded towards my bag with a big grin on his face. I loved how the left side lifted more than the right. "What'd you get?"

"I'm the proud new owner of my very own eye and ear protection." I waved the matching purple set in front of his face to show them off.

"Nice color." He chuckled, then reached for the ear muffs. "Good choice."

"Thanks. Grant helped me pick them out."

On the range, Jack set out a couple of different guns for me to try. He said I should try as many as I could and make notes of what I liked, and didn't like, about each one, so I'd be better prepared when I was ready to buy my own. He must have made a mental note of the gun I shot the best, which was also the one I liked the most, and had me shoot it the rest of the day. The SIG p320 fit my hand perfectly, and I liked how smooth the trigger felt.

"Ready to take your shooting to the next level?" Jack asked.

"What? I'm barely good enough at this level."

"You're too hard on yourself." He brought in my black silhouette target, took it off the hanger and held it up to his body. "See where the holes line up with my body?" He made a circle around the holes. "Any hits in the body are good defensive shots."

Without thinking, I put a finger through a hole and poked his ribcage. It seemed strange to me to hear I didn't have to hit the bullseye to be effective.

"That's a lung shot." Jack gently pushed my hand away. "Lung shots stop threats."

I met his eyes. "But–"

"Will you please listen to me," he pleaded, "and trust I know what I'm talking about?"

"I do trust you." It shocked me to say it, and even more so to believe it. I didn't trust many people and didn't know when I'd started trusting him.

He smiled. Something in his eyes seemed to say he knew I didn't give my trust easily.

"Thank you." After a brief pause, he changed the subject. "Want me to show you how to shoot like an action hero?"

"Um, yeah, I'll never be that good." I hadn't seen a lot of action movies, but they did the impossible in the few I had seen.

"True, no one is. But you can learn to shoot better faster with a little guidance and practice."

Jack taught me how to use the trigger reset and encouraged me to practice it for the rest of our time.

When I looked at my last target, I did a little happy dance. "Holy shit!" I pointed at my best target yet.

"I don't want to say I told you so, but," Jack grinned and emphasized every word as he pointed at me, "I told you so."

God only knows why, but I put my hands on my hips and stuck out my tongue like a petulant child. *Poor Jack, he must think I'm crazy.* There was something else in his expression too, but I couldn't put my finger on it, so I let it go. I was too excited to think about it.

He laughed, then pulled me into a loose hug. "You're adorable."

I gave him a quick squeeze before pulling away and looking back at my target. "I can't believe I did it. But it was only ten feet, so I guess it's not too impressive."

"Fucking Hell, Meg." I flinched at his words. Jack must have noticed, because he softened his tone. "You should feel good about how much you improved today. Stop finding reasons to put yourself down. Please."

"Okay." I paused before adding, "but I'm not wrong I-"

"Yeah, you are." Jack sounded exasperated. "I moved your target out to fifteen feet while you were loading your mag."

"You did?"

"I did. Do I need to tell you again to feel good about how well you did today?"

"You just did." I looked at the floor, my shoulders sagging. I hated to think I'd upset Jack.

"Hey," he lifted my chin, "You did great today."

"Thank you."

Chapter 16

Jack

As we were leaving, I blurted out. "It's too late for coffee. Can I buy you a beer instead? To celebrate." Damn it, I'm supposed to keep it professional. *If she says no, just accept it.*

"I don't know. I should probably go home."

"Come on, Meg, you've earned a treat for all your hard work today." I ignored my advice. I had beer with my friends all the time, it was nothing special.

She hesitated before replying, "Okay, but it's my treat. Especially since this felt more… lessony than the other times."

"Lessony? Is that even a word?"

"Hey if Shakespeare can do it, so can I. Seriously though, is everything okay? You seem–"

I cut her off, hoping to diffuse her concern. "Teachery? Hey if you can do it…" I wiggled my eyebrows to lighten the mood. It didn't work.

"I was going to say serious."

I thought I'd done a decent job of keeping it light and fun. Guess not. "Sorry. Guess I'm still a little jacked up after last weekend." I lied. Now wasn't the time or place to tell her what I'd learned.

"Okay." She didn't sound convinced.

"Where are we going so I can buy you a beer?"

I raised an eyebrow when Meg ordered water. "Are you really going to celebrate with water?"

She shrugged. "I've tried beer a few times, but have never found one I like."

"Trust me?" I asked, grinning. I was treading in dangerous waters but couldn't stop myself.

Meg nodded, then turned to the server and smiled. "I'll have a water too."

I asked our server for two flights of their most popular beers. "We'll try them together. Each flight is four beers, so there's bound to be one you like."

Meg tried a tiny sip of each of the eight beers. It was cute how she scrunched her face up after tasting most of them. The only one she thought was "pretty okay" was the pumpkin amber ale. *Noted.* She said she didn't think she could drink a whole glass, so I slid the sample towards her. "Here. You can drink the rest of this one. It's about a quarter of a beer."

"You don't want it?"

I laughed as I dragged the seven remaining samples towards me with my arms. "Oh, I think I'll be fine."

I picked up a random glass, tilted my head towards the one in front of her, and waited for her to pick it up.

"To a job well done." I touched my glass to hers, then tapped it lightly on the table before tilting it back.

"Thanks." Meg said before taking a sip. Then she sniffed the beer. "It smells like pumpkin pie. Who would've thought a beer could taste like dessert?" She looked at the beer flights in front of me. "Do you want to order a real beer?"

"I'm good. These may be small, but they're real." I said, as I finished another sample. "Add them all together and I have a full beer. Though I wouldn't recommend mixing them together in one glass." I shivered in exaggerated disgust.

She laughed and drank some water before picking up her beer again. Relief washed over me as she relaxed a little more. Our conversation flowed effortlessly until I asked her if she was practicing the self-defense stuff she'd learned in class. I knew from experience few did—they didn't think they'd ever need it. But Meg knew she might.

"Sort of. I don't have pads or a partner, so I only practice the movements."

"It's more than most people do." I held my hand out for a fist-bump and smiled when her small fist touched mine. "Now that you've found a gun you like, do you think you'll buy yourself a SIG?"

She started fidgeting. I'd tried to keep it casual, but ended up sounding more intense than I intended.

"I don't think I'm ready yet." She wouldn't meet my eyes, so I dropped the subject.

We made small talk while I finished the rest of my samples. I wasn't ready for our evening to end, but she'd closed herself off again. *I need a better tactic if I'm going to get her to open up to me.*

I walked her to her rusty, beat up SUV. *I hope it runs better than it looks.* The idea of her car being unreliable made me nervous.

I stalled to buy a few more minutes. "Oh hey, I almost forgot to ask. Are you going to the Wyatt Foundation fundraiser dance next weekend?" Even though I already knew the answer. Ma expected everyone from Grannie's to volunteer, even if only for a couple of hours.

"Yeah, Mary," she corrected herself, "Your mom asked me to work the raffle table with Beth. I think it'll be fun."

"So you'll be wearing a cute cowgirl costume?" Ma ordered cowgirl costumes for everyone at Grannie's and had insisted Dad and everyone at SSI wear matching cowboy costumes. My dick jumped at the thought of her in cowboy boots and a short skirt. *I wonder if she'll braid her hair?*

"I will. Your mom said you guys are dressing up, too."

"We are." I rolled my eyes, then laughed. I didn't really mind. Ma hosted the fundraiser near Halloween each year. She loved holiday and said the festive atmosphere put people in a giving mood.

"I guess I'll see you at the fundraiser."

"Yup, unless I need a caffeine fix."

She smiled and opened her door. "Thanks Jack."

As I watched Meg pull away, I thought about how the day had gone. I was happy to hear she was practicing moves from the class, and her shooting skills were improving with each lesson. I almost corrected myself out of habit, but who was I kidding? They were definitely lessons. Meg relaxed more each time we hung out, and I was loving it.

I'd do my best to keep my relationship with her professional, but wasn't sure how successful I would be. Because every time I saw her eyes sparkle when she smiled or laughed, my heart did a little dance.

Chapter 17

Meg

I thought about asking Jack why he seemed so serious when we said goodbye, but I chickened out. I was afraid of upsetting him. When I asked him earlier, he shrugged it off and said it was because of the attack. I guess I could understand that, but something felt different.

I was probably overreacting. *I'm sure he'll be back to normal next time.*

The next day at work, Beth asked me how my range date with Jack went.

"I had fun. Jack said I'm getting better." I didn't want to sound arrogant, so I added, "I don't think I'm very good. And it's not a date," I corrected her, "he's teaching me how to shoot."

"Me thinks the lady doth protest too much." Beth chuckled.

Damn it. I was afraid this would happen. If Beth thinks I have a thing for Jack, then Mary probably does, too. I didn't want things to get weird at work because people were gossiping about me and Jack. He wasn't interested in me, so even if I wanted something to happen, it wouldn't. Jack wouldn't want to be with someone like me. I have too much baggage, too many secrets.

"We're just friends," I said, keeping it simple.

"Alright." She paused, bending down to grab a bag of beans to restock after the morning rush. "Would you say yes if he asked you out?"

Why can't she let this go? Any sane girl would say yes to Jack. He was gorgeous, nice, fun, and protective. But I didn't want to think about it because he was just being nice to me. He said it himself, he'd help anyone who worked for his mom. "He won't. Besides, I'm still settling in and not ready to date yet."

Hopefully, she'd let it go. I really didn't want to think about how perfect Jack was, or all the reasons he shouldn't ask me out, or why I'd have to say no even if he did. I couldn't risk putting him in danger. Luckily, she didn't have a chance to ask any more questions because customers walked in.

Beth came back from her lunch break looking flustered. When I asked her what was wrong, she said her babysitter had canceled.

"It'll be impossible to get a replacement so late. Which means I have to cancel my date." Poor Beth, she didn't go out often.

"That sucks." After thinking about it for a second, I said, "I'd be happy to babysit so you don't have to cancel your date." I didn't have any plans and could use the extra cash.

"Are you sure? I don't want you to change your plans." Her voice was hopeful.

I laughed. "My only plans are reading a book while I eat dinner. It'll be more fun to hang out with Chase."

"Thank you. You're a lifesaver!" She squeezed the air out of my lungs with her hug. "He'll be excited you're filling in. He likes you. None of his other babysitters color with him."

It felt good to help Beth. She'd been so nice to me, and we were becoming friends. In some ways, I could imagine her being the nosy aunt I'd never had. At least that's what I thought it might be like from the books I'd read. I kind of liked it.

Chapter 18

Jack

Monday after work, Jamie, AJ and I took our newest team member, Doug Sharpe, out for a beer to get to know him a little better. We went to our favorite local sports bar and sat at a high top. The rich smell of deep fried food made my stomach growl. The steady hum of background noise filled the room, punctuated by the occasional shouts from fans watching their favorite teams on the big screen TVs. It was the perfect environment for the four of us to relax and to get to know each other.

AJ and I swapped military stories with Doug, while Jamie shared stories about his time with SWAT. It was the natural camaraderie that comes from shared experiences in the trenches. We might have served in different branches, but we all belonged to the same brotherhood.

We ordered a second round of drinks and some appetizers to share.

"Dude, she's totally into you." AJ elbowed me.

"Who?"

"Who?" Doug mimicked. "Our waitress practically threw herself at you." He was a few years older than the rest of us, but it didn't matter, he fit right in. Doug was a communications specialist in the Air Force, and had recently transitioned to civil life. He'd worked as a civilian contractor for Chicago PD before applying to SSI.

"Dude. How did you not notice her?" AJ asked, shaking his head. His eyebrows practically reached his hair line.

I shrugged and took a long pull from my beer. Jamie and AJ had rarely seen me pass up an opportunity to flirt with a pretty server, especially if she was flirting with me.

She returned with our drinks and served me last. "Here you go." She leaned in close, brushing against my arm as she put a fresh beer down and slowly picked up my empty bottle. I gave her a once over as I thanked her. She was pretty. Her long blonde hair was in a bouncy ponytail, and her low cut top showed off her cleavage.

I watched her walk away, glancing down at her long legs, then turned back to the table and picked up a menu.

"So, what do you think?" AJ nudged me after she was out of hearing distance. I could feel the weight of Jamie's stare. I lifted my head and stared back. My lack of reaction didn't amuse him. More accurately, it was the reason I wasn't reacting.

Doug leaned his six foot four frame back, whiskey in hand, as he watched the exchange between me and AJ. His face was a mask except for the hint of amusement in his eyes, suggesting he could tell there was something going on, even if he didn't know what.

In true wingman fashion, AJ was encouraging me to ask her out. I'd do the same for him if the situation was reversed.

"She's pretty." I agreed absentmindedly. My phone buzzed, and I instinctively picked it up. A text from Meg.

I felt them watching me as I read her brief text. When I felt myself grinning at my phone, I neutralized my expression. I didn't want them asking questions. AJ cleared his throat. Jamie frowned. Doug looked at me, then Jamie, picking up on the quick, silent exchange taking place between us. He squinted his eyes and raised his left eyebrow in question. I should be happy Doug is so perceptive. Awareness and good intuition are great qualities for an SSI team member, but once again I was reminded that I didn't enjoy being on the receiving end of it.

AJ was the first to speak. "So, I'm guessing that text is why you have zero interest in the hot blonde throwing herself at you?"

Of course, he called me out. "What? No. Just a friend."

AJ coughed 'bullshit' into his hand. Doug's laugh sounded like a snort. Jamie didn't speak.

I opened my mouth to give him shit, but our server brought our food. After emptying her tray, she gave me a "come up and see me sometime" look and asked if there was anything else I wanted.

"No, thank you." I answered, while avoiding eye contact with the guys. I picked up my beer and turned to Doug.

Needing to change the subject, fast, I asked, "So Doug, you a Cowboy's fan?"

"No." He deadpanned. "But I like their cheerleaders."

"Who doesn't?" AJ added as he raised his beer. We all raised our drinks and toasted.

"I'm a Bears fan. Born and raised in Chicago." Doug added, preventing AJ from waxing poetic about cheerleaders. We all cringed in mock pain. The Bears hadn't had a good season in quite some time.

"Cubs or White Sox?" Jamie asked him.

"Go Cubs Go." Doug sang his answer. We talked more about sports, something else we all had in common.

It was a good night getting to know Doug. We were happy to have him on our team. His tech and communication skills put the rest of us to shame and they'd come in handy as we continued to grow and take on more complex cases.

Chapter 19

Jack

Ma closed Grannie's early so she could set up for the third annual Wyatt Foundation Fundraiser–Halloween Dance, co-hosted by Grannie's and SSI. Mom and Dad had started the foundation after Phil, Beth's husband, died in the line of duty. Its purpose was to help the families of fallen police officers. We'd finished our SSI assignments early, so Ma drafted us to help carry in supplies and hang decorations.

I was carrying in the first of many boxes, listening to AJ carry on about wanting to meet a cute girl at the dance. When I got to the door, I stopped, frozen in my tracks. Meg was dancing with Chase. She wasn't in her costume yet, but Chase was, and he looked adorable as Woody. They were laughing and singing along to The Monster Mash. My heart skipped a beat or two as *mine* raced through my mind. It wasn't like me to be so possessive, but with Meg, it felt different.

Natural. I admired her quiet strength, fierce independence, and determination. I wanted to make her mine. And because she was in danger, the need to protect her consumed me.

"Dude, what's the holdup? Stop blocking the door." AJ nudged me with his foot.

I was frozen in place, my heart pounding against my ribs as I stared. I loved seeing her so relaxed, so happy. *I am so fucked*.

AJ pushed me with his box. "Move it Sheppard."

"Right, sorry." I sucked in some much needed air and shook my head to clear it as I moved into the dining room and looked for a place to set down the box.

Meg glanced up at the commotion and met my gaze. Her lips puckered as she sang along, "Ah ooo."

My palms got sweaty and my heart pounded in my ears. *Think about something else, anything but how kissable Meg's lips are. It's going to be a long day.*

She stopped dancing and sent Chase to help his mom. I smiled as she walked towards me.

"You didn't have to stop on my account." Great, I sounded like a fourteen-year-old in puberty. *Dude! Get it together.* I heard AJ snicker and looked up to see him raise an eyebrow in question. "What the fuck, Sheppard?" was written all over his smirking face.

"Haha, you guys need any help?" Meg asked.

"Nah, let us do the heavy lifting." I glanced over her shoulder at AJ, who was making kissy faces in our direction.

I balanced the box with one arm and flipped AJ the bird. I was going to kill him for this.

"Jackson!" Mom yelled from behind the counter.

"Sorry Ma." I gave Meg a sheepish grin and shrugged as I whispered, "Oops."

I nodded in the direction I was going, hoping she'd walk with me instead of returning to Chase.

"How's your arm?" She asked while we walked.

"It's good." I set the box down and lifted my arm to show her the bandage. "Stitches come out next week."

"Then get back to work. Those boxes won't carry themselves in." Dad wasn't nearly as concerned about my injury as Meg was.

"Yes, sir." I winked at Meg. "Nothing but a pack mule."

Chapter 20

Meg

I glanced in the bathroom mirror one last time before going back to the dining room. I didn't look too silly in my cowgirl costume. The jean skirt hung to my knees, a few inches above the top of my boots. The red and white checked button-up shirt fit tight and was thin enough to see through, so I had a white tank top on underneath. I let the cowboy hat hang on my back.

I couldn't wait to see Jack in his cowboy costume. I wondered if he'd be wearing chaps. A vision of Jack looking sexy as sin dressed as a cowboy, chaps and all, invaded my mind. *Damn it, I have to stop thinking about him. I can't let it happen.* I couldn't risk getting involved with anyone.

I looked around the dining room as I walked to the raffle table I'd be working with Beth. I told myself I wasn't searching for Jack, but I totally was. Grannie's place looked completely different once it was fully decorated and lit up with orange and purple twinkle lights. We'd pushed all the tables together near the walls and set them up to display the raffle items. The center of the room was clear and people were mingling about. There'd be dancing later. From my position at the raffle table, I could see the entire shop. I should feel safe with all the police officers around, not to mention Jack and the other guys from SSI, but I still felt better knowing I could see everything and everyone. I learned a long time ago not to depend on anyone else for my safety.

Mary had transformed the coffee bar into a boozy bar for the night with Jamie, Jack and AJ bartending. She had beer and wine, and soda for kids and adults who wanted alcohol free options. There was regular drip coffee too, but they wouldn't be making any fancy, or "Frou Frou" as Jack called them, drinks tonight.

I watched the room come to life as people arrived, some in costume, others in uniform. Mary and John seemed to know everyone, which shouldn't surprise me since they both grew up here. A sense of nostalgia washed over me. Could a person have nostalgia for something they never had, a loving family and a tightknit community, but always wanted? My head was a mess as I watched a uniformed police officer greet John with a handshake and a pat on the shoulder before giving Mary a big hug.

The coffee shop buzzed with energy.

Beth and I tapped our feet to the eclectic mix of Halloween and country music while we sold raffle tickets. I took advantage of the 5 for $20 raffle ticket deal because someone had donated a SIG p320c and I wanted to win it. It was just like the one Jack let me try, and the one I liked the most. If I won, it'd save me over six hundred dollars! I probably wouldn't. I never won anything. But it was worth the twenty dollars to try, plus the money was going towards a good cause.

I was people watching when I saw Jack standing near the door, talking to a couple. Damn, he looks good in his costume. No, not good. Good wasn't nearly strong enough. Great, amazing. *Sexy*. I felt the heat rise in my cheeks as my gaze wondered from the blue plaid shirt that hugged his muscular back to his rock-hard ass framed by brown leather chaps.

Beth chuckled beside me. "He looks good, doesn't he?"

I felt her watching me as I stared at Jack. I shifted my focus to the table to hide my embarrassment.

"Yeah, he, uh, they all do, especially Chase." I nodded in his direction. "He's adorable in his Woody costume. It's cute how he wanted to match the guys in their cowboy costumes." I didn't think she'd buy it, my lame attempt to change the subject.

"Mmm hmm." Nope, she didn't buy it at all.

She didn't get to say anything else because someone asked to buy some raffle tickets. I turned my attention back to Jack. He used his beer to tip his cowboy hat, a big sexy grin on his face. I forced myself to wave and breathe. I'd intended for it to be a normal full hand wave, but gave him one of those silly finger wiggling waves instead.

A little while later, Jack sauntered over to the raffle table, took off his cowboy hat, and bowed with a theatrical flourish.

"Howdy ladies." He turned to Beth. "Mind if I steal Meg for a dance?" The orange and purple lights hanging over the raffle tables caused the gold specks in his amber eyes to sparkle.

"Not at all," Beth answered before I could say no.

This was bad. I would probably embarrass myself again by tripping over my feet or stepping on his toes.

"Go." She gave me a soft push. "Have some fun."

Jack held out his hand as I stepped around the table. My small hand tingled when he grasped it in his big, strong one.

"I don't know how to do any of these dances." I protested as he led me to the dance floor. People were lining up for a line dance as an upbeat country song started playing.

"It's easy. Follow my lead."

Jack held my hand as he talked me through the steps, only letting go when we had to turn. Despite knowing I shouldn't, I missed his strong, warm hand every time he let go. By the middle of the song, I had learned most of the steps and didn't need Jack to lead anymore. But I'd never admit it because I wanted him to keep holding my hand.

Why are you doing this to yourself? I would never forgive myself if something happened to him because I couldn't keep my distance. He deserved better than to be dragged into my mess. A mess that was getting messier by the minute as my mind and my body argued about what to do.

I laughed as Jack hooked his thumbs in his belt and exaggerated the steps while singing along. I thought about doing it too, but was afraid I'd look like a fool. When he reached for my hand again, I didn't resist. It felt good. I wanted to convince myself he was only being nice; it'd be safer for everyone if it were true, but it was getting harder to do.

I tried to pull my hand free when the song ended so I could return to the raffle table, but Jack didn't let it go. He spun me around and pulled me in. At five-foot-five, my head only reached his chest. He wrapped his right arm around my back and gently held me in place.

"I should get back to the table." I didn't pull my hand away or even lift my head off his chest.

"Beth has it covered. Relax and dance with me. Please."

I looked over at Beth. Part of me wanted it to be true so I could stay in Jack's arms, and part of me wanted Beth to need me so I could avoid being so close to him.

Beth mouthed, "Enjoy," as she lifted her wineglass.

No use fighting it. "Okay, one more."

He pulled me in closer and entwined his fingers with mine as we swayed. I tilted my head so I could see Jack's face. His eyes crinkled at the corners as he flashed me a toothy grin. *He has an amazing smile.* The tension drained from my body as I released a soft sigh.

He brought our joined hands up to his chest, bringing our bodies closer still. I could feel his chest rise and fall with each breath. It felt safe, being this close to him. His muscular arm wrapped around me and his clean pine and leather scent filled my nose. I wondered what his stubble would feel like if I reached up and touched it. *What would it feel like to kiss him?*

No point in lying to myself. I wanted to be here with him. I could hear the rhythmic beat of his heart as I rested my head against his chest. He rested his chin on my head as his chest lifted in a soft sigh. I closed my eyes and released a sigh of my own.

What a mess. I needed to stay away from him. *It's the right thing to do.* But I wanted to relax in the warmth and comfort of his embrace.

But I can't relax. I enjoyed being with Jack, but I couldn't let my guard down, not while Sullivan was still alive.

Yet here I am, standing in the middle of a noisy, crowded room. And I'm not scared or nervous. I feel… safe.

My breath caught in my throat, and my back stiffened. Safe? I pulled back, shocked by the reality. I couldn't remember the last time I felt safe.

Jack squared his shoulders. "Meg, what's wrong?" His voice was thick with concern, his muscles tense as he scanned the room. He looked back at me. "Are you okay?"

My heart skipped a beat. Jack was ready to face whatever, whoever, had scared me. No questions asked. He felt me stiffen, assumed it was from fear, and started searching for the threat. No hesitation.

He was ready to face the threat, to protect me. I could see it in his eyes, feel it in his tense muscles. So different from the other men in my life.

"Nothing. I freaked myself out a bit." My voice sounded shaky, so I smiled up at him to convince him I was okay.

He tilted his head and squinted his eyes. I watched as he scanned the room again. He relaxed when he saw the other men of SSI hanging out and chatting. If there was a threat, they'd all be on high alert.

"What'd you freak yourself out about?" Jack asked as he pulled me closer. He placed my hand on his shoulder and wrapped both his arms around me. I leaned my head against his chest again and listened to his heart as he placed both hands on my lower back. The warmth of his hands through my thin shirt sent shivers up my spine and butterflies dancing in my stomach.

When I didn't answer him, he nudged me. "Meg?"

"It was nothing." I lied. "I thought I saw a ghost." My chuckle sounded forced.

He laid his cheek on top of my head. My heart did a little jig when I felt a soft kiss along on my forehead, right at the edge of my hairline. His stubble felt rough on my skin. *Maybe he does like me.* I released a soft sigh, content in the moment. I was so worried about putting Jack in danger, but what if he could handle it?

Maybe I can do this.

Chapter 21

Jack

Meg didn't move away when I put my hand on her lower back as I walked her back to the raffle table. I swept my hat off my head and gave Beth a deep bow. "Much obliged."

I asked if I could bring them anything, hoping to have an excuse to come back sooner rather than later. Unfortunately, they were fine, so I snaked my way through the crowded room and relieved Jamie at the bar.

"So, not keeping your distance?" Jamie asked, handing me a fresh beer.

Right to the point. If his tone was any indication, I was about to get a talking to.

"It was just a dance. It's not a big deal." My eyes drifted to Meg as I answered him. I didn't want to be standing here talking to Jamie. I wanted to drag Meg somewhere private, pull her head back by her braid and kiss her until her knees went weak. Thinking about it made my blood flow south and my heart race. *Down, boy, it's not happening tonight.*

"Right." Jamie waved AJ over. "Can you man the bar for a bit? I need to talk to Jack."

"Yeah, I got it." AJ raised his eyebrows at me. I could practically hear his thoughts—you're in trouble.

I was. And apparently Jamie didn't think his lecture could wait until the party was over.

"Thanks." Jamie said before leading me to mom's office and shutting the door to give us some privacy. I leaned against the wall and waited for him to speak.

"You're playing with fire." Jamie warned me as he carefully leaned up against Ma's organized desk.

I put my hands in my pockets. "You don't have to worry. It was just a dance." I was trying too hard, so it didn't surprise me when he called me out.

"So you said." Jamie paused. "I saw the look in your eyes when you were dancing with her. And I saw the kiss. From where I was standing, it didn't seem like no big deal." He made air quotes.

Jamie watched me, searching for clues in my expression and body language. One drawback to having a family full of cops. We're all experts at reading people, especially each other, so I knew he could see right through me, despite my efforts to keep my face neutral and my voice even. I gave up the pretense.

"It felt like the natural thing to do." Jamie waited patiently while I took my hat off and ran my fingers through my hair, causing it to stand on end. "I can't explain it."

"Try, because you'll have to explain it to Dad, too." He sounded more compassionate than upset. I hadn't expected him to switch from boss mode to brother mode so quickly. He wasn't technically my boss since we were equal partners, but he was fully vested and I wouldn't be until after the new year.

I was prepared for a lecture. *Defending myself is easier than explaining myself.* I loved working with my family, but sometimes it sucked having them in my business twenty-four-seven. They rarely intervened in my private life, but they were now. Because for the first time, my personal and professional lives were overlapping. I sighed. How could I explain it to him when I wasn't sure I understood?

Maybe I could find the answer if I didn't censor myself. "When I got home from Austin, she surprised me with a hug. She was open and vulnerable for the first time because she was worried about me. I could see it, feel it. And her hug, it felt," I searched for the right word, "it felt right and I didn't want to let go."

"I get it, but are you sure this isn't because you're intrigued? Or because she needs help and you want to protect her?"

"No. I mean, I want to protect her, but that's not it. It's, fuck man, I don't know." Why was this so hard? "I felt something the day we met, but dismissed it as physical attraction. Then, in the self-defense class, her fierceness and determination captivated me. When I heard her ask about shooting lessons, I felt like I had to volunteer. I hadn't expected anything to come of it, but the more time I spend with her, the more I… the more time I want to spend with her."

"Any chance you can pull back, at least for now?" At least he wasn't telling me to back off.

"I don't know. Maybe." I shrugged. I wasn't sure I could. My willpower was non-existent when I was with Meg. "When that guy came at me with the knife, one of my first thoughts was of Meg. I'd completely forgotten it until she hugged me. When we were dancing tonight, I didn't want to stop." My voice was barely above a whisper as I admitted how I felt.

"Listen, I get it, but-"

"Thanks." I cut him off.

He put his hand up. "I'm not the only one who saw you with her on the dance floor. Dad's going to want to talk to you about this later." He paused before adding. "Ma too, though I suspect that'll be a much different conversation." He knew as well as I did that mom 'had a feeling' about me and Meg.

He was right, about all of it. I shook my head and laughed. "Yeah." Ma's reaction would most likely be the exact opposite of Dad's. I'd worry about ma later. It wouldn't be easy, but I had to hold myself back. It was the right thing to do. I could ask her out once we removed the threat.

"I'll talk to Dad. You know I'd never do anything to hurt the company, right?"

"We do, but you're not logical when it comes to Meg."

"Hmph." I wanted to argue, but he was right.

"Does she feel the same way about you?"

"It's hard to tell. She'll start to relax and open up, but then tense up and shut down with one wrong word. I think she likes me, and wants to trust me. But she's scared."

"I assume you haven't told her you're digging into her past." I shook my head back and forth. "You should," Jamie said. "Because she's going to find out eventually, and if it comes from anyone but you, you'll lose any trust you've built."

"I know. I have to figure out how to bring it up. And then convince her I, we, want to help her." I confessed, "It's harder than I thought it would be. Any suggestions?"

"Keep it simple. You tried to find her on social media to friend her. You noticed a few things that worried you, so you did a quick search, thinking she had a stalker or something. It's an edited version of the truth. But you need to tell her now before too much time passes. If you're lucky, she won't be too pissed."

"And if she is? What do I do if she decides she can't trust me?" My voice hitched as I stood up straight. "What do I do then?"

"I don't know. It's a tricky situation. But you're not alone. I may not think it's a good idea for you to date her, at least not until we know more, but I'll support you whatever you decide."

He stepped away from the desk and pulled me into a brotherly hug.

"Thanks man." It felt good knowing I had his support.

"Anytime, little brother, anytime." Jamie patted me on the shoulder as we walked back to the dining room.

Jamie thanked AJ for covering as we stepped back behind the bar. I couldn't stop thinking about what Jamie had said; he made sense, and I knew it. So why hadn't I told her? *Because I'm afraid she'll freak out and stop trusting me.* The smart thing to do would be to keep my distance until I could remove the threat.

AJ stuck around after we relieved him. "Dude, you gonna ask out that Meg chick, cause if you don't, I think I will."

I squared my shoulders as I turned to challenge him, practically growling, I said, "Watch it, Janerek."

AJ flung his hands up in mock surrender. "Damn Sheppard. Relax, I was just giving you shit." I was as surprised by my reaction as he was. I knew he was giving me shit, it's what we do, but I'd totally lost it. Over a joke.

I relaxed my shoulders. "Sorry man, I don't know what's gotten into me."

When Jamie coughed 'bullshit' behind me, I turned and glared at him.

"I might not have my fancy PI license yet, but I have eyes Sheppard, and it's obvious you like her. A lot. So man up and ask her out." AJ's advice was the opposite of Jamie's, and in direct opposition to my father's orders. Because AJ was a friend, not a parent or business partner, and he didn't know how serious Meg's situation was.

AJ took a pull from his beer and tilted his head in Meg's direction. "Before someone else does."

A man I'd never met was flirting with Meg. *Mine.* Neither AJ nor Jamie said anything while I attempted to burn a hole in the back of his head with my eyes. After a second, I took a deep breath and counted to ten. I had no right to claim Meg. Or be jealous because some asshole was hitting on her. I had literally just decided to take things slow.

"Listen, I know you don't want a repeat of what happened with Ana." AJ misunderstood my hesitation, but he knew less about Meg's situation than I did, so I couldn't tell him why I was holding back. "But I'm telling you, Meg's nothing like her. And she's into you. I can see it, hell anyone with eyes can see it." He gestured to Jamie and then the crowd. He grabbed me by the shoulder and turned me to get my full attention. "Ana used you from the beginning, but Meg has never asked you for anything. And Ana never, not once, looked at you the way Meg does."

AJ was right, Meg wasn't manipulative like Ana. She hadn't shared a lot, but she hadn't lied to me either. At least, not that I knew of. She had a good heart, a sweet laugh, and I didn't think she had a malicious bone in her body.

I nodded slowly, then chugged the rest of my beer as I leaned against the back counter to watch Meg. My shoulders relaxed when the guy hitting on her walked away. Meg giggled, sharing a joke with Beth. When she looked up and caught my eye, she flashed me one of those rare bright, shining smiles that reached her eyes. It felt like an arrow struck me smack dab in the middle of my heart.

I tilted my head, touching my empty beer bottle to the rim of my hat, and smiled. I was a picture perfect example of calm, cool, and collected.

I'm totally and completely fucked.

AJ patted me on the shoulder. "I have a feeling she'll be worth the risk." Luckily, Dad saved me from having to answer when he waved AJ over. He was taking advantage of the party to introduce AJ and Doug to friends from the local and county police departments. It never hurt to have friends with badges.

After the party ended, Ma hugged Meg and thanked her for helping. When Meg asked if she should stay and help clean up, Ma told her not to worry about it, "Go home and get some rest. The guys can handle it."

Yup, we were pack mules alright. Not that we minded, we got paid in coffee, the best damn coffee in Texas.

Meg looked tired, but happy, as she walked towards the door. Her bag slung over her shoulder, her work clothes hanging out. I took a minute to appreciate how cute she looked with her skirt swishing around her knees as she walked.

"Meg, wait, I'll walk you to your car." I called out as I jogged towards her. Just because I wasn't sure what my next move would be, didn't mean I couldn't be a gentleman.

"Thanks Jack, but I'm across the street." She pointed to the lot where she had parked. "I'll be fine."

"True, but Ma'd kill me if I didn't make sure you got to your car safely. You don't want to be responsible for my death, do you?" I was laying it on pretty thick, but it made her laugh, and the sound was music to my ears.

"Okay, fine, but only because I don't want you to die." She laughed as she answered. "Though I find it hard to believe your mom is half as violent as you make her out to be."

She didn't think I was serious, but she'd never seen my mom go all drill sergeant crazy on us.

I opened the door and placed a hand on the small of her back. Her skin felt warm under her shirt as I led her out. I probably should have removed my hand once we were outside, but I didn't. She stiffened, but she didn't pull away. After a second, her back muscles relaxed under my hand. I didn't bother hiding my goofy grin as I walked her across the street.

When we reached her car, I reached over her shoulder and put a hand on her door to stop her from opening it. When she turned towards me, fear flashed in her eyes.

"What?" she asked.

It broke my heart to see how skittish she was. It also made me go all primal with the need to beat the men who'd hurt her into bloody pulps.

I gave her a big grin, hoping to put her at ease. Her shy smile was all it took for my heart to overrule my brain. I did what I knew I shouldn't. "So, when are you going to let me take you out on a proper date?"

Her jaw fell open. Time stood still as I stood there holding my breath, waiting for her to answer me.

"A date?"

"Yes. A date. We get dressed up, I pick you up, take you to a nice dinner, we share a bottle of wine. A date." I hadn't intended to ask her out, but since I had, I was going all in. "And maybe if I'm lucky, I'll get a kiss goodnight."

Meg's breath caught in her throat. She licked her lips and whispered, "Um, soon, maybe."

My dick twitched when she bit her lower lip.

I ignored the maybe and stepped back. "Friday?" I didn't trust myself to be so close and not kiss her. God knows I desperately wanted to.

She hesitated and furrowed her brows. "No. I–"

I straightened up and stepped back. "No?" Why did that hurt so much? I studied my boots so she couldn't see my disappointment.

"No, not No like never No." She stumbled over her words in a rush to get them out. "No, as in not Friday. I told Beth I'd watch Chase."

"Oh," was all I could say as relief flooded my senses. I took a deep, calming breath and smiled. She wasn't saying no.

I could hear AJ in my head, "Dude, for fuck's sake, ask her out already." I listened to his advice and asked her out properly.

"Meg, will you go out with me on a proper date next Saturday?"

"Yes." Her voice was barely above a whisper as she stared at my boots. I lifted her chin so I could see her eyes when she answered. "Meg?" I didn't want to question whether she really wanted to go on a date, or if she said yes because she was afraid to say no.

Meg met my eyes. "Yes, I'd like that." Her voice was soft and genuine, her smile reached her eyes.

We stood there for a few seconds, not saying anything. I'm sure we looked like a couple of awkward teenagers on our first date. "I, uh, I should get back and help clean up."

I reached for her door handle, moving close enough to kiss her again. Her cucumber mint shampoo was intoxicating. *You can't kiss her.* But I wanted to more than I wanted my next breath. Meg drew in a ragged breath and I gave up. One hand moved to her waist, as the other moved to her chin. I gently turned her until we were facing each other. I moved slowly, giving her the option to pull away. To say no.

She didn't.

Demonstrating control I didn't know I possessed, I asked, "God, Meg, do you have any idea how badly I want to kiss you right now?"

Her breath caressed my lips as she whispered yes. It was the only permission I needed.

I leaned in.

A horn blared as my lips touched Meg's. She jumped back and whipped her head toward the sound. I dropped my hand from her face.

The moment was gone. Ruined.

Meg was still staring in the direction the horn had come from. "Hey," I turned her face towards me, but her eyes stayed focused on the road. "Meg, are you okay?"

"Yeah, it just scared me a bit." I could see the fear in her eyes when she finally looked at me. "I should probably get going."

I knew I couldn't recover the moment. Which was probably for the best. Meg deserved to be kissed properly and was worth waiting for.

"Alright." I said as I stepped back and let my hand fall from her waist.

Meg opened her mouth and I could tell by her worried expression she was going to apologize. She had a bad habit of apologizing for things that weren't her fault.

I nudged her under the chin. "Hey, no apologies."

I leaned in and gave her a chaste peck on the cheek. "Goodnight." Then I stepped back and opened her door.

"Goodnight." Meg flashed me a smile as she tossed her bags onto the passenger seat.

I held the door open, one hand on the roof. "Text me when you get home." I didn't wait for a reply. I pushed the door closed and waited for the click of her door lock before stepping back.

"Dude, where'd she park, Canada?" AJ called out from his perch on a ladder. I was about to risk my mother's wrath by telling him to fuck off, but he kept talking. "Or did you decide to bail on helping us take down the decorations?" I flipped AJ off before walking over to my mom to ask what she wanted me to do.

She'd probably want to talk before putting me to work, having seen me with Meg. Her mom-intuition was stronger than any cop or investigator's instincts.

"Ma, what do you need me to do?" I asked as crossed the room.

"Where are you taking Meg on your first date?" she answered my question with one of her own.

"I'm not sure yet." I put my arm around her shoulders and laughed. "Any suggestions?"

I knew she'd ask me about Meg, but I hadn't expected her to do it in front of everyone. I might have tried to play it cool or deny it, but it was useless. She didn't need her mad intuition skills when I'd been acting like a lovesick teenager all night.

"I know you'll pick the perfect place." She stood on her toes and gave me a motherly peck.

It felt a little weird having my mom encourage me to date Meg while my dad discouraged me from doing the same. I hoped it wouldn't be an issue. The last thing I wanted was them arguing about it.

She handed me a box. "Go on, help AJ pack up the decorations. We'll talk later."

I made my way to the table AJ was dropping decorations on and started putting them in the box. I intentionally avoided making eye contact with him.

AJ pushed me in the shoulder with his foot. "Can I assume from your stupid grin you grew a pair and asked her out?"

I shook my head in mock exasperation. "Yes. Happy now?"

"Yup." AJ climbed down the ladder and put his hand on my shoulder. "Sorry I brought up Ana. It didn't occur to me Jamie might not know what happened."

"No worries, he knows a little. I was too embarrassed to share the ugly details when it happened, and then it faded as I focused on adjusting to civilian life and working at SSI."

"So I guess this means I need a new wingman." AJ teased me as he closed up a box. "Seriously though, I'm happy for you."

"Thanks."

Chapter 22

Meg

My brain was on overdrive the entire twenty-two minute drive home.

A date. We have a date next Saturday. I couldn't do this. I couldn't date my boss's son. *Oh my god, I can't believe I almost kissed him.* I'd never wanted to kiss anyone as much as I wanted to kiss him. It's a good thing we got interrupted, even if it had scared the hell out of me. He was so close, and he smelled so good, and I couldn't think about anything but his lips. Those stupid lips and his stupid grin. I bet he's a great kisser. *We have a date, and I don't have anything to wear. I need a dress. And shoes, I can't wear sneakers with a dress.*

Was I really going to do this, go on a date with Mary's son? Would she be mad? Should I really be doing this when I know I might have to pack up and run away again? Should I cancel? I should probably cancel.

I didn't cancel. I could have done it at any time in the last week, but I couldn't bring myself to do it. *So here I am, waiting for Jack, who'll be here any minute to pick me up.*

On Monday, Jack had stopped by Grannie's to tell me he'd pick me up at six for our six-thirty reservations at Hank's Steakhouse. He said I should dress in layers because after dinner he was taking me to a concert in the park. It sounded like the perfect first date.

On Tuesday, Mary had told me I won the SIG. I couldn't believe my luck. In my excitement, I hugged Mary. Luckily, she didn't mind and hugged me back. I had texted Jack as soon as I got home to tell him and ask if he wanted to go with me to pick it up on Thursday. I didn't tell him I was nervous about going to the gun store alone.

Jack sent a congratulations gif, and an apology. He couldn't go on Thursday because he'd still be working in Dallas. "I'd love to take you Sunday, unless you can't wait that long." I told him I could wait, I wasn't in a hurry. It was probably obvious I wanted him to go with me. *Why couldn't I tell him the truth, that I'm nervous and want his help?*

Because you don't feel comfortable asking for help. You don't trust people. Because people can't let you down if you do it all yourself. But Jack was different. I trusted Jack to keep his word.

Except for a few text messages while he was on stakeout, we hadn't seen or talked to each other since he told me his plans for our date.

Nothing in my closet was date worthy, so I went shopping at a cute boutique consignment shop I'd found. They had reasonable prices, and a perfect, gorgeous emerald green, knee length dress in my size. My black pumps were new, because I didn't like buying used shoes. The only necklace I owned, a Celtic knot heart pendant with an emerald teardrop dangling at the bottom, accented the dress perfectly. I sent a thank you prayer to my grandmother; it was the last gift she'd given me before she died.

I grabbed a thin black embroidered scarf from my closet, thinking it would be enough if it cooled off. I hung it near the door so I could grab it on my way out.

After several failed attempts at a sophisticated up do, I left my hair down. I rarely had a reason to do anything fancier than a ponytail or a messy bun, so I wasn't very good at doing my hair. My make-up was simple: smokey eyeliner, mascara, and my favorite pink tinted lip gloss.

I jumped when I heard the knock on my door. Five-fifty-four. Of course, he was a few minutes early. I chuckled at the thought, like I knew him so well. "It's Jack." A thousand humming bird wings fluttered in my stomach. I was as nervous as I was excited. I liked him, and he seemed to like me. But I'd been wrong before. Guys acted like they were interested in me, but what they really wanted was a free coffee, to copy my homework, or have a one-night stand.

I'd been a nervous wreck all week, alternating between excitement and fear whenever I thought about tonight. Even as I was shopping for my dress, I thought about canceling. I hemmed and hawed until it was too late. *So here I am.* I smoothed down my dress as I stepped up to my door, wondering if I was making a huge mistake.

I checked the peephole out of habit to verify it was Jack before removing the door stop alarm, unhooking the chain, and unlocking the dead bolt. I pulled the door open halfway, too embarrassed to ask him inside. My rooms were clean, but dingy from years of use and neglect, and in desperate need of an update.

Jack was holding a bouquet of bright daisies, pale yellow roses, and other yellow and orange flowers. The heady fall scent filled my nose as he handed it to me.

"Hi." I choked out as my gaze shifted from the flowers to Jack. He was breath-taking, literally. I couldn't breathe. *He's out of my league. I can't believe he wants to take me out.*

I took a second to appreciate how good he looked. He wore a dark sport coat over a pale mustard button-up shirt, which brought out the gold flecks in his eyes. The top button was unbuttoned, revealing a hint of chest hair. The snug fit of his black pants showed off his muscular thighs. Jack waited until I finished my appraisal and met his eyes before saying, "Hi."

I shifted on my feet as he scanned me from head to toe and back again. "You look amazing."

I clutched the flowers in front of my chest, enjoying the sensation of his gaze tingling across my skin. No one had ever made me feel like that before. "Thank you."

"Should we put those in a vase?" Jack asked.

I brought the bouquet to my nose and inhaled the warm fall scent. "They're beautiful."

"Beautiful flowers for a beautiful lady."

Time ticked by as I stood there, holding the flowers in front of me like a shield, searching my brain for something intelligent to say.

"I assume there's vase is inside." Jack said.

"Right, yes." I snapped out of it and stepped back. I didn't want to invite him in, but I couldn't think of a good reason to say no. At least it was clean. *Thank God it's temporary and I won't have to be embarrassed much longer.*

Jack shut the door behind him and waited. I knew he'd assess my rooms while I pretended to search for a vase. After a few seconds, I put the flowers on the counter. "I'll find a vase later. We don't want to be late." I didn't want to admit I didn't have a one. I could buy one tomorrow or just use glasses.

Jack opened the door and held it for me. "After you."

"Thank you." Jack turned towards the parking lot while I locked the door, almost like he was standing guard.

Jack opened the truck door and steadied me when I struggled to step up. "Have I told you how amazing you look?"

"Thanks," I blushed, "You look great too."

Chapter 23

Jack

"Are you excited about picking up your gun tomorrow?" I asked as I pulled out of the parking lot.

"I am." She paused and looked out the window, then turned back to me. "And a little nervous. Thank you for coming with me."

"Happy to help." I sat up straighter, thrilled she wanted me to go with her. I made a mental note to pack my cleaning kit so I could teach her how to clean her new gun before shooting it. "If you want to take it for a test run, I can stick around."

"That'd be great. Thanks. I know it's the same as the one you let me shoot, but this one will be mine and I'm excited to try it. Is that weird?"

"Not at all. I still get excited when I buy a new gun." I flashed her a quick smile before turning back to the road.

We made small talk the rest of the short drive to the restaurant. Meg told me she was searching for a studio apartment and had found a couple she wanted to check out.

"Good to hear. I can check out the crime history of the areas you're looking, if you'd like." I was glad she was apartment hunting. The extended stay wasn't ideal.

"Thanks. I'll let you know which places I'm interested in."

I told her about my last stake out job. "It's never as glamourous as it appears in movies. We're trapped in a car, sometimes for several days, staring at the same things and eating nothing but take out. At least this time AJ was with me, so it wasn't too bad." A guy had hired us to find out if his wife was cheating. I was happy to report we hadn't found any evidence of her being unfaithful.

I told Meg to wait while I ran around to open her door for her. I wiped my hand on my pants before reaching up to help her. Her small, warm hand fit perfectly in mine; I didn't let go as we walked to the restaurant.

It was upscale but not too formal. I chose it because the dark stained wood panels on the pale green and ivory walls, and soft lighting from simple chandeliers and wall sconces, gave the place a romantic vibe.

Meg's head darted right and left and back again as she took it all in. "This place is amazing."

I wondered if this was her first romantic dinner. It was petty, but I felt honored to be the first. She deserved to be spoiled and if she let me, I'd spoil her every day.

I walked behind Meg as the host showed us to our table. The way her skirt hugged her ass and swished across the back of her knees as she walked was mesmerizing. Her emerald dress fit snug at her breasts and waist, then flared out. It highlighted her soft curves and was the perfect balance of flirty and sexy. The soft lace peeking out at the bottom of her knee length dress matched the lace at the sleeves and neckline, adding to the allure. My pulse quickened as I imagined Meg wearing a lace bra and matching panties underneath. My eyes wandered down her fit legs to her feet. She was wearing black pumps with short, thick heels. I wondered what she'd look like in four inch fuck-me heels? *Think about something else.* I forced my gaze up to her thick straight strawberry blond hair, which flowed like a pink waterfall down her back. All I wanted to do was run my hands through it and pull it until her head tilted back, exposing her neck to me. *I need to rein in my imagination before it runs away with me.*

She didn't hesitate or glance over her shoulder as she sat in the chair I pulled out for her. It was a boost to my ego to realize she finally felt safe with me as I sat across from her, making sure I had a clean line of sight to the door. I expected her to glance over her shoulder, and was surprised when she only did it once or twice before our wine and appetizer arrived. Maybe she finally believed I could, and would, stop any threat.

I couldn't help staring as I appreciated her simple makeup and how it let her natural beauty shine through. *If I'm lucky, I'll get to smudge her shiny pink lip gloss at the end of the night.*

Our conversation flowed easily while we waited for our food. I answered her questions about my older sister, Jamie's twin, Madeleine, and my youngest brother, Jaden, who were both still serving in the military. "Madi's a Navy Corpsman stationed in Louisiana. She's getting her MSN so she can be a nurse practitioner when she retires."

"MSN?"

"Master of Science in Nursing." She nodded her thanks. "Jay's a Marine, stationed in the middle east." As a Marine Raider, he couldn't always tell us exactly where he was or what he was doing.

Meg talked a little about her grandmother, who had helped raise her. She blinked back a tear when she told me her grandmother had died when she was fourteen, but she didn't talk about anyone else in her family. I knew enough to understand why, so I didn't ask. I wanted her to relax and enjoy our date. Meg was sharing a little more each time we got together, and I trusted she'd share more when she was ready.

After the meal, I encouraged Meg to order desert. She said she was too stuffed to eat any more, so I ordered a piece of their famous Death by Chocolate cake and asked the server to pack it up to go with two forks.

"Their cake is to die for. We can enjoy it later."

My insides melted when she laughed at my pun.

We had to park several blocks away from the already crowded area, unfortunately it wasn't well lit. I opened Meg's door and helped her out before grabbing a blanket and a small red cooler from the back seat. When I saw her look around nervously, I reached for her hand and whispered into her ear. "I've got you."

Chapter 24

Meg

Jack slowed down as a group of boisterous teens walked around a corner, heading in our direction. They pushed each other back and forth, hooting and hollering, and throwing pumpkins they most likely stole from a nearby porch. When they noticed us, they crossed the street to have a little fun, cat-calling and whistling.

I clutched Jack's hand, my feet rooted to the sidewalk.

Jack pried my hand out of his and stepped in front of me, putting himself between me and the rowdy teens.

From my position behind him, I could see two of them, clearly the boldest of the bunch, as they separated themselves from the group and aggressively closed the distance. My heart started racing and I couldn't get enough air in my lungs.

"It'll be okay." Jack whispered as put the cooler and blanket on the ground. "Stay behind me." He kept his eyes on the advancing teens as he spoke.

I did my best to calm myself down, but I could feel my heart pounding against my ribs. The metal clasp of my purse dug into my hand as I clutched it in a death grip.

I watched as the teens stopped short in front of Jack, their eyes suddenly bugging out of their heads. I followed their focus and saw Jack's right hand hanging at his side, near his pistol and Private Investigator ID. His jacket had been concealing his pistol until he slid it back.

"Duude, you a cop?" One of them asked, slurring a little as he pointed at Jack's waist.

Jack answered with a question, "Have you boys been drinking?" Jack's deep, authoritative tone caused them to take a step back. I saw the moment they realized they'd picked the wrong guy to fuck with.

"Nah man, we're cool, just having a little fun." They backed away, with their hands up, towards their already fleeing friends.

Jack waited until they were out of sight before turning his attention back to me. "You alright?"

I nodded but couldn't answer. I needed a few minutes to get my heart rate back to normal.

He pulled me into a quick hug, turning us so he could see the direction they'd run. My breathing slowly returned to normal as his strong, warm arms surrounded me like a protective blanket.

Stepping back, I finally answered him. "I'm okay." My nervous energy caused me to babble, "Wow, you sound so different when you're all business." I tried to play it off like they hadn't just scared me half to death. "Is it legal for you to say you're a cop?"

"They made an assumption. I neither confirmed nor denied it." He winked before picking up the cooler and blanket. To say I was grateful the encounter hadn't escalated to violence was an understatement. Groups of teenage boys could easily turn violent, especially when alcohol was involved. It could have been so much worse.

I couldn't hide my shaking hands and Jack noticed. He didn't mention my anxiety, but asked if I wanted to skip the concert.

"Would you mind?" I wiped my sweaty palms on my dress. "I feel so bad."

"I don't mind." He reached for my hand. "Please don't feel bad."

When Jack walked me to my door and asked to use the bathroom, I couldn't say no. I prayed he wouldn't pay too much attention to the stained split pea soup green carpet in my bedroom or the things on my nightstand. *Who am I kidding? Jack is stupidly observant and won't miss any details. I should've put my knife and book in the nightstand drawer.*

Jack didn't stay long. He said he had to go after I pulled back when he tried to kiss me. Not that I didn't want him to. I did, but my nerves got the best of me.

I walked the few feet back to my kitchenette after locking my door, picked up one of my mini bouquets, held it up to my nose and inhaled deeply.

Jack didn't know it, but he'd made my twenty-fourth birthday the best I'd ever had.

Even if the date ended a little crazy, and might be our last one. I took one of the glasses of flowers into the bedroom with me. I wanted to see them first thing when I woke up.

The smell of alcohol and cigarettes on his breath as he hovered over me made me gag. I struggled to pull away, but he pinned me in place with his fat, sweaty body. Drops of sweat fell on my cheek as he lowered his head to bite my neck. I whimpered softly, trying not to cry out in pain. Tears ran down my cheeks, but I wouldn't scream and give him the satisfaction of knowing he was hurting me. I squeezed my eyes and prayed it would be over soon.
   Suddenly I'm being crushed by his excessive weight and struggling to breathe.
   I woke up screaming.

Chapter 25

Jack

I wanted to kiss Meg goodnight without prying eyes, so I asked if I could use her bathroom. Doug had installed cameras on the dash of the beat-up brown sedan parked at the end of the lot. Jamie was reviewing the recorded footage several times a day. I didn't have access to the feed or recordings, and that was okay. Watching her door felt a little too stalker-creepy, and I wasn't that guy. Doug made sure the camera wouldn't have a line of sight into her apartment. The goal was to watch for suspicious activity, not spy on her.

My gut clenched when Meg hesitated before inviting me in. I hoped her hesitation was because she didn't want me to see her bedroom, on the way to her bathroom, not because she didn't want me to come in at all.

I'd scanned Meg's bedroom on my way to the bathroom. I wasn't trying to be nosy, but it was a habit to scan any room I walked into. The baby vomit green carpet was the ugliest I'd ever seen. Ignoring the rest of the cheap decor, I glanced at the nightstand. My chest swelled with pride when I noticed the flashlight and fixed blade knife. *Defensive tools staged throughout her apartment. She won't be an easy target for anyone.*

She also had a book in every room. The one on the nightstand was probably a romance, given the image on the cover. *She really does love to read.*

Meg was arranging the flowers in four tall glasses when I came back from the bathroom. "Note to self: bring flowers in a vase on our next date." I fake whispered as I stepped up to the counter separating the living space from the kitchenette.

She laughed without taking her eyes off the flowers. "I can hear you. And you don't need to bring me a vase. The glasses work fine, besides now I can have the flowers in the living room and the bedroom." Meg stopped fussing with the flowers and looked up. "Wait, you want to go on a second date?"

"Did I give you any reason to think I might not?" I didn't think I had.

"No, but–" Meg lowered her eyes, but not before I saw the uncertainty in them, "I kinda ruined this one."

Without thinking, I walked around the counter and closed the distance between us. I gently grabbed her by the shoulders and turned her so she was facing me. I took the flowers out of her hand and put them on the counter before lifting her chin until she lifted her eyes to meet mine.

"No, you didn't. It's normal to be shaken up after a scary situation." I desperately wanted to kiss away her fear, so I leaned in. I was close enough to feel her soft breath on my lips when she tensed up and pulled away. My hands fell to my sides. *She doesn't want me to kiss her.* That stung. I put my hands in my pockets and stepped back, staring at the floor while I regained my composure and hid my disappointment.

"I should go."

Meg walked me to the door. "Thank you for a great night. I'm sorry I cut it short."

I opened my mouth to tell her to stop apologizing, but knew it was useless. My smile didn't reach my eyes as I answered, "It's okay, we can go another time." Meg was giving me mixed signals, so I wasn't sure if she'd agree to go out with me again, but hoped she would.

I hugged her goodbye and waited until I heard her door lock click before walking to my truck.

I was halfway home before I realized we hadn't set a time for our range date on Sunday, so I called her. I hadn't expected her to answer, but was grateful when she did. Maybe it meant I still had a chance.

"Hey. I know I just left, but we didn't plan a time for our range date."

"Oh yeah, sorry."

I was tired of hearing her apologize for things that weren't her fault. I thought about saying something but didn't bother. She was already carrying more than enough guilt, and I didn't need to make it worse. "No worries, I forgot too." I paused before asking, "So, what time should I pick you up?"

"I don't have any plans, so whenever you want."

I ignored the lack of enthusiasm in her voice; it'd been a long night. "Let's get an early start, then grab lunch after. How about I pick you up at nine?"

"Sounds good." She paused. "Thanks for going with me."

"You're welcome. Goodnight Meg."

"Goodnight."

I didn't like how the night ended. It wasn't her fault. And it wasn't my fault. Fucking kids. I told myself she'd feel better after a good night's sleep. And started thinking of ways I could make tomorrow special for her.

Chapter 26

Meg

Between the nightmares and my excitement, I couldn't sleep. I was excited about picking up my gun but wasn't sure what to expect from Jack after disappointing him last night. With plenty of time before Jack picked me up; I scrambled some eggs and sprinkled them with grated cheese. After eating, I washed the dishes, then moved my flowers, taking time to enjoy each mini bouquet. A reminder of the good part of our date.

Before my anxiety could take over, I picked up my book. Reading was better than staring at the clock. *I still can't believe I'm picking up a gun, my gun, today.* After a few chapters, I heard a knock. Using Jack's business card, I marked my place and set the book aside before walking to the door. I peeked through the peephole as he called out, "It's Jack."

"Just a second." I removed the door alarm, undid the chain, and unlocked the dead bolt so I could open the door. I started rambling before he closed the door. "Thanks for picking me up. Sorry again about last night. Let me grab my bag. Is it okay if my stuff is in a girlie tote bag? I mean, it's only my hat, eye and ear pro right now, but after today I'll have a gun too. Can I put a gun in a flowery tote? Will the gun feel weird? Like your guns are probably happy in your serious black tactical bag but-" I cut myself off as Jack walked towards me. I was a little nervous before he got here, but not crazy, rambling nervous. But now that he was here, it felt so real. I'd own a gun after today. *How crazy is it that two months ago I'd never even shot a gun and after today I'll own one?*

I swallowed my excitement, knowing I couldn't forget the reason I needed a gun, Patrick Sullivan.

Jack closed the distance between us and pulled me into a loose hug. "You're adorable. I don't think it'll care what bag it's in, but we can always ask it." His grin did funny things to my insides.

Shaking off my thoughts of Sullivan, I admitted, "I'm a little nervous. Is that weird?"

"No, it's pretty normal. Come on, let's go." He grabbed my bag and carried it to his truck while I double checked my locks.

"I forgot to tell you last night. I like your door stop alarm." He nodded at my door.

Of course, he noticed it. "Thanks. A girl can never be too careful. This place isn't the worst, but it is a little shady."

"A little shady? It's shady as fuck, Meg. Shady A.F." He opened my door and helped me climb in.

"Is that your professional opinion?" I tried not to sound too serious, but the crack in my voice let me know I'd failed. Was the motel worse than I thought?

"Yes." He said, his tone less relaxed. "I'll feel better when you live somewhere safer."

"Me too." I took a chance and opened up a little more. "I started looking for a furnished studio. There aren't a lot of options here, so I need to expand my search towards Fort Worth. I don't think many people like to move this close to the holidays, so I may have to stay here a while longer."

"Let me know if you need any help."

"Thanks. Another option to make it affordable is to find a roommate."

Jack's hands clenched the steering wheel. Was he mad I was thinking about finding a roommate? That didn't make any sense. It didn't matter. I could never move in with someone I didn't know, therefore didn't trust. Hell, I barely trusted the people I knew. "But I'm not sure I could. You know? Move in with a total stranger."

Jack's hands relaxed and he let out a breath before replying, "Yeah, I get that."

When we got to the range, Jack hopped out and grabbed his range bag and a long black case before walking around to open my door. I hadn't waited, so he opened the back door and grabbed my tote bag instead.

"That's a mighty big pistol you got there," I said, staring at his big black bag.

He grinned. "It's a rifle. I need to zero my new scope."

"Right, of course, zero your scope." I had no idea what he was talking about.

"I'd be happy to explain what it means during lunch." Jack grinned and winked.

It took about thirty minutes for me to get through the process of picking up my gun. Jack dropped his bag off in a classroom and came back just as Grant wished me a happy belated birthday. I thanked Grant and prayed Jack hadn't heard him. He didn't say anything while we walked back to the classroom, so I assumed he hadn't. Relief washed over me—I didn't want him making a big deal out of it.

Jack took my gun apart for me, explaining each step along the way. Thinking there'd be a million pieces; it shocked me how easy it looked. Then he put it back together and told me to try. I failed. It wasn't nearly as easy as he made it seem. With a lot of help from Jack, I finally did it.

This time, Jack had reserved side-by-side lanes instead of the quieter, private training lane we'd used before. He told me he wanted me to get comfortable shooting with normal range noise, plus I could shoot without him hovering over me. He said it like it was a bad thing; him being right next to me. It wasn't, especially since I wasn't sure I was ready to do it alone, but he assured me he was right next door if I needed him. He asked me if I had any questions before leaving me alone.

I can do this. I have to, if I'm going to use a gun to protect myself.

Chapter 27

Jack

Meg took her time, her shooting rhythm slow and controlled. I listened to her shot cadence and did a mental clap when I heard the smooth rhythm of a controlled pair with a well-manipulated trigger reset. Glancing at her target, I could see she was still dropping her shots low left. I made a mental note to help her correct it later.

I shot a couple of mags through my back up ankle gun, to remind myself what it felt like, before switching over to my Glock 19 and practicing head shots on a hostage target.

I peeked around the lane divider in between mags to check on her, grateful she was focused on practicing and didn't notice me.

After thirty minutes, I uncased my rifle so I could zero my new scope, a tedious but necessary task.

After a stretch of silence from Meg's lane, I stepped back, intending to lean over and check on her, and almost bumped into her. This time, I was the one too focused to notice her standing at the divider, watching me shoot.

"All done?" I asked.

"Yup, out of ammo." She reached over and grabbed one of her targets. "What do you think?"

"Looks good." I said, glad she was smiling. She'd seemed nervous when I picked her up, but I hadn't been sure if it was because she was getting her first gun today, or about seeing me after last night. I didn't want to think it was because of me. "You want more ammo? I've got plenty."

"No, I'm good. Thanks."

"Alright, give me a few minutes to finish up and we can go grab lunch."

"Okay. Does it bother you if I'm watching?" she asked.

"Nope, I didn't even know you were there." I turned back to the bench and finished my mag. I placed the rifle on the bench and turned to Meg.

"You want to try it?"

"Um, I don't know. It seems complex."

"Nah, it's just like your pistol." Her eyebrows shot up in disbelief. I winked. "Like a big pistol. It's easy, I did all the hard work already. All you need to do is point and shoot."

Meg hesitated. "Maybe next time." She stepped back and watched as I cleared the rifle before packing it up. *Next time.* I liked the sound of that.

"You make it all look so easy," she said after we left the range and took off our ear pro.

"I've been doing this a long time, and had lots of training and practice, but I was a beginner once, too."

When we were all done, I suggested a nearby pub instead of our usual café for lunch and was happy she agreed. I was hungry for more than a pastry and a coffee, and since I was going to pay, I didn't have to worry about stressing her budget.

I ordered a bacon cheeseburger and a beer and Meg ordered a Cobb salad and water. I almost teased her about ordering rabbit food but decided against it, figuring she'd feel self conscious. Walking on eggshells sucked, but after last night, I was worried she'd pull away instead of opening up more.

Meg told me she loved her SIG and asked me what zeroing meant. I explained the process as simply as I could.

"Make sense?" I chuckled at her cute scrunched-up concentration face.

"I, uh, I think so, maybe." She laughed and shook her head. "No, not really."

Our server arrived with our food and we both dove in. I laughed at myself for thinking her salad would be rabbit food. They loaded it with chicken, bacon, hard-boiled eggs, cheese, and avocado. I was almost jealous.

When I asked Meg if she planned to carry her gun or use it for home defense, she said she didn't think she was ready. "I don't have nearly enough training or practice yet."

"I'm happy to help. I can teach you how to draw from a holster too. Piece of cake."

"Right, easy for you to say. And how many you're-training-me-but-its-not-a-lesson lessons will it take?"

"Funny." I sipped my beer to buy myself a second. *We're dating, so I didn't have to pretend anymore.* She might want to pay me, but I wouldn't let happen. "You can call them whatever you want. They're all free. A perk of dating me." I winked and flashed her a playful grin. I took another sip of my beer and hoped she wouldn't tell me we weren't dating.

"Another perk." I waved our server over and handed him my credit card before Meg could protest. "Lunch is on me."

"So now I can't even repay you by buying you lunch?" Her voice held a hint of annoyance.

"Meg, I've told you, you don't have to pay me. I enjoy our range dates. But if it makes you feel better, I'll let you buy me a coffee next time."

She fiddled with her fork. I had a feeling she wanted to say something but was holding back. "Meg, what is it?"

She wouldn't meet my eyes. "Nothing."

"It's not nothing." I reach across the table and held her hand. "Please?"

"I wasn't sure you'd want to see me again, or help me anymore, after I ruined our date." My jaw clenched as I watched her blink a few times quickly.

Dammit, she has nothing to feel guilty about. "Meg, you didn't ruin anything." I squeezed her hand, hoping to re-assure her.

Chapter 28

Meg

I replayed the day in my mind as Jack drove us back to my apartment. He'd been helpful, but not overbearing. He let me shoot alone, trusting I could do it safely, but stayed close in case I had questions. Then he bought me a lunch to celebrate. It was the perfect day. And he said we're dating. *But what if Sullivan finds me and I have to run away again? What if I get too comfortable and let my guard down? What if Jack realizes I'm not worthy of him?*

When Jack dropped me off, I invited him in. It was the least I could do. We sat on the couch and talked about movies and books. I intentionally sat on the opposite end, leaving plenty of space between us. He didn't move closer, but he turned so he was facing me. After a while, we started talking about college. He'd taken virtual classes, earning his BS in Criminal Justice from Texas State. I told him I'd attended a community college in southern Indiana, then slipped up and told him I had almost enough credits for my associate's degree, but had to move before finishing. *Shit, I shouldn't have said that. What if he wants to know why? This is why it's dangerous for me to get too comfortable.*

"What was your major?" Jack asked when I didn't volunteer more.

"Business Management." I thought that'd sound boring to someone who saves people for a living, but he said, "That's cool."

"Yeah? Thanks." I glanced down to hide my embarrassment and didn't remind him I hadn't earned my degree.

He reached over and lifted my chin. "You keep surprising me, Meg." My cheeks got warm as he held my gaze. Jack leaned forward a few inches, never breaking eye contact, like he wanted to kiss me. My heart thumped in anticipation. *I can't.* I broke eye contact and turned away. "I, um, Thanks." Jack leaned back and sighed. *I hate myself right now.* He wanted to kiss me. I wanted him to kiss me. *But it can only end badly.*

"I should get going." Jack stood up and reached a hand out to me to help me stand.

"Okay. Thanks for helping me today, and for lunch." I wanted him to stay but couldn't ask him to. Nor could I blame him for wanting to leave. I'd ruined today just like I ruined our date last night, all because I was afraid to let him kiss me.

"Anytime." His smile didn't reach his eyes. He probably won't want to see me anymore. *I should feel relieved, so why don't I?*

Chapter 29

Meg

I had Monday off, so I went to Fort Worth to search for apartments, hoping to find a furnished one I could rent since I didn't have money to buy furniture. My phone chimed as I was shutting down the library computer.

Hey Meg, You busy tonight?

I hesitated, trying to think of why he'd want to know.

No.

Want some company?

I wasn't sure what to do. I wanted to see him, but didn't think it was a good idea.

Sure. Is everything okay?

> Yup, just want to stop by and say hi.

> Does 6 work? I'll bring pizza.

> 6 is good. You don't have to bring anything.

> Extra cheese, right?

I laughed. I didn't know why I bothered trying to stop him. He never listened.

Jack knocked on my door at five fifty-seven. "It's Jack." He was always a few minutes early, and he always announced himself. I knew I could count on it and would probably assume he was standing me up if he was ever late.

All thoughts drained from my mind when I opened the door. Jack had a backpack slung over his shoulder, a large gift bag in one hand, and a pizza box, with a gorgeous flower bouquet on top, in the other.

"What is all that?"

"Heavy, can I come in?" His devilish grin made my heart skip a beat.

"Right, of course, sorry." I stepped back, opening the door wider so he could fit through. "You didn't have to bring food. I could've made you something."

"I know, but it wouldn't have been very gentlemanly of me to invite myself over and then expect you to cook." He winked.

That wink. It was silly of me to think I was special. He probably winked at everyone.

"Table or living room?" Jack asked as he put the bag down and locked my door. He inhaled. "Mmm. Smells good in here."

"I'm baking cookies. The table. I'll grab plates. Sorry I don't have any beer or wine or, well, anything except coffee or water."

"No worries, I brought both. Do you have wine glasses?"

"No, sorry." I checked the cupboard. "I don't actually have any clean glasses. They're currently full of flowers." I laughed to cover up my embarrassment. "We can use coffee mugs, or I could wash some glasses." I smiled at the mini bouquet I'd placed on the counter.

"Mugs work. I'm not picky."

"Cool." I passed plates and empty mugs over the counter separating my kitchen from the dining area and living room. I filled two more mugs with water from the pitcher in the refrigerator and carried them in.

I almost dropped the cups of water when I saw the pink and white carnations in a gorgeous crystal vase sitting in the middle of the table with a colorful Happy Birthday balloon sticking out the top.

"Jack?" I couldn't move my legs as a million questions raced through my mind. *How did he sneak in a vase? How'd he set it up so quickly? And without me seeing? How did he know it was my birthday? When did he go shopping for flowers?*

Jack stood there and waited for me to take it all in. A smug expression plastered on his face.

"How?" was all I could ask as I shook my head.

"I overheard Grant wish you a happy belated birthday, so I did some sleuthing to find the date."

"Sleuthing?" I said it as a joke, but must have sounded worried. I saw concern flash across Jack's face before he chuckled and said, "Not exactly sleuthing, I asked my mom." He took the mugs from my hands. "Happy Birthday."

"Thank you," I whispered. Overcome with emotion, I blinked back tears before they could spill over. "This is so sweet. But you didn't have to get me anything."

"I know I didn't have to. I wanted to. Why didn't you tell me on Saturday it was your birthday?" He was standing in front of me again. I craned my neck to look up at him as he brushed a few strands of hair off my face and tucked them behind my ear.

"That would have been weird. 'Hey, I know it's our first date and all, but it's my birthday.' I didn't want to make it weird."

He pulled me into a hug, laughing. "When you put it that way." He pulled back a little and gave me a quick peck on the forehead. "Let's eat before it gets cold."

He was so sweet. And gorgeous. His dark gray polo showed off his muscular chest and arms. And he smelled good, clean with hints of pine and leather. He wasn't making it easy for me to keep my distance.

He helped me clear the table before refilling my wine mug and grabbing himself another beer, and walking to the couch.

"Come here, sit. I have one more surprise for you." I opened my mouth to protest, but he cut me off. "Nope, don't say it. Sit down, accept your birthday gift, and say thank you."

He held his hands in front of him, as if praying, before adding, "Please."

There was no point in arguing, so I nodded and sat down. It felt weird having someone spoil me. I kind of liked it, and that scared me. *Don't get used to it.*

Jack handed me a gift bag. "Sorry it's not wrapped better."

"Seriously?" I laughed at him. "You brought me dinner, wine, flowers, and a gift, and you're apologizing for not wrapping it better?"

Jack shrugged. He sipped his beer as he watched me open my present. I stared down in confusion at the pink and purple camo fabric, my brain trying to figure out what I was looking at. I pulled it out and shrieked as I recognized the shape.

"Oh my god, you bought me a pink and purple camo range bag. I love it!" I leaned over and gave him a quick hug, in case my words hadn't properly expressed my gratitude. "Thank you, Jack. It's perfect." It was smaller than Jack's but big enough to hold my gun and gear. Lifting it up to examine it, I said, "It's heavier than I expected."

He nodded towards the bag. "Look inside."

I did; inside was a cleaning kit, two extra magazines, and a box of ammo. And a book. *I can't believe he bought me a book too.*

"Thank you." I looked down to hide my tears, even though they were happy ones. Crying over happy stuff pissed me off. It was stupid. "You're so sweet. This is one of the most thoughtful gift I've ever received." I put the range bag to the side and hugged him. I felt a tear slide down my cheek as I pulled away and tried to wipe it away without Jack noticing. Of course I failed. *Seriously, he notices everything.*

He didn't need to know I hadn't received a birthday gift since my grandmother died nine years ago.

He reached over and gently wiped away a second wayward tear before pulling me close and wrapping his arms around me. I sighed when he kissed the top of my head. "Tell me about the most thoughtful."

After a short pause, I said, "My grandmother gave me this," I lifted the Celtic knot heart pendant I wore on our first date, "For my fourteenth birthday, she said it matc- she wanted me to remember her when I wore it." I paused, remembering how my world fell apart the day she died. She'd practically raised me and while I didn't know it then, she'd also been protecting me. "I think she knew she was dying. She passed a few months later."

"I'm so sorry." He caressed my back.

"Thank you." I didn't want to talk about it anymore, so I changed the subject. "When did you have time to do all this? Didn't you work in Dallas today?"

"I did." I felt his shoulders lift. "And while I was there, I did a little shopping."

"Thank you, but you really shouldn-"

Jack put a finger over my lips. "I wanted to."

Jack told me stories about his mom while we relaxed on the couch.

"Haha, you act like your mom's a crazy woman, but she's been nothing but kind and generous to me. I don't think she'd ever be mean to anyone."

"Because you've never been on the receiving end of a verbal smack down by Mary Sheppard," he pointed at his chest, "but I have."

"You probably deserved it." I laughed.

Jack feigned offense. "I never!"

I crossed my arms and raised my left eyebrow. "Never?"

"Well, maybe once or twice." He grinned.

I peeked over his shoulders at the flowers sitting on my table. "Thanks for making my birthday so special."

"You're welcome. Let me know if you'd rather have the bag in another color. I'll exchange it."

"Oh no, I love it. It's perfect. Soooo, what did you do to deserve a, what did you call it, a verbal smack down from your mom?"

"I don't always like to play by the rules," Jack said, as if it explained everything.

I raised my eyebrows and lifted my hands. "And?"

He explained that when they were growing up, Jamie and Madi were the good kids (well behaved, good grades, color inside the lines type of kids); he was the rule breaker (easily bored, always questioning things, a color outside the lines type of kid); and Jaden, their youngest brother, was the rebel (breaking the rules to see if he could get away with it, a draw on the walls kind of kid).

"Wow, you really like the coloring metaphor." I laughed as he shrugged.

"It fits."

"So, being a PI is perfect for you. I'm guessing it's never boring."

"It can be but it allows me to use my natural sense of curiosity and need to question things… for instance, why would someone," he gently lifted my chin so we were staring into each other's eyes, "with gorgeous green eyes cover them up with brown contacts?"

I tried to pull away, but he held me firmly in place. He brought his other hand around and lifted my pendant. "Your grandmother chose it because it matches your eyes. That's what you started to say, isn't it?"

"How do you-? When did-" My heart was about to beat out of my chest. *HOW?*

"Your contact shifted while you were rubbing your eyes and I saw a flash of green. I half doubted what I'd seen until you mentioned, or rather didn't mention, what your grandmother said."

This was a conversation I didn't want to have. I couldn't talk about my contacts or why I wore them. "Oh." I tried to get up, but Jack held me firmly, but gently, so I couldn't run or hide. I tried changing the subject. "You don't miss much, do you? You learn that in PI school?"

"Oh, no you don't. I'm not letting you change the subject."

I inhaled and counted to five. How could I explain why I wear colored contacts without revealing my secret?

"Fine," I huffed out, "I got annoyed with everyone noticing my eyes aren't the same and teasing me about it. So I got colored contacts and now it's not an issue." I sounded more defensive than I intended, but damn him for ruining an otherwise perfect day with his questions.

"Will you take them out, your contacts, not your eyes," He grinned. "So I can see them?" Jack asked softly. "Please."

Jack always seemed to sense when I was uncomfortable, and used humor to lighten the mood. He couldn't know how close I was to freaking out right now. At least I hoped he didn't.

None of this made sense. Why was he so interested in me? Was it because I didn't tell him anything? He was smart, kind, and understanding. He could have any woman he wanted, so I couldn't imagine what he saw in me. *My life is a mess.* A big, ugly, dangerous mess.

"Okay." I whispered after a moment's hesitation. He'd been so nice to me I didn't think I could say no. A small part of me didn't want to.

Chapter 30

Jack

I sat, tapping my feet, impatient to see what she was hiding behind those brown contacts. Her eyes were expressive even with the contacts, so I could only imagine what it'd be like when she removed the curtains to the windows of her soul.

I didn't have to wait long before Meg came out and sat down beside me. When she lifted her gaze to meet mine, my heart stopped dead in its tracks.

It wasn't the color; they were a gorgeous shade of emerald green, or because they didn't match; and one had specks of pale blue. It was the raw vulnerability.

Meg sat at the edge of the couch, clasping her hands together. It didn't take a professional to see how scared she was to be exposing herself. I understood why she hid her eyes; they stood out, making it much harder for her to hide.

She might be on the fence about dating me, but she'd shown me a level of trust beyond measure. It was humbling. I vowed then and there I'd protect her regardless of what happened between us.

I sucked in an exaggerated deep breath. "Jesus, no wonder you hide your eyes. They're lethal weapons."

"At least it's original." Her fake laugh was like nails on a chalkboard. *Dammit, I want her real laugh back.*

"What is?"

"Your reaction. Most people see them and make fun of me."

I couldn't imagine anyone doing that, but then I remembered. *That's not the real reason.* "They're not that bad. Sure, one has some blue spots the other one doesn't, but they're not completely different colors. I like them, they're gorgeous."

"Thank you." Her cheeks turned the cutest shade of pink. *I wonder if she flushes like that during sex.* I mentally slapped myself to bring myself back to the conversation.

"Are they corrective?" I wanted to know if she'd be willing to take them out when we were alone, because now that I'd seen her without her contacts, I never wanted to see them again.

"No, just a shield against getting noticed." She shrugged, clearly uncomfortable again.

"Your eyes are stunning. Would you mind if I asked you to take them out once in a while?" She flinched, so I quickly said, "Only when we're alone?" I wanted to hear her laugh, or at the very least see her smile, so I added, "The contacts, not your eyes." It was cheesy, but it worked.

"Maybe." Her shy smile was hard to read. I wasn't sure if she was teasing me or not, but considered it a win either way.

I thought I was getting better at reading her, but she was all over the place lately, flirting one moment and backing off the next. She challenged my PI skills and my confidence in them. "Thank you."

I wanted to kiss her, but was worried she'd pull away again and I didn't want to lose the progress I'd made tonight. I could be patient for a little while longer.

"It's getting late. I should go." I said. "Can I see you Wednesday night?"

"Um, okay. Yes."

"I'll pick you up after work. Dinner at my place, I'll cook."

"What about Jamie?"

"He's out of town until Friday."

Her shoulders relaxed in relief. "Do you guys ever work from your office?"

"Dad's the only one who spends any real time in the office. The rest of us are out doing the real work." I laughed. "Don't tell him I said that."

"I promise." She crossed her heart, laughing and shaking her head. "I almost forgot. Wait here." She came back with a large, colorful tin. "I made you cookies."

The tin was still warm, beckoning me to open it and try one. I licked my lips as I took one out. "These smell delicious." I popped the peanut butter chocolate chip cookie in my mouth. "Mmm, thanks," I mumbled around a mouth full of gooey goodness. I closed the tin and put it in my backpack. The cookies were good, but it was her proud smile that filled me with warmth. "Happy Birthday Meg." I wanted a proper goodbye kiss, but chose the safer option of a hug and a kiss on the forehead.

She squeezed me back before stepping back and making eye contact. "Thank you, Jack, for everything."

I waited until I heard her lock click before going to my truck. I had thought there might not be an us, but after today, hope bloomed again. *And I only have three days to think of a way to break through her shell.*

Chapter 31

Meg

"How do you like your steak?" Jack asked from the patio, where he was manning the grill. I was in the kitchen staring at his faded jeans, admiring how they showed off his ass and thighs, instead of making the salad. It'd been a few days since I let Jack see me without my contacts. I trusted him and when he asked me if I'd take them out for our dinner date today, I agreed. But I had them in my purse in case we went out.

"Medium-well."

Jack clear his throat theatrically. When I looked up, he pointed the tongs at me. "That is an insult to these here fine steaks. Most I can cook these bad boys is medium."

I laughed at his exaggerated drawl. "Why'd you ask if I don't have a choice?"

"Because I hadn't expected you to use such foul language." He shook his head. "Medium well."

"Wow. Foul language? Insulting the steak? Don't you think you're taking this a tad too serious?" I walked to the screen door, so we didn't have to keep yelling at each other.

His drawl was even more pronounced as he said, "No ma'am, here in the great state of Texas there is no such thing as being too serious when talking about steak."

I walked outside and put the salad on the table before standing next to him. "Well, okay then, medium it is." My best attempt to mimic his drawl was mediocre, at best. "I wouldn't want to insult the steaks," I pointed to the grill, "or the great state of Texas." I swept my arms wide.

"Good girl." He nodded.

"Should I apologize to the steaks?" I tried to sound serious, I really did, but I busted out laughing instead. "And the great state of Texas."

I'd almost said no when Jack asked me over for dinner. I was still worried about putting him in danger if Sullivan came for me, but I didn't want to seem ungrateful after all he'd done. Standing on his patio, cooking together and joking around, I realized I was glad I'd said yes.

Jack squinted his eyes at me. I had a moment of panic before he wiggled his eyebrows. "Not necessary." He snapped the tongs at me before turning back to the sizzling steaks.

"So, Mr. I-Take-My-Steaks-Far-Too-Seriously, how do you cook yours?"

"Medium rare. Of course." He tested the doneness by tapping them with the tongs.

"Of course." I mumbled under my breath and rolled my eyes.

"Hand me a plate, please." He plated the steaks and the foil wrapped potatoes before turning off the grill. He served me, then sat across from me.

"So, have you always eaten your steaks overcooked?"

"I don't eat steak very often." I didn't want to ruin the evening by talking about my lack of money and/or my mother's lack of cooking skills.

"Well, prepare yourself for a culinary delight." Jack winked.

I used to think winks were silly or cheesy, but when Jack winked, I felt all gooey inside.

I cut a small bite and raised my fork. "I can't eat with you staring at me."

"Sorry. I want to see your reaction when you take the first bite of the best steak you've ever eaten."

"Fine." I pulled the bite off my fork and chewed thoughtfully.

I thought about shrugging and saying it was okay, but I couldn't hold back the happy yummy sounds as I chewed. It really was the best steak I'd ever had.

"That good, huh?" Jack smiled and shifted in his chair.

"Yes." No point in trying to lie. "It's delicious."

Jack laughed when I apologized to my steak.

We talked while we ate, keeping the conversation light. Jack didn't ask me about my family, which was good. I trusted him, but still wasn't ready to open that can of worms yet. I worried he'd bolt if I told him about my family, my past.

Jack refilled our wineglasses, careful to only pour me a half serving, before collecting the dirty dishes and taking them into the kitchen. He refused to let me help. "This is a date. I can't let you do all the work."

"You haven't let me do any of the work." I wasn't sure how I felt about him calling this a date. *I have to make up my stupid mind.* Did I want to date him or not? I couldn't keep going back and forth. It wasn't fair to Jack.

I gave up when Jack said, "Wrong, I let you make the salad, and that's all I'm letting you do."

The weather was perfect, so we sat on the patio chatting and sipping wine after dinner. As the sun set, Jack listed some movies for me to choose from: "John Wick, Ever After, The-"

I cut him off. "You have Ever After?"

"I do now." He grinned. "You mentioned it's one of your favorites, and I figured I should probably have something to watch that isn't an action flick."

"Thanks." I gave him my biggest, toothiest smile. I wasn't used to this. "He's too good to be true." *Shit. Did I say that out loud?*

"I'm not. I assure you I have my share of flaws. Ask anyone."

Yup, I most certainly did, and now I wanted to die. I picked up my wineglass and studied the contents.

"I'm guessing you've dated a few jerks who didn't do nice things for you."

"You could say that." I continued to stare at my wine. I hadn't dated many guys. Not that it mattered; I wasn't thinking about them.

"Come on, let's go watch Prince Charming save Cinderella." Jack stood up and offered me a hand.

"Cinderella saves herself in this one." I whispered, my voice as distant as my thoughts. I blinked twice, turning my attention back to Jack. "It's one reason I love it so much."

"Tell me Prince Charming at least helps?"

"You'll see."

Jack laughed out loud near the end when the prince arrived too late to save Cinderella. "You didn't lie. Cinderella saved herself."

"What'd you think?" I asked, as the credits rolled.

"Definitely not your typical fairy tale. I can see why you like it though, Cinderella's a badass in this version."

Which was exactly why I loved it. "I'm glad you liked it."

It was still early, so Jack suggested we watch another movie. I let him pick, and wasn't surprised he chose an action flick.

I screamed myself awake, the terror from my nightmare clinging to me.

Where the fuck am I? Panic filled every cell in my body. My heart raced in my chest. When I heard my name, I just about jumped out of my skin.

It took my fear-addled brain a second to recognize Jack's voice. "Meg, what's wrong?" Jack kneeled in front of me. The ambient light from the TV allowed me to see the worry in his eyes.

I exhaled sharply. "Jack?"

"I'm here." He was rubbing my arms and shoulders. "Are you okay?"

"Yeah, I had a nightmare. I didn't know where I was when I woke up. Sorry if I freaked you out."

Jack sat on the couch, wrapped his arms around me, and held me close. "It's okay. You're okay. You fell asleep watching the movie." He lifted my chin and looked into my eyes. "Do you want to talk about it?"

"No, not right now, but thanks. I think I'll, um, go get some water." Jack's intense scrutiny was a little too much to handle while I was still upset. He was only trying to help, but I couldn't talk about it.

"You stay here. I'll get it for you."

"Are you sure?"

He stood up. "I'm sure."

I looked at the clock: twelve-thirty. *How long was I asleep?* The last thing I remembered was the opening credits.

I got up and walked to the bathroom so I could splash cold water on my face and wash away the memories clinging to the edges of my mind.

Will I ever be free from him? I stared in the mirror. After a few seconds, I reminded myself, *Jack's waiting for you.* I patted my face dry and went back to the living room.

He handed me a glass of water after I sat back down. "Will you tell me about your nightmare? It might help to get it out in the open, take away its power."

"It was nothing. Just my over-active imagination." I could tell he didn't believe me and was grateful he didn't push it. I stared into my glass, wishing I could drown my embarrassment at the bottom.

After a few seconds of awkward silence, Jack asked me if I wanted him to take me home.

"Do you mind? I feel bad that I keep ruining our dates." I blinked back my tears, but couldn't prevent my voice from wavering.

"Please don't apologize. I understand."

For the next few minutes, he sat next to me and rubbed my back, reminding me of my grandmother when she would comfort me, as my mind spun out of control. *He can't possibly understand the nightmares that terrorize me.* He didn't know they were memories of abuse and rape. *And he never will.* Because I couldn't live with the shame. And he'd probably drop me like a hot brick if he ever found out.

"Let me grab my keys and I'll take you home."

"Okay."

Chapter 32

Meg

The next morning, I was almost late for the first time since starting at Grannie's. "Sorry I'm late." I said to Beth as I ran to the back and put my purse in my locker. Beth chuckled. "Relax, you're not late."

"Thanks." I caught my breath as I tied my apron. "I hate cutting it this close."

After getting everything ready to open, I made myself a latte with an extra shot. Mary and Beth often reminded me free drinks were a perk of working here, but I'd always felt too self conscious to make anything other than a regular coffee or tea. Today was different—I needed the extra boost after being awake all night.

"Late night?" Beth asked as I put the lid on my drink. I took a sip and let the warm, rich vanilla latte coat my throat. Comfort in a cup. "I didn't get much sleep."

"Well, good for you," Beth said. The first thing I saw when I looked up was the wicked grin on Beth's face. Did she know I had a date with Jack last night? *Oh My God, does she think I was up all night with him?* I blurted out, "It wasn't like that. I had bad dreams."

"I'm sorry. I was hoping it was because you had a great night with Jack." Beth squeezed my shoulder.

"It was a fun night." I didn't dare say anymore. It had been until my nightmare had fucked it up.

Beth was about to say something else when the door opened and the bell chimed. When she called out over my shoulder, I turned so I could help our customers.

My breath caught in my throat when I saw Jack. His steel grey suit highlighted every inch of his perfect body. His purple tie shimmered against his crisp white dress shirt. Warmth flooded my cheeks. *And I thought he looked good in his jeans last night.* I forced my gaze back to his face in time to see him turn away from AJ and Doug. His eyes held mine as he walked over to the counter. I practically drooled.

"Hi Beth." He nodded in her direction without breaking eye contact with me. "Hey Meg, can I talk to you for a sec?"

"I, uh, I can't, I'm working." To hide my flushed cheeks, I organized the counter.

"Go on." Beth gave me a little push. "I got this."

"Thanks." I moved around the counter, painfully aware everyone was watching us. Did they know we had a date last night? Or how it ended? *Damn it.* This was one reason I didn't want to like him or trust him. Nor did I want to keep embarrassing myself. I was failing miserably on all accounts.

Jack held out his hand for me. "Hi." When I put my hand in his, he tugged me into his arms. I forgot about my embarrassment and everyone else in the room as I wrapped my arms around his waist. I wanted this so damn bad. And I was tired of being afraid of everything and everyone. *Jack hasn't given me a single reason to distrust him.*

"Hi." The soft country music drowned out my answer.

"How are you this morning?" His chin was comforting on my head. "Did you sleep okay?"

My head was resting directly over his heart, but I couldn't hear or feel his heartbeat. I flexed my hands a little on his back and realized he felt… hard, flat. I tapped on his back, then pulled back a little and tapped on his ribs before making eye contact. "Are you wearing armor?"

AJ and Doug choke back their laughs, but Jack didn't bother. "As a matter of fact, I am."

I scrunched my eyes together, making my forehead wrinkle, and pursed my lips to the side. "Why? I mean, I know you're not jousting, which is the first thing that comes to mind when I think of armor. You'd be a knight in hidden armor instead of shining armor." My nervous laugh sounded like a cackle. "But seriously, why do you need to wear armor?" The idea of Jack getting shot short-circuited my brain, and I couldn't stop the steady stream of stupidity spilling out of my mouth. If I hadn't been so worried, I would have remembered sooner that Jack had a dangerous job. "You aren't planning on getting shot, are you?" Thank God there was no one else was in the café because I'd said that a little louder than I probably should have.

"No, I don't plan on getting shot." Jack laughed. "Wearing a vest is standard procedure for security detail."

I looked at his arm. "You didn't plan on getting stabbed."

"Burn!" AJ said at the same time Doug said, "Ouch!" Jack rolled his eyes. "I did not get stabbed. And I wasn't working when it happened."

"Oh." Did it matter if he was working or not? I wouldn't have thought so.

Then he led me to the corner and asked again if I was sure I was okay. I nodded. "I am."

"Good." He paused. "I'm sorry I didn't wake you up sooner. I should have realized it might confuse you if you woke up alone."

"It's not your fault." The bell above the door chimed. When I turned and saw John, I jerked my hands away from Jack. "I should get back to work." I hurried away before he could reply.

John greeted AJ and Doug before turning his attention to Jack. "Shouldn't you be on the road?"

"Yes, sir, just grabbing a coffee for the drive."

John greeted me. "Good morning Megan." He was the only person who called me by my full name, and I hated it. It always felt like he was judging me and finding me unworthy. *I have enough doubts of my own, sir. I don't need you making me feel worse.*

"Hello Mr. Sheppard." I tried to sound calm, but my voice squeaked like a mouse. I stared at the floor as I hurried to the register. He wasn't as intimidating with the counter between us.

Mary came around the corner. "Don't scare my barista, John." She playfully swatted him on the arm.

"Yes, ma'am." John pretended to rub away the pain, but was smiling the entire time.

"Hi Ma." Jack said as he walked towards her.

"You clean up nice Jack." She straightened his tie for him. "I make handsome children, don't I?" Her face glowed with pride, and Jack blushed. For a second, I could imagine Jack as a kid, being embarrassed by his mom.

"From the looks of it, I'd say John had a lot to do with that one," Beth answered, laughing as she looked from John to Jack.

Jack was a younger, taller, friendlier version of his dad. *So that's what Jack will look like in twenty-five years? Not bad.* I listened to them as I poured their coffees, wishing I could feel as comfortable around John as Beth did. It's not that I expected us to be friends, but I wished he'd stop looking at me like he wanted me to disappear. His features softened when he smiled at Beth. "Thanks for the credit. Mary likes to forget I had a part in making our children." He put his arm around Mary and kissed her temple. The love in her eyes as she looked up at him could have lit up the café.

When Jack walked up to the counter and handed me his credit card, Mary called over, "On the house today, Meg. Can you pour one for John too?"

"Of course."

Jack grabbed the coffees. "He's not as scary as he seems. I promise." I didn't believe him, but nodded anyway. He put the coffees down, leaned over the counter, and placed his warm hand over mine. "He's a good guy. You'll see." He stood up to his full height when John cleared his throat. "I gotta run. I'll call you later, okay?"

"Okay."

He handed out the coffees before leaning down and giving his mom a peck on the cheek. "Thanks for the coffee, Ma."

"You're welcome. Be safe."

After everyone left, Beth said, "From his expression, I'd say your second date went well."

"Yeah." I wished I could talk to her, but I didn't want to explain why our date ended badly. I was also worried about over-sharing. It'd be weird talking to her about dating her best friend's son. If *we're still dating*. I already regretted letting everyone see how much I liked Jack, knowing they'd ask questions and make it even more awkward for me.

"How's Chase doing?" Changing the subject to Chase when I didn't know what to say usually worked. Beth's expression told me she'd let it go, for now. "He's doing great. He's decided he wants to play t-ball in the spring. I think it'll be fun for him."

"I can't wait to see him play." I didn't have to fake interest. Chase was a great kid.

"And I'm sure he'll love having you there." She paused. "You could bring Jack too. Chase looks up to him."

"Maybe." I smiled.

Chapter 33

Jack

As I was standing near her door waiting, I convinced myself I could stay professional during our range date. *Is it a date?* I wasn't so sure. I'd been getting mixed signals. One minute she'd be warm and trusting, the next she'd shut me out. And she pulled away every time I tried to kiss her. I couldn't tell if she wanted me to ask her out again, or just be her friend. My plan was to keep it professional today, to be her friend, until she made it obvious she wanted more. *I can do this.*

"Let me grab my range bag." Meg laughed as she slung it over her shoulder. "I sound so fancy, 'my range bag', like I know what I'm doing."

We hadn't seen each other since I stopped by Grannie's to check on her before my assignment, when I'd fucked up and acted more like a boyfriend than a friend. During our talks and texts, I fought the urge to flirt and kept it friendly.

Today, Meg seemed a lot more relaxed as she buzzed around, gathering her bags. She walked up and hopped her last step so she was standing less than a foot in front of me; her cucumber mint shampoo invaded my senses. "Ready."

I inhaled sharply at her nearness. Meg's playfulness was adorable and I couldn't help but chuckle and shake my head. *She's not making this easy for me.*

It was a hell of a lot harder than I'd expected to keep it friendly, but professional, at the range. More than once I thought she was flirting, and I desperately wanted to believe she was, but I wouldn't let myself flirt back until she made it clear she wanted to be more than friends. I didn't want to push myself on someone who wasn't sure she wanted to be with me. Holding myself back when I wanted to flirt back was exhausting.

After we finished, Meg asked if I wanted to grab a coffee at our usual place. I said yes, but only because it was part of our ritual, and I wanted to learn a little more about her. Not because I wanted to spend more time with her. *Liar.*

It surprised me when Meg voluntarily told me more about her herself—I'd been trying for weeks to get her to open up, but she kept secrets better than most spec ops guys I knew. She shared a few stories about growing up in Massachusetts and how much she hated the cold winters. "One reason I chose Texas." I couldn't blame her. I loved living in the south. *But that wasn't the real reason. Will she ever tell me?* It didn't matter. I knew why she'd moved. Which reminded me I still needed to tell her what I knew. Since we were just friends, it should be easier. *I'll do it today. But not here, not now. When I drop her off would be better.*

Her eyes sparkled as she told me more stories about grandmother, her father's mother, teaching her how to cook after school. I listened to her explain how her grandmother would swat her hand with a rubber spatula for sampling raw cookie dough. "She's the reason I like to cook." Nostalgia, gratitude, and sorrow fought for space in her eyes.

"I got in trouble for the same thing. Cookie dough is hard to resist." I had to keep reminding myself this wasn't a date. It may have taken me longer than I cared to admit, but I had to accept that she might not want to date me. She didn't trust me enough to share more than a few bread crumbs. I was sure her opening up today was a fluke, like taking out her contacts, and she'd push me away again tomorrow.

I chickened out. It wasn't my proudest moment, but I couldn't bring myself to ruin her good mood when I dropped her off. I was still kicking myself for being a coward when I pulled into my driveway and saw lights on in the house. Jamie must have hopped an earlier flight home from Boston.

I paced the kitchen while I waited for him to get out of the shower. As soon as he walked in, I asked. "What'd you learn?" I opened the fridge to grab myself another beer. "Beer?"

"Hi. It was a shitty flight. Thanks for asking."

I really didn't need his bullshit right now. "Hi James, how was your flight? Would you like a beer before you tell me what you learned?" I laid the sarcasm on thicker than peanut butter.

"Yeah, thanks." He grabbed the beer. "What's up your ass?"

"Nothing. Just fill me." I didn't want to spill my guts, or tell him Meg confused me, or admit I'd turned into a coward.

"I'll tell you what I can." He couldn't tell me everything, and I fucking hated it.

He'd gone to Boston to talk to the FBI Agent in charge of Sullivan's case, Frank Jones, because he wasn't willing to discuss it over the phone.

My stomach dropped when Jamie told me Jones confirmed that Meg, as Margaret Graham, had made the 9-1-1 call resulting in Sullivan's arrest. Sullivan was a big time crime boss involved in Human Trafficking, and Meg had turned him in. *This is really fucking bad.* I had so many questions. How did Meg get messed up with him? Did she witness a crime? Was she a victim? Was it because of her father? Jamie knew more than he was telling me but, despite the empathy I could see in his eyes, he wouldn't answer my questions.

"You weren't lying when you said her eyes are unforgettable." Jamie said, having seen them for the first time in photos from the investigation files. "Is she still wearing the contacts when she's in public?"

"Yeah." I chugged half my beer.

"Good. Sullivan hasn't made a move yet, but she should still be careful. I snapped pictures of anyone entering or leaving his house while I had it under surveillance. I'll match them up with the list of known associates Jones provided."

"Thanks, I appreciate it."

Jamie nodded. "Of course. Have you told her?"

"Not yet." I ran my hand through my hair, *because I'm a coward*. "But I will soon."

"The sooner the better, Jack. This is bigger than we thought."

I snapped, "I said I'll take care of it." I didn't like being reminded of my earlier cowardice, or that I was being left in the dark.

Jamie ignored by jackass attitude. "Has she opened up anymore?"

"A little, but not with anything that'll help us." I explained, "She only shares big-picture, general information. She mentioned her parents were alcoholics and drug addicts, but shrugged it off like it was no big deal."

I'd known all along Meg might be the minor who turned Sullivan in, and might be in more danger because of it. Men like Sullivan always wanted revenge and would go to any lengths to get it. It was killing me knowing Jamie had information about her past, information I could use to help her, but wouldn't tell me. My stomach felt like it was lined with rocks.

"You okay?"

"Yeah. I'm thinking about how much I want to hang these bastards by their balls." I left the rest out because I couldn't admit I wasn't handling any of this well and risk getting benched.

"Right there with you, brother." Jamie raised his beer in agreement. "Have you told her how much you like her?"

I almost choked on my beer. "I, no, we've only had three dates, and they didn't end well. I'm pulling back, giving her some space so she can figure out what she wants."

"Riiight." Jamie didn't even try to hide his amusement. "She might be scared, but she likes you. And it's obvious to everyone who knows you, you've fallen for her."

I stared at him over my tipped beer but didn't trust myself to say anything.

He grinned. "So, when are you going to ask her out again?"

I felt the heat rise in my cheeks. I didn't blush often, but having Jamie call me out on my feelings for Meg caught me off guard. Damn him, bringing all this back up. I'd barely come to terms with backing off, which I'd expected him to support. Now he was encouraging me to ask her out. *What the actual fuck?* I wanted to wipe the shit-eating grin off his face.

"Why the change of heart?" I asked, instead of dealing with my feelings.

"Because I want you to be happy." His voice had the tone he used when he was thinking about Isabelle, missing her. I studied him for a second, waiting to see if he'd say more. He tipped his beer instead.

"Well, it may not happen. She's giving me mixed signals." I shrugged away my disappointment. "At least Dad will be happy." I meant it to sound like a joke, but it came out snarky.

"It's not like that and you know it."

I did. Dad was fine with me dating Meg, just not while we were researching her past. It was the circumstances, not Meg, that he didn't like. Which I understood, I didn't like them either. "I know." The perks of having a family full of police officers. They can do things like help you solve the mystery of your gir- your friend's past. Of course, the downside is they notice everything, and don't shy away from calling you out on your bullshit. Like Jamie just did.

"Speaking of Mom and Dad, you coming to dinner?"

"Yeah, but Ma'll be disappointed. She wanted me to invite Meg, but I couldn't." I finished my beer. "It didn't feel right since we're not dating."

"You should talk to her. You can always take it slow, just don't give up."

Everyone around me was giving me mixed signals, and I didn't like it. What a fucking mind fuck.

Chapter 34

Meg

I invited Jack over for dinner Tuesday after work, and fully expected him to ignore me when I told him he didn't have to bring anything. He had a bad habit of trying to pay for everything. It was weird and a little unnerving. I'd always fended for myself and while I liked the idea of someone wanting to take care of me. *Hell, I've longed for it my entire life.* I didn't like that he felt like he had to. Or the idea of being indebted to someone. Jack didn't expect anything in return, but Sullivan had forced me to rely on him for everything those weeks he'd held me, and while he'd showered me with gifts, they'd come at a hefty price.

Anytime I tried to address it, Jack would dismiss it and say, "It's who I am," and that it was normal for a man to want to take care of the woman he cared about. I didn't know what a normal relationship felt like, so I tried to let go of my discomfort. So far, I wasn't doing a good job.

Thankfully, the only things Jack brought were a bouquet of red and white carnations and a six-pack of beer.

The flowers were gorgeous; I held them to my nose and enjoyed their scent as I carried them to my bedroom so they wouldn't have to compete with the rich smell of freshly cooked bacon.

Jack asked if he could help, but it was almost done, so I told him to relax while I finished. He popped open a beer and leaned against the wall. "What's for dinner? It smells great."

"Baked macaroni and cheese with bacon. It was one of my favorites to make with my grandmother." The recipe called for a pound of thick cut bacon, chopped, and five different cheeses. It was thick, rich, and gooey, and mouth-wateringly delicious.

I told Jack to sit while I filled two bowls and served us.

"Looks delicious." He took a bite, closed his eyes and made happy food noises as he chewed. He opened his eyes and caught me smirking. "What?"

"You have cheese in your beard."

He laughed and wiped his chin with a napkin. "Did I get it?"

I nodded and did a little happy dance in my head because he liked it. I was worried he'd think it was too cheap to be good.

Jack asked about my grandmother, starting with simple, easy to answer questions about the culinary delight, as he called it, in front of us.

It wouldn't hurt to open up a little, as long as I didn't reveal too much about my parents, or talk about the abuse and Sullivan. I wasn't ready to share that yet. Jack was already protective and a little over-bearing, trying to take care of me all the time. And I didn't want him feeling sorry for me, or to give him an excuse to be even more protective. Or worse, a reason to run away.

"My grandmother would babysit me when my parents were at work, or when they were drunk." He already knew they were alcoholics and drug addicts. "Sometimes I'd stay as long as a week or two and she'd let me help her make dinner. She taught me how to cook and to sew." My best memories were of the times I spent with my grandmother. I'd always felt safe and loved when I was with her and would have lived with her full time if I could have.

Jack didn't say anything as I talked. I could only imagine how odd it must've sounded to someone with a close-knit family to hear me say I wanted to live with my grandmother instead of my parents. It surprised me he didn't ask about it, not that I'd tell him. I'd been hiding my past for a long time and was quite good at it.

"Your grandmother sounds like an amazing woman."

"She was. I miss her. Things were so much better when she was alive. She prote- she took care of me."

"Did things get worse with your parents after she died?"

I looked at my half-eaten dinner and hunched my shoulders. I really didn't want to talk about them.

"Meg, please don't do that."

"Do what?"

"Close yourself off," Jack answered.

"Sorry." I said to my plate, not daring to meet his eyes, knowing I'd upset him. I couldn't handle his disappointment.

"Don't apologize. I want to learn more about you, but you push me away anytime I try."

"I'm sorry." I said, then met Jack's eyes. "It's just, I don't like talking about my parents." I couldn't hold eye contact with him.

"I've noticed." Jack gave me a warm smile. "I'm here to listen, if you ever want to talk. Okay? No judgement. I promise." He didn't push me for more answers, but I knew he'd ask again, eventually.

When I didn't answer, Jack reached across the table and covered my hand with his. "Meg?"

I looked back up, expecting to see pity or irritation, but saw a compassion instead.

I didn't know what to say, so I nodded and said, "Okay. Thank you."

We finished our meal in relative silence. I appreciated his willingness to listen. I really did. But I wasn't ready to share, and I was worried he'd eventually start demanding answers. He'd be upset if I didn't share, but I knew he'd walk away if I did. My childhood was a shit show, and my teen years were even worse. Could a guy like Jack want to be with a girl as broken as me?

Maybe it's normal for him to ask so many questions. Just because the few guys I'd dated in the past hadn't wanted to know more about me doesn't mean it was wrong for Jack to ask. *I mean, I want to know more about him.* Though I rarely asked him any questions because he was an open book and would answer any, and all, of them. But then he'd expect me to answer his. Which was only fair.

Jack helped me clear the dishes and offered to help me wash them. I told him I'd wash them later as I got him another beer and refilled my water.

Before we watched the movie, Jack asked if we could talk. My breath caught in my throat. *Is he going to break up with me? Are we–*

Jack interrupted my thoughts. "I want to make sure we're on the same page." He swallowed hard. "About us."

I clutched my water. "Okay." I didn't have enough time for the negative thoughts to form before Jack started.

"I like you, and I'd like to keep seeing you."

I looked up at him with my mouth hanging open, then quickly closed it. *What a relief, I thought for sure he was going to break up with me.*

"We can go as slow as you'd like." He reached over and pried one of my hands off my glass. "But I need you to talk to me. I don't want to guess what you want from me."

"I'd like that too." I whispered as I squeezed his hand. "You're sure you don't mind taking it slow?"

"I'm sure." He put his hand under my chin and gently lifted my face. "Can I please kiss you now?"

I almost choked on my spit. Jack was full of surprises tonight. Not trusting my voice, I nodded because I'd been fantasizing about his kisses since the day we met. Slowly, he leaned in and pressed his lips to mine. He held us there, his warm hand cupping my face. His beard rough on my skin. His lips gentle, undemanding.

His actions let me know I was in control, and I wanted this.

Jack groaned when I parted my lips and deepened the kiss. It didn't last long, but kissing Jack was everything I dreamed it would be.

I pulled back, breaking the kiss. My chest heaving as I tried to catch my breath.

Jack's grin stole what little breath was left in my lungs, but I didn't care. We were officially dating. And he said it was okay to take things slow.

We settled on the couch to watch a movie on Jack's laptop, since I didn't have a DVD player. I told him he could pick the movie, and he surprised me by choosing Princess Bride.

"Madi made me and Jamie watch it with her a couple of years ago. I thought you'd like it. Have you seen it?"

"Yup, but I don't mind watching again." I could watch it a thousand times and never tire of it.

Every so often, Jack quoted Wesley, making my heart skip a beat. It was silly, but I loved hearing him quote the movie's hero.

We chatted off and on throughout the movie, quoting the occasional line and making fun of the silliness. Jack grabbed me as the first fire spurt happened in the swamp scene, making me scream.

"Don't worry, I'll save you, princess," Jack whispered in my ear. He didn't sound like he was joking.

"I don't need saving," I mumbled.

Jack paused the movie and turned my face towards him. "What was that?"

"You don't have to save me, Jack. I can take care of myself."

"I know you can," Jack pulled me in for a hug and kissed the top of my head, "but is it so wrong that I don't think you should have to do it alone?"

I shrugged, but didn't pull away, too afraid he'd see the fear in my eyes. He kept one arm around me and turned the movie back on.

I sighed. I could do it on my own, but it felt nice having someone who wanted to help me.

My huge smile lingered as I cleaned up after Jack left. We'd talked and were officially dating. No more guessing. And we had our first kiss, which was swoon worthy. He also asked me to go to his parents' for Thanksgiving dinner, but I said I wasn't sure. This was all so new, and I was worried I'd feel awkward around his family. Besides, I didn't think his father and brother liked me very much, though I wouldn't tell him that.

I went to bed expecting to have sweet dreams about Jack. I didn't.

I woke up drenched in sweat, my heart racing out of control. In my dream, I was being chased down a hallway and every time I thought I was about to reach the door and escape, the hall would get longer.

Chapter 35

Jack

I called Meg before she left for work the morning after our first kiss to make sure she was okay. Her voice sounded distant when she answered. *I hope she hasn't changed her mind.* When I asked her what was wrong, she said nightmares were keeping her up. I repeated my offer to listen if she wanted to talk about them. She didn't. I wanted to push, but had promised to take things slow. We talked for a few more minutes. I relished the sound of her laughter when I made my best, not very good, Wesley impressions. She sounded more like herself by the time we hung up.

It had been a week since we talked, and had our first kiss. We hadn't gone out on a date since, choosing to spend our time together at her place. I didn't mind. Meg was more relaxed when we were alone, plus she'd take her contacts out, which made hanging out in her motel room worth it.

Luckily, she was looking for a new place, so we wouldn't have to see the ugly carpet much longer.

Meg hesitated when I asked if Jamie could join us for dinner at my place. *Does she think I plan on having my big brother chaperone our date? Or is she worried he doesn't like her?* Whatever her reason, she agreed after I assured her he'd only be there for dinner. "Jamie's dying to try your bacon mac and cheese after I bragged about how good it was." Dinner would be a good chance for them to get to know each other.

It started sprinkling as I finished grilling our burgers. I set them on the table and called for Jamie, who was reading in his bedroom, then grabbed beers for me and Jamie and a glass of water for Meg since she still wasn't a big beer fan.

"Hey Meg. How's it going?" Jamie was still concerned about the circumstances surrounding my relationship with Meg, but he was happy I found someone I liked enough to invite to Thanksgiving. Holidays are a big deal in our family. I wasn't sure asking her was the right thing to do after promising to take it slow, but my mom wanted me to invite her. I promised Meg I'd respect her decision.

Our conversation was relaxed while we ate. Eventually, it wandered to Thanksgiving dinner. It was bound to happen. When Jamie asked Meg if she'd be joining us, she hemmed and hawed. I watched in awe as Jamie talked to her. He gently coaxed until she gave in and said, "Maybe." I might have doubted she meant it if it wasn't for the smile in her eyes. Until that moment, I'd fully expected her to say no.

Meg told us it had been forever since she'd had a real family holiday meal, which I knew was before her grandmother died.

"Did your mom not like to cook?" Jamie asked.

"Too drunk is more like." Meg answered, her voice thick with pain. I saw panic cross her face when she realized she hadn't censored herself.

"I'm sorry." Jamie said, "Ma would love for you to join us." Then corrected himself so the full weight of the invitation was clear, "We all would. Ma always cooks enough to feed a small army."

"Which is good, because we eat like a small army." I laughed. "Especially when Jay is home." Jay was tall like me, but thicker, and could eat his body weight in turkey and stuffing.

Jamie and I shared memories of the mass quantities of food we could eat when we were all active in school sports. And how holiday meals hadn't been the same since Madi, Jay, and I had joined the military. Video chatting was now an important part of our holiday tradition.

"Speaking of Madi," Jamie interrupted. "Did Jack tell you she's coming home for Thanksgiving and is dying to meet you?"

"Really? Why?" Meg asked her plate. My heart ached; it should be obvious why my sister wanted to meet her. God, I hated the people who hurt her. She deserved to be loved, spoiled, and happy. *I'll remind her every day if she gives me the chance.*

Jamie did a double take. "Did she really ask me that?" To Meg, "Because she wants to meet the only girl Jack has ever invited to Thanksgiving."

"Oh." The color inched up her cheeks. "I don't know. I mean, we've only been on a few dates. Won't it be weird?"

"No. Besides, no one should be alone on the holidays," Jamie said. I nodded in agreement.

"It's not a big deal, I'm used to it." Meg's voice didn't waver, but she wouldn't make eye contact with either of us as her shoulders slumped.

"When was the last time you had a traditional stuff-your-face-until-you-hate-yourself Thanksgiving dinner?" Jamie asked.

"It's been a while, not since…" She shrugged. I didn't think she'd offer more than that. Talking about her grandmother always made her sad and introspective, and she rarely included her parents. Not that I blamed her. She hadn't told me much about them, but they sounded like horrible people and worse parents. They deserved every day they spent in jail.

"Since before they went to jail?" *Fuck.* I hadn't meant to say that out loud. *Fuck!*

Meg went stone still. She clenched her teeth and slowly set down her fork as she stared at her plate. I could almost hear her mind going a mile a minute, trying to remember if she'd slipped up and mentioned her parents going to jail. I held my breath as I waited for her to say something. Jamie made eye contact and I shook my head back and forth, a pit in the bottom of my stomach. There was nothing I could say.

"How?" Meg's voice was barely audible.

Still trying to find the right words, I didn't answer immediately. Meg's teeth ground together and her knuckles turned white as she clenched her fists.

The chair scraping across the floor was the only sound as she stood up. "How do you know that?" Her hard, bitter voice sliced through my heart like a hot knife through butter.

I looked at Jamie, panic-stricken. I'd fucked up. Big. I needed to answer her, but I didn't know how. Jamie's expression was loud and clear, "be honest".

"Meg, please. I was worried. Some things seemed off. I thought you might be in danger, so I did a little research."

"What the fuck Jack! A little?" If looks could kill, I'd be dead. "If you know about my parents going to jail, you did a hell of a lot more than a little." She called me a liar with her air quotes.

Shock, fear, and anger fought for space as it sunk in that I knew about her past. She couldn't know I was being kept in the dark about most of it. I knew her real name, and about her parents' arrests and the FBI helping her relocate, but not much else. I started to tell her, but she cut me off.

Anger radiated off of her. "Did you tell Jamie?" She clipped her words.

Wanting to keep Jamie out of it, I said, "I, please Meg, I wanted-"

"What the fuck Jack? What right do you have digging into my past?" She whipped her head around and leveled Jamie with a glare, annunciating every word. "Did He Tell You?"

Jamie met Meg's blazing eyes. "I-"

She cut him off as she swung back to me. "Of course you did."

Jamie had told me, but I didn't think she'd care about the distinction. I waved Jamie out of the room. This was my fuck up to fix, and he didn't need to be here for it.

Instead of correcting her, I tried to explain my reasons. "I was worried you had a stalker and wanted to protect you." I could hear my guilt and fear in my shaky voice.

"Protect me? By sneaking around behind my back? By lying to me? What am I? Some poor victim you get to feel good about saving?" Meg held her arms at her side, opening and closing in fists. She looked like she wanted to punch me.

"Please…" My tears welled up and threatened to spill over. I could handle her anger, but not the pain behind it. I'd betrayed her trust, lied by omission. She may never forgive me. *But I have to try.*

"Please what Jack? Trust you? I don't fucking thinking so."

"I only wanted to–"

"What Jack, protect me? Be the fucking hero?" Meg threw her hands in the air. "I should've known better."

She didn't bother to wipe away the tears flowing freely down her cheeks. She leveled me with an expression that would turn a lesser man to stone. "Sullivan," she shot daggers at me, "I'm guessing you know who he is? He said he wanted to protect me. He lied too, but at least I expected it from him."

Meg turned and stalked towards the door.

"Meg, wait." My voice cracked. "Please." I couldn't let her leave, not without telling her the truth.

"No. We're done." She grabbed her purse. "I should have known better." She slammed the door behind her.

My heart ached as I watched her march to the end of the driveway without looking back. Jamie came back after the door slammed shut. When I turned towards the door, he held me back. "Don't. You'll make it worse."

"I have to. I can't let her walk home in the rain." There were a thousand reasons I didn't want to let her walk away. A million things I needed to apologize for, but my fucking brain fixated on the rain.

"Let me take care of it." He squeezed my shoulders before grabbing his keys. "I'll make sure she gets home safe. We'll talk when I get back."

Chapter 36

Meg

Rain drenched my clothes as I stood at the end of the driveway. *I should have driven.* But I'd trusted Jack, and broke one of my safety rules: always drive yourself. *God, I'm so fucking stupid. I should have known better.*

I wasn't looking forward to walking in the rain, but I wanted to create some distance before calling a cab. The walk would help me work off some of the anger raging through me.

"Meg, wait." Jamie called out as he jogged down the driveway, an umbrella in his hand.

"Go away."

"I can't. I won't." He opened the umbrella and handed it to me. "Please take it."

"I don't need your help." I brushed wet hair off my face.

Jamie sighed. "I know you're hurt and pissed off, and you have every right to be. And I get it. You don't want to talk to

Jack right now, but I want to make sure you get home safe. Will you let me drive you home?"

"No." I turned and stomped away.

"Meg, it's too far to walk, especially in the rain. Please?" I could hear him closing the distance behind me.

"How do you know it's too far?" I turned and glared at him. "Of course you fucking know. No, I don't want a ride, and I don't want to hear anymore bullshit right now." I stalked down the sidewalk, splashing through the shallow puddles, not caring if the rain ruined my shoes. A few minutes ago, we were all sitting at the table, talking and laughing like they hadn't dug up the worst parts of my life.

"I swear, I won't say a single word. Let me drive you home." He caught up and stepped in front of me. "Please."

"If I say no?"

"I'll follow you to make sure you get home safe. I'll be out of your hair faster if you let me drive you."

I wanted to say no, but it was a long walk. If he was going to follow me anyway, I might as well accept the ride, as long as he didn't talk to me. "Not one single word?"

"Not one." He crossed his heart.

I stared at him as rain dripped down my face and drenched my clothes. I didn't trust him to keep his mouth shut, but I was soaking wet, and knew he meant it when he said he'd follow me. "Fine." I snapped, too mad to be polite or grateful. I turned and stalked towards his SUV. When the door clicked, I ripped it open, climbed in, and slammed it shut.

"Tha-" I whipped my head around and gave him a look to melt flesh off bone. He held up a hand in surrender. *Smart man.* Jamie turned the heat on and directed the vents towards me. It wouldn't be enough to dry me off, but it was enough to warm me up.

I sat on the far edge of the seat, with my head pressed against the cool window, and cried. I didn't care if he could hear me when I started mumbling, "So fucking stupid. Should have known." I sniffled. *Never again.*

Without lifting my head from the window, I asked, "Why?"

I assumed Jamie would know I was talking to him, but he didn't answer. I turned and stared at him, waiting for him to acknowledge me, then repeated the question. "Why?" My voice shook with pain and anger.

Jamie pulled over before answering calmly, "He did it because he thought you had a stalker, and he didn't want to lose you the way I lost my wife."

I sucked in a breath. Even in my anger, I couldn't be a bitch to him about losing his wife. "I'm sorry that happened," I whispered as I leaned my forehead against the window again, "but it's not an excuse to betray my trust."

"Thank you. And you're right."

"He should have asked me."

"He should have, but would you have told him the truth?" Jamie's voice was neutral, but it sounded like an accusation and it pissed me off.

I snapped at him. "I don't have a stalker, is the truth."

Jamie raised an eyebrow. "Technically no, but you are hiding Meg, from someone who wants to hurt you. It's no less dangerous." He paused. "Would you have told him that, or stuck with the technical truth?"

This time, the accusation was intentional, and I flinched. Then got pissed. *How dare he?* I barked, "No, because it's none of his fucking business!"

"You're wrong-"

I didn't want to hear anything he had to say, so I cut him off. "Fuck you." I mumbled, "Fuck you both." Jack had betrayed me. The sadness and regret shattering my heart were almost as strong as my anger.

Jamie put the truck in drive and turned onto the road. For a few minutes, the rain on the windows was the only sound other than my sniffles. It occurred to me they probably told Mary. I asked softly, "Does Mary know?" I couldn't stand the idea of Mary knowing.

"No, we told her someone might come asking about you, and asked her to let us know if anyone does. She needed to know, for her safety as well as yours."

I nodded, grateful Mary didn't know my history. Then it occurred to me John must know. *At least now I know why he doesn't like me.* I didn't say anything for the rest of the ride. Jamie parked in the spot closest to my door, but didn't turn the engine off. He reached up, grabbed a business card from his visor and handed it to me. "If you need anything, please call me."

I didn't take it. "Thank you for the ride," I said as I climbed out of his truck. I didn't look back before closing my door and securing all the locks. How could I have been so blind? I knew better than to trust anyone, to get too close, but I let my guard down and took a chance. *A mistake I'll never make again.*

Not wanting any reminders of Jack in the apartment, I gathered up all the flowers he'd given me before changing out of my wet clothes. I was going to throw them in the trash, but threw them outside so I wouldn't have to see them. After changing out of my wet clothes, I sat down to write a to-do list. My hand trembled as I listed the things I needed to do in the next couple of days so I could leave Weatherford as soon as possible.

> Cancel my appointments to see potential apartments.
> Give Mary my two-week notice.
> Go to the library and find a new city to live.

I opened the safe and counted my cash, chastising myself for getting comfortable with Jack. Never again. Once I counted my savings, I wrote a moving budget. Which didn't take long since I only had a few expenses. Tears flowed freely down my face, but I didn't care enough to wipe them away. *I'm going to miss Mary and Beth.* I decided not to give Mary my new address after I moved, even though it meant forfeiting my last check. If I gave her my new address, Jack would know where I was and I didn't want him showing up on my doorstep. The harsh sound of my laugh cut through the room. *Don't be stupid.* He could find me easily if he wanted to. *He won't.*

I stared at my list through tear-filled eyes for a few more minutes before taking a hot shower. Having a plan to leave

Weatherford, and Jack, helped me feel a little better. *I've started over before, I can do it again.*

It was going to be a long two weeks.

As the hot water washed over my body, I forced myself to ignore the voice in my head. *You work for his mom. You won't be able to avoid him if he comes in.* I thought about quitting without notice, but had too much respect for Mary. The hot water washed away a fresh wave of tears.

Chapter 37

Jack

I fucked up. If I'd listened to Jamie and told her what I'd learned, this wouldn't have happened. I wore a path on the hardwood floor between the dining room and livingroom while I waited. My jaw ached from clenching it. Jamie sent me a text when he dropped Meg off so I'd know she got home safe. I appreciated it, but needed to know what she'd said during the ride. If he thought there was even the slightest chance she might forgive me. And if I was being totally honest with myself, I needed my big brother's support.

I heard the garage door close and rushed down the hall. "What'd she say? How pissed off is she?" I demanded. "Will-"

Jamie put up his hand. "Not much. She's pissed. Very pissed. But judging from her body language, she's more hurt than angry. Though she only expressed her ang-"

"What exactly did she say?" I practically barked when I cut him off. Jamie raised his eyebrows. "Sorry." He'd done me a favor and didn't deserve my attitude. The only person I should be mad at was me.

"She wanted to know why you lied." Jamie ushered me back down the hall, grabbing a towel on the way. "She needs time to calm down before she'll talk to you." He rubbed his hair dry. "I answered her as best I could, but she wasn't ready to hear the answers."

"Fuck." I stared down at our half-eaten meals on the table. The evening had gone to hell in the blink of an eye. "How do I fix this, Jamie? I can't lose her." I had just accepted how much I like her.

"I know." Jamie patted me on the shoulder. "Give me a second to change out of my wet clothes, and we'll talk."

I grabbed two beers from the fridge and carried them into the living room. The mess in the kitchen could wait—the mess I'd created with Meg couldn't.

Jamie and I talked for hours, mostly about Meg and Isabelle, love and loss.

It broke my heart all over again, hearing Jamie's voice crack when he talked about her.

I grabbed us a couple more beers and told Jamie the ugly, embarrassing truth about my breakup with Ana.

"It's different with Meg. She needs my help, even if she won't admit it, but she refuses to ask for it. She doesn't want anything from me, not like Ana. I know Meg thinks I have a hero complex, and maybe I do, but there's more to it. I'm at peace when I'm with her, Jamie, and…"

"You love her." It wasn't a question.

Do I? Jamie waited while I thought about it. "I do." It was the first time I'd admitted to myself. I ran my hand through my hair, causing it to stand on end, before leaning forward and resting my head in my hands. "How do I fix this?"

"You'll find a way." I appreciated his confidence in me, but right now I wasn't feeling it and I needed his advice. We talked some more while we cleaned the kitchen, each half eaten meal a painful reminder of how badly I'd fucked things up.

Grief, fear, and loss weren't the easiest subjects to share, but by the end of the night, I felt closer than ever to Jamie.

I sat at my desk Monday morning, ordering flowers for Meg while I waited for my dad. The bouquet was like the one I'd brought her on our first date. I had it sent to Grannie's, with a note that said: I'm sorry. Jack.

I was dreading my upcoming meeting with my dad, knowing he'd read me the riot act. Which I deserved. At least Jamie had been sympathetic when he lectured me. Unlike AJ, who hadn't pulled his punches and made sure I knew I was a "fucking idiot" who had "royally fucked up" before saying anything useful. The flowers had been his suggestion. "It'll show her you're thinking about her, while still giving her the space she needs."

My phone rang as I was putting my credit card back in my wallet. "Hi Ma, wha-"

"Don't you 'Hi ma' me. What the hell happened? Meg just gave me her notice!"

I flinched and held the phone away from my ear.

"Fuck." I swore, then quickly apologized, so she wouldn't have another reason to tear me a new asshole. Even though I deserved the verbal smack down. *If Meg could see this, she'd understand my healthy fear of my mom.* I would have laughed if I hadn't been so worried Meg would never talk to me again.

Of course, my dad walked in at that moment. *It's going to be a long day.* He sat down in front of my desk and made a hand gesture at AJ, who quietly left the room.

"I'll let it slide this time." Mary softened her tone. "What happened Jack? She looked devastated when she gave her notice."

"What reason did she give?" I asked as Jamie walked in. He sat next to dad. I switched to speaker and put my phone down. I wouldn't be getting any privacy today.

"She said things aren't working out in Texas, and she needs to move on."

Dad and Jamie exchanged a look.

"She didn't say it was because of me?" It didn't surprise me. I couldn't imagine Meg telling my mom I was the reason she was leaving.

"No, but what else would it be? You said you had a fight, but this is more than a fight."

"I fu- messed up," My voice caught in my throat as my mom's words sunk in: Meg's leaving. "I thought I'd have time to fix it."

After a brief pause, she asked, "What can I do to help?"

I swallowed down the lump in my throat, preferring it when she was acting like an angry mama bear. Her sympathy made it too real.

"Thanks Ma, but there's nothing you can do. I have to fix this myself."

Before hanging up, she reminded me she was there if I needed to talk.

After I put my phone down, my dad spoke up, "I just got an earful from your mother. Care to fill me in on the why?"

This day was going to suck ass. "Jamie didn't tell you?" What I couldn't ask was, weren't you listening?

"I want to hear it from you."

I relived the events as I told him what happened and waited for his lecture.

I didn't get one. Instead, he gave me the same advice as Jamie: "Give her time."

What the fuck? When had he changed his mind? I knew he didn't have anything against Meg, but I still hadn't expected to get through the day without a lecture from him. I embraced my good luck instead of questioning it. "Time is a luxury I don't have."

Dad said, "She feels betrayed, and won't hear anything you have to say until she calms down. You'll make it worse, not better, if you try to rush it."

He was right, and I could practically hear Jamie saying, I told you so. He'd taken every opportunity to remind me it was a bad idea to get involved with Meg, and an even worse one to lie to her.

I wasn't sure I could sit around and do nothing without going crazy. Especially since I didn't have any big assignments this week and paperwork could only keep my mind occupied for so long.

Ma called on Tuesday to confirm they had delivered the flowers. "She seemed pissed after reading your note," she paused, "she threw it away and left the flowers in the break room."

Not surprising. I hadn't expected her to forgive me just because I sent flowers.

I ordered another bouquet for Wednesday. I didn't want to be pushy, but my schedule was tight if I was going to stop her from leaving.

This time I sent pink and white carnations with the note: Can we talk? Jack.

Ma called to confirm the delivery and tell me Meg had the same reaction. I'd hoped for a different one. When I asked my mom for advice, she echoed dad and Jamie: "Give her time." Why did they all think I could afford to wait?

My desperation grew as I thought about how fast the days would fly by.

Chapter 38

Meg

I got up early on Sunday and ate a quick breakfast before driving to the library. Knowing I needed to find a new place to live, quickly, and needing to stay busy or go crazy had me hyper-focused on my to-do list.

Tears rolled down my face off and on during the drive. I was still angry at Jack, but right now, the sadness was stronger. My dreams of a happy future in Weatherford shattered to pieces. I hated the thought of leaving, but couldn't stay.

I wiped away my tears with the back of my hand. *I knew I'd regret getting attached.* The more I thought about Jack, his lies and betrayal, the angrier I got. I let the anger replace the sadness. It was easier to deal with.

I'll get over it, eventually. I was a survivor, and this wasn't the first time someone I thought I could trust hurt me. *But it will be the last. Never again will I be dumb enough to trust anyone.*

My tears were dry by the time I parked. I didn't need a mirror to know my eyes were red and my cheeks blotchy from salt. I stopped in the women's room to wash the tear stains off my face.

I checked my emails before searching for a new town. There were a few new emails from my mother. I scanned them. They all said the same thing: we miss you and want to be a family again. *Again? We were never a family.* Why did everyone lie to me? I moved them to her folder.

I emailed Agent Jones, asking if there was anything I should know because my mother was emailing more than normal and it made me nervous. Agent Jones would tell me if there was anything I should be concerned about, but I couldn't get rid of the feeling something wasn't quite right. I added a quick note to let him know I was moving again before hitting send.

I gave Mary my two-week notice first thing Monday morning. She seemed surprised and disappointed. When she asked why, I told her I was leaving because Texas wasn't working out for me. There was no way I'd tell her the real reason. Thankfully, she accepted my notice without asking a lot of questions.

"If you change your mind, I'd be happy to keep you on." Mary said, as I stood up to leave. "You've been a great addition to the Grannie's family."

"Thank you." I said, hoping I could hold back the tears long enough to escape outside. I didn't want her to see me cry.

I'm going to miss working here. Beth and Mary were both so kind and supportive, like the aunts I'd always wanted. I doubted I'd be lucky enough to find a job I liked as much as this one again.

How am I going to get through the next two weeks without crying every time I come to work?

Gratefully, Mary didn't mention Jack, although I assumed she knew what had happened.

Jack didn't contact me. It's not like I expected him to show up and apologize, or beg for a second chance, but it surprised me he hadn't called or texted. My emotions switched back and forth between disappointment and relief. I didn't want to talk to him, but I had hoped he'd at least try to apologize. *Just proves I was right—I don't mean anything to him.*

I wasn't angry anymore. *Well, not as angry.* I was still angry with myself for letting my guard down and trusting him. *Now I'm paying the price.*

Beth didn't ask about Jack either, but she said, more than once, she'd be there for me if I wanted to talk. I could have used a friend, but I couldn't talk to her about this. She might be my friend, but she was Mary's best friend.

Another reason I couldn't stay in Weatherford; the Sheppards knew everyone. It didn't matter if I liked the town or my job. No, I needed to make a clean break and start over somewhere new.

I didn't know where I was going yet, but I had two weeks to decide. *Maybe Colorado. I could find a tourist town and hide among the throngs of people coming and going all year long.*

An hour before my shift ended, a delivery guy walked in carrying flowers. My stomach sank when he announced, "Delivery for Meg." *Great.* Only one person would send me flowers. The bouquet was a copy of the one he'd brought for me on our first date. The note said: I'm sorry. Jack.

Fighting back tears, I carried them to the break room without making eye contact with anyone. I ripped up the card and threw it in the trash. When my shift was over, I left the flowers on the table. I couldn't stand the thought of seeing them.

I was a wreck all day Tuesday. It was hard to do my job while trying to be invisible, and it took all my energy to smile at the customers. Jack didn't ask me if I got the flower and I didn't bother to tell him. During my break, I went for a walk instead of sitting and reading like normal, so I didn't have to see the flowers sitting there, taunting me.

I didn't get a delivery on Tuesday, and for the second day in a row, no one from SSI came in to pick up coffee.

I felt a little better on Wednesday. Not good, but at least I wasn't a nervous wreck. Beth and Mary still avoided talking to me about Jack, which I appreciated. My shift was half over when the same flower guy delivered more flowers; a bouquet of pink and white carnations, like the ones he surprised me with for my birthday. I blinked back tears as I thought about how happy I was that day.

"Meg, why don't you take your break," Mary said softly.

"Thanks." I picked up the flowers and carried them to the break room.

This note said: Can we talk? Jack.

I didn't want to cry, but couldn't stop the tears from sliding down my cheeks. Jack's note was a simple, polite request. No begging, no explanations, no demands. I didn't want to feel sad anymore, so I got mad that he was sending them to Grannie's, where everyone could see them.

At least he hadn't delivered them in person. The last thing I wanted was to do was deal with Jack in front of his mother.

The soft knock on the door frame snapped me out of the cyclone of thoughts spinning around in my mind.

"Can I come in?" Mary asked.

"Of course." I wiped my eyes before looking up at her. "Am I late?"

"No, I'd like to talk to you about Jack, if that's okay."

I nodded. It wasn't, but I didn't think I could tell her no.

"I don't know the details about what happened, so I won't defend him," Mary said. "But I know he cares deeply about you, and I know he's sorry."

I couldn't hold back my anger. "He should be." I was about to apologize for being rude, but Mary didn't give me time.

"I'm sure you're right," she paused, "but I know my son. Whatever he did, he meant well, even if it doesn't seem like it right now."

The clock ticked away the seconds as I tried to think of something to say, but soon gave up. "I should get back." Wow, that sounded lame. Mary was my boss and wouldn't punish me for making me late.

"Will you do me a favor?" Mary asked.

"Yes." I answered without hesitation, then hoped I wouldn't regret it. I liked Mary and hated that I had to move because of what happened with Jack. *Exactly why I didn't want to get involved with him.*

"Will you consider everything you know about Jack, and how you felt when you were with him before giving up?"

She was asking a lot. Only time would tell whether I meant it when I said, "Okay." I put the note from Jack in my pocket, doubting anything would change. Not only had Jack's betrayal reminded me why I couldn't trust people, but Jamie had told me I put Mary in danger. I wouldn't be able to live with myself if anything happened to her or Beth.

"Thank you for hearing me out."

"You're welcome."

Not wanting them as a reminder at home, I left the flowers in the break room at the end of my shift. I wished everyone a Happy Thanksgiving as I walked out the door.

After my shift, I showered faster than normal, eager to get to Fort Worth. Guilt washed over me for lying to Mary, though it wasn't a total lie. I could help but think about Jack, and how comfortable and safe I'd felt in his arms. *Which is why his betrayal is so devastating.* The lie was the part about forgiving him. I didn't think I could ever forgive him or trust him again.

It wasn't easy searching for a new place to live with tears blurring my vision.

Chapter 39

Jack

It was a family tradition to hunt on Thanksgiving morning and I usually loved the quiet bonding time, but this year I couldn't stay focused and was relieved when it was time to go home and get cleaned up.

Despite how miserable I felt, I was looking forward to seeing Madi, even if it meant having to explain why Meg wasn't there. Madi was eager to meet her and would want to know why she wouldn't get to, and what I did to mess it up. My family was supportive, but that didn't mean they wouldn't hold me accountable or give me shit.

"You ready?" Jamie interrupted my thoughts.

"Yeah. I'll drive separately," I said, without making eye contact.

"Want an escape option if it's too much?" He knew what was coming. I'd need to man up, swallow my pride, and own my shit.

"Nah, I want to be free to leave if…" I shook my head. "Never mind. Let's go."

"If Meg wants to see you?"

"She won't." I sighed. "But yeah."

When I pulled up in the driveway, dad was in the garage, dressing his deer. The only catch of the morning. Jamie never had a clean shot, and my heart wasn't in it.

When I asked dad if he needed help, he said, "I'm good. Go in and see your sister. She's waiting. Impatiently."

His expression told me all I needed to know.

After a round of hugs, we gathered in the kitchen to help Ma. Madi updated us on her degree and career, and we all raised our glasses to celebrate her promotion. She told us she was single again, even though it was a mutual break up because he transferred overseas.

"Speaking of relationships," Madi pointed her knife at me, "you want to explain to me why I'm not meeting Meg today?"

"I'm sure Ma filled you in." My eyes never left the knife. I wasn't worried she'd stab me, but it was easier than seeing the accusation in her hazel eyes. The only feature she shared with Jamie, despite being twins.

"I did no such thing. I only told her Meg wasn't coming because you had a misunderstanding." The air quotes around misunderstanding were less than subtle.

"How much of that is on you?" Madi's accusation was stronger than her question.

Jamie coughed around a laugh. Madi didn't beat around the bush, never had. She learned early on how to handle her three rowdy younger brothers. Jamie might only be a few minutes younger, but it didn't matter to Madi. She always referred to herself his big sister.

I sighed. Time to fess up. Bite the bullet and get it over with. I stared down at the vegetables I was no longer chopping. "All of it. I wanted to help her, protect her, so I dug around into her past." I looked up at her. "But I didn't tell her."

"Oh Jack." Madi's tone was somewhere between I'm sorry and you're an idiot.

"I thought she had a stalker. All the signs were there." After Isabelle's murder, a potential stalker was a serious and personal issue for us. "I should have talked to her, but I didn't. Instead, I asked dad and Jamie to dig deeper, thinking I could help her without her knowing." I shook my head and made eye contact. "I fu-screwed it all up. She thinks I betrayed her trust, and in a way, I did."

"Are you in love with her?" Madi's sympathetic tone didn't help me feel any better. I preferred it when she was giving me shit. It was easier to handle. I'd fucked up and deserved their lectures and judgement, not their sympathy.

I could hear a pin drop as they waited for my answer.

"I don't know, I-" Jamie cleared his throat. Great, just what I didn't need, an external conscience. I glared at Jamie. "Yes." I looked back at Madi. "And now I'll never get to tell her because I'm an idiot. Even worse, she's still in danger tand," my voice cracked, "I can't protect her."

"No, but we can." Dad had snuck in during my confession. "She may not want your help, but we'll still monitor the situation and we won't leave her to deal with this alone. If her past comes knocking, we'll answer the door." He patted me on the back.

"Damn straight." Jamie chimed in. Overcome, I blinked back my tears. Unable to find words strong enough to express my gratitude, I simply nodded.

Dad saved me the trouble. "Smells good in here." He kissed Ma on the cheek. "I'm hungry enough to eat a deer." He changed the subject with his favorite Thanksgiving dad joke before patting me on the shoulder and going to shower.

Madi wrapped me in a big-sister hug. "You'll figure this out. You're good that way."

"Thanks." I lifted her feet off the floor with my return hug. "I needed that."

After over-eating and putting away the leftovers, we headed to Dad's office to video call Jaden. He didn't have much time, so the call was brief, but filled with love. We were grateful we could talk to the youngest Sheppard and see for ourselves he was alive and well.

I texted Meg after I helped wash the dishes. I didn't think she'd reply, but I had to try.

Happy Thanksgiving.

I sent the message, then stared at my phone. Any response was welcome, even if she told me to fuck off. At least I'd know she was okay.

"A watched pot never boils." Madi plopped down on the couch beside me. "Tell me about her."

I sat for a moment, deciding where to start, but before I could, my phone buzzed. The tension drained from my shoulders.

You too.

Better than I'd expected. I could feel the weight of Madi's stare as my thumbs hovered over the screen. She leaned over and read Meg's reply. *Really? My sister has no shame.*

"You too. That's all it takes to make you smile?" I hadn't realized I was.

I put my arm around her shoulders and squeezed. "She's safe." I smiled. "And she didn't tell me to fuck off."

I ordered more flowers, Madi suggested adding chocolates or a cute teddy bear. I took her advice and ordered both.

Chapter 40

Meg

I made myself a turkey sandwich for Thanksgiving dinner. I wanted to do more research, but the stupid holiday meant the library was closed.

I tried reading, but the protective and passionate hero reminded me too much of Jack, so I stopped. The last thing I wanted to think about was Jack. But I couldn't stop myself.

I thought about our time together: the lessons he insisted weren't, the fundraiser dance, our first date, his sweet birthday surprise, our first kiss, the way I felt when I was with him.

I cried. Not pretty crying like women in movies. No, this was tears streaming down my face, snot running from my nose, ugly crying. I took a hot shower to wash away the tears and clear my head.

Of course it didn't work. Did I really think a shower could erase my pain? I berated myself before finally admitting I missed him. It still hurt, but I was calmer and could think about it more logically.

It still pissed me off that he'd snooped around and uncovered my past. But he only did it because he was worried. Which made sense. Anyone coming after me might be a threat to his mom and he couldn't, wouldn't, take that risk. And his concern about me having a stalker shouldn't surprise me, not after hearing what had happened to Jamie's wife.

Maybe I could forgive him for looking up my past, but could I forgive him for lying? I was more angry he didn't ask me or at least talk to me after he found out, than I was about him involving Jamie and his dad. After all, they all worked together, and they'd be worried about Mary, too.

Was Jamie right? Was I as guilty as Jack? I never lied, but I'd kept secrets from him, hid the truth. Jamie had asked if I would've told Jack the whole truth if he asked. *Probably not. I would have lied to keep my secrets hidden. I have before.*

I kept a lot from him, especially in the beginning. I didn't want him getting involved, or feeling sorry for me, or thinking less of me because of what had happened. But I had been opening up to him, sharing my past on my own terms. I would've told him, eventually.

How long has he known? I thought back to the lesson when he seemed more serious… *He's known for a while, but hasn't treated me any differently.* And now he was respecting my space by not visiting Grannie's or calling me.

My phone buzzed.

Happy Thanksgiving

My thumb hovered over the send button after I typed my reply. Did I want to open this door? I wasn't sure, but I hit send anyway.

You too

Those two words didn't commit me to anything. Stared at my phone, I waited to see if he'd reply. I wasn't sure if I wanted him to.

Maybe I should talk to him, let him explain.

Chapter 41

Meg

On Friday, there was a box of chocolates along with the bouquet of red and white carnations. The note said: Please? Jack

On Saturday, there was a small soft brown teddy bear hugging an emerald green crystal vase filled with white roses. His note said: I'll wait. Jack

I left the flowers at Grannie's but took the cards, chocolate, and teddy bear home with me.

My anger was cooling off with each bouquet, each note I received. It wasn't the gifts, but his actions. His patience.

He hadn't contacted me, except for one text on Thanksgiving. He'd given me space and hadn't visited Grannie's during my shifts. His notes were simple—no begging, no dramatics. Jack was patiently waiting for me to change my mind. To listen.

On Sunday, I went to the library to continue my search. I'd tried twice before, but couldn't read through my tear-filled eyes and had given up. Anger and pain at Jack's betrayal made my brain useless, and it didn't help that I compared every place I found to Weatherford. I couldn't help it, I liked it here. Would I feel as welcomed anywhere else? *Focus. You have one week to find a new town to call home.*

After I got home, I did my laundry and started packing. Sadly, it didn't eat up a lot of time. I hadn't unpacked half my boxes, because the motel had been a temporary solution.

I picked up the notes from Jack and placed them on the counter beside the small, smiling teddy bear. I smoothed out the crinkled notes and lined them up in order.

Can we talk? ~Jack

Please. ~Jack

I'll wait. ~Jack

Jack was usually talkative, charming, expressive, but the notes he sent with the flowers were none of those things. Yet they made an impact. Maybe because they were so simple. He wasn't trying to convince me of anything. Well, except to talk to him. He could have sent one bouquet, begging and pleading, and then dropped it.

But he didn't. Instead, he reminded me he was thinking about me often, while respecting my space.

Damn it. *I need to stay mad.* Leaving would be easier if I was mad. But I wasn't. Not anymore. I'd had a lot of time to think about everything that happened, and the more I thought about, the more I realized Jack wasn't the only guilty one.

I didn't know when I changed my mind, but I had. And I was ready to talk to him.

Could I forgive him? *I'm not sure.* I'd decide after we'd talked. *If I leave without talking to him, I'll regret it.*

I picked up my phone and typed as fast as I could, then hit SEND before I could chicken out.

> If I agree to talk, it has to be somewhere neutral.

Jack responded a few seconds later.

> Tell me where and when.

> Are you available tomorrow night?

The coward in me wanted him to say no.

> Yes.

I suggested Starbuck's at four-thirty. It was the only place I could think of. I waited for him to make a joke about Mary killing him for going to a different coffee shop.

> I'll be there.

It felt like snakes were slithering in the pit of my stomach. I'd agreed to see Jack tomorrow night, and knew I'd be a nervous wreck until it was over.

After work on Monday, I kept myself busy by scrubbing the shower walls and behind the toilet, wiping down the cabinet doors and cleaning the grease filters above the stove. If I stayed busy enough, I wouldn't have time to over-think about my meeting with Jack. It didn't work.

I almost canceled a dozen times throughout the day, but controlled the impulse. I wanted to hear what he had to say, even if it wouldn't change the outcome.

Jack sent a text at three-thirty to confirm and I lost my last chance to back out when I sent my confirmation.

Knowing he'd try to beat me to it, I arrived early so I could buy us coffee. Jack arrived a few minutes after I sat down, holding a single white rose. *He looks so tired.* His usually neat beard was long and shaggy, and he had bags under his sad eyes. I fought back the urge to stand up and hug him.

"May I?" Jack asked before sitting.

I nodded and slid his coffee across the table.

Jack smiled, not his usual grin or a wide smile, but the sad smile of a person remembering something that used to make them smile. "Thank you."

He handed me the rose before picking up his coffee.

"Thank You." Tears filled my eyes as I stammered, "I, uh-" Everything I'd wanted to say drained out of my head. The buzz of people carrying on conversations around us filled the awkward silence between us.

Jack finally spoke up. "Meg, I'm sorry. I let my ego get in the way, and I hurt you. I have no excuses for not talking to you about Sul-" Jack glanced around. "Everything."

"Why?"

"Why didn't I tell you?"

I nodded and sipped my coffee to hide my face, my tears. This was a lot harder than I thought.

"Because I thought I could fix everything, protect you, without you knowing. I thought it'd be easy. I'd find your stalker, scare him off. He'd go away, and you'd feel safe." Jack paused, running his hair through his hair.

He sounded genuine, but I wasn't ready to trust him. "But?" He'd tried to tell me all of this before, but I stormed out of the house, too pissed off to listen. Today I was calmer, willing to listen, and I wanted to understand, needed to know why he'd betrayed my trust.

"But while I was trying to figure out who he was, I noticed some things in your background didn't fit." He paused and ran his hand through his wavy brown hair as he glanced around the crowded dining room again. "Are you sure you want to discuss this here? I want to be completely open, but I'm worried others will hear me."

"I don't know where else we can go and not have the same issue." I didn't want to go to my apartment, and he lived with Jamie. Neither place was neutral.

Jack was quiet for a minute as he thought about it. "We could go to my office. I know it's not neutral, but it's not personal either. I can shut my door so we have privacy." After a brief pause, he added, "It'd also give you the opportunity to ask Jamie or my dad questions I can't answer."

I thought about it. It wasn't ideal, but he was right; it'd be more private. Then I wondered what questions I could have that he couldn't answer. "Alright, I'll meet you there." It wasn't ideal, but it was a better option than having strangers overhear my ugly secrets.

Jack sent me the address before walking me out. I felt the absence of his hand on my back, and missed it, when held the door for me.

I shook my head. *I'm not supposed to want him touching me.*

Chapter 42

Meg

I didn't see anyone as Jack walked me to his office. It had two desks and four leather chairs clients could use. He pulled out a chair in front of his desk and offered me a seat. Organized chaos was the only way to describe Jack's desk. Stacks of files covered with colored post-its lined the front edge. A monitor stood off to his right with a keyboard in front of it and on the left was a closed laptop and a coffee mug with the SSI logo on it.

After offering me a water, Jack picked up where he'd left off, not leaving out any details as he explained how he asked for help after noticing the red flags. He said Jamie and his dad had learned my birth name after a facial recognition program matched a current picture of me to a junior high school photo. I always knew that might happen, but had counted on most people not caring enough, or having the ability, to do it.

I played with my water bottle as he told me everything I'd been too pissed to hear the night I walked out.

"SSI is monitoring Sullivan and watching for strange activity at Grannie's and your apartment."

I almost choked on my water. "Did you just say you're watching my apartment?" My knees pushed the chair back when I jumped up. "What the fuck Jack?"

"I'm not. I swear. But yes, there's a camera set up to monitor the parking lot."

"So you are watching me." My voice cracked with shock and anger.

He held his hands up. "No." He rubbed his face. "We're not. I'm not. My dad and Jamie are the only ones with access to the footage, and they can't see inside your apartment." He pleaded, "I swear, it's just a safety precaution. I can have one of them show you the feed if you want."

"I would." I sat back down with a thump and crossed my arms over my chest. It wasn't what I needed to focus on, but I was too shocked to let it go. "So your dad and Jamie, they know everything?"

"Yes."

That was all he had to say? I mocked him. "What, no apology?" It was petty, bitchy, but I couldn't help it, hearing they were watching my apartment had thrown me for a loop. I'd come here to talk to him, to hear him out, but he wasn't making it easy for me to stay calm enough to listen.

"You don't need to hear me say I'm sorry again. I am, but you need answers, not more apologies." Jack paused and ran his hands through his hair, making it stand up on end. He'd done that a lot today. "Here's the thing. I want to work this out with you if you'll give me a chance. I also want to help you. But right now, those two desires are at odds because I can't answer all your questions, but my dad and Jamie can, but that means we can't talk about us." He stood up and walked around his desk until he was standing in front of me. "Tell me what you want, or need, me to do and I'll do it."

I wanted answers, but also wanted to understand why I wasn't as pissed off at him as I thought I would be, as I thought I should be. But he couldn't answer that question for me. He'd lied to me, spied on me, and betrayed my trust, so I should be mad. But my strongest emotions were pain and shock, because I hadn't expected it from him. He'd been kind, patient, generous, and caring. *And apparently, he's been protecting me from Sullivan.*

If I was being completely honest with myself, I hadn't been honest with him either and after everything he'd done for me; he deserved the truth as much as I did.

"Meg?" Jack sounded nervous.

I searched his eyes. He wasn't hiding his pain or fear, and it floored me to see he wasn't handling this any better than I was.

I needed to know what they'd learned. Everything else could wait.

"I'd like answers, please. What about AJ & Doug? What do they know? How involved are they in all of this?" My heart raced in my chest. I wasn't sure I wanted to hear the answer, but I needed to.

"Not much, less than I do, actually. Doug set up the cameras, and he and AJ are monitoring the feed from Grannie's." He must have seen me cringe because he quickly added, "But not your apartment. Do you want me to ask them to come in too?"

I couldn't answer right away. *Do I want to talk to all of them?* No, I didn't, but I'd decided on the ride over I'd tell Jack the truth. All of it. I hadn't planned on talking to anyone else at SSI, but since they already knew, it didn't matter. I didn't have any secrets here.

I nodded, then added, "Yes. Please."

My feet tapped out a quick rhythm as I waited for Jack and the rest of the SSI guys.

Jack handed me another bottle of water when he came back, then suggested I move to his chair so I could see everyone. I stared at my shoes as I walked around his desk, grateful it provided a barrier between us. AJ sat at his desk, Doug sat in a chair in front of him, turning it so he faced me. Neither of them spoke. Jack sat in front of his own desk off to the right, and John and Jamie moved chairs into the space between Jack and Doug.

John's voice was all business. "Thank you for being willing to talk to us. We'll answer any questions you have."

"Thanks." My voice trembled as regret and fear set in. I clasped my hands under the desk to hide them. *You can do this.* I cleared my throat. "I'd like to see the view from the camera in my parking lot." My voice squeaked, so much for sounded strong.

Jamie opened his laptop, then brought it over so I could see the screen. The feed showed most of the parking lot, including my door. Jack hadn't lied; they couldn't see inside my apartment. "Where is it?"

"In the brown sedan parked at the end of the lot," Doug answered. "I made sure we couldn't see inside your apartment."

"Thanks, I guess." I slammed the laptop closed.

Jamie sat back down.

"You know about Sullivan?" I asked the room.

I saw John and Jamie nod and assumed AJ and Doug had as well.

"You did this, helped me, even though I didn't ask for it? Even though I can't pay you?" It was a lame question, but I couldn't sort through the chaos in my mind to find a better one.

They nodded and murmured, "Yeah." John's yes stood out.

My knuckles turned white as I clasped my hands in my lap. "Is there anything I should know about Sullivan right now? Like, has he left Boston?"

"He's still there. We'll tell you if anything changes," John answered.

"Right." I nodded as I replied, glancing at everyone except Jack. I wasn't sure I could stay strong if I looked him in the eye.

I took a sip of water, put the bottle down, and hid my shaking hands under the desk. "You're still helping me? Even though Jack and I broke up?"

I saw Jack flinch in my peripheral vision.

"Yes. And we'll continue monitoring things." John's response was direct. "If you decide you don't want our help, we'll remove the camera from the parking lot and stop monitoring your parents. But we'll continue to monitor Sullivan until enough time has passed that I no longer believe he's a threat to my family."

It was my turn to flinch as the color drained from my face. I knew Sullivan might connect me to Grannie's, but I hadn't thought Mary would be in any real danger. I was his target, so there was no reason for him to hurt her. But if John thought he was a threat, then he probably was.

"I'm so sorry, Mr. Sheppard. I didn't think I put anyone else in danger. There's no reason for him to hurt Mary." What had I done? "I'd never," I fought back my tears, "I wouldn't." But I had. "I did everything I could. He can't leave Boston and shouldn't be able to find me." I sucked in air as I wiped the tears off my cheek. "And he hasn't." I met John's brown eyes.

"Yet," John said. "It wasn't hard to figure it out, and if we can do it, so can he."

That wasn't what I wanted to hear. "I know." I choked out the words. More tears ran down my face. *Jack really should keep tissues on his desk.* I wiped my face with my hands and took a deep breath. *Why did I think I could do this?* Everything he said was making things worse.

I can't do this alone. They already knew everything and were already helping me. I didn't want them to stop, but I wasn't good at asking for help. Not good? I was awful at it. *Because I'm afraid to ask.* I sucked in a deep breath and spat out the words before I lost my nerve. "If I accept your help, can we set up a payment plan?"

Jamie and Jack spoke up, telling me I didn't have to pay. *They don't understand.* "I, I have to. I can't be in debt, not to anyone, I just… I can't." This mess was because of my father's debt, and Sullivan always reminded me I owed him a debt.

"We'll work something out," John answered. For the first time, I was grateful he didn't like me.

I nodded. "Thank you." I didn't know how I'd pay them, but I'd figure it out.

After a few long seconds, I turned to Jack. He was watching me quietly. *I can't believe he did all this to help me.* I'd been such a fool. And a bitch. I'd assumed the worst without ever giving him a chance to explain.

I clenched my fists to give myself courage. "I'm sorry I freaked out on you. You're the first person I've trusted since my grandmother. When you said you wanted to protect me, right after telling me you knew about my past, I snapped." I closed my eyes and inhaled. "Which isn't a normal response. Most people would be grateful, but," *You can do this.* "Sullivan always told me he was protecting me." I talked to my feet. "Fucking asshole protected me alright. He didn't let anyone beat me, and he didn't let me get addicted to drugs. He only drugged me when I had a 'date'." I didn't think they needed the air quotes to understand what I meant, but I did it anyway.

"Fuck." Someone hissed at the same time someone else said, "Bastard." I didn't know who said what because they spoke at the same time. It didn't matter. I could feel the anger in the room, and knew it wasn't directed at me.

I met Jack's eyes. "When you said you wanted to protect me, I heard his voice. I couldn't separate you in my mind."

"Jesus, Meg, I –"

Not wanting to lose my nerve, I cut him off. "I know you're not like him. I do. And I'm sorry I wasn't more open with you. I didn't dare–"

"Meg, please–"

I ignored him and rambled on. "I'm not saying it justifies your actions. It doesn't. But I guess we both had our reasons." I sniffled, no longer trying to hold back my tears. "I tried to stay away from you Jack, God knows I tried. But you were so damn charming, and persistent. I tried to keep you at arm's length, I did. But then I didn't want to anymore, even though I knew I should. I figured once you saw how fucked up my life is, you'd give up. But you didn't. You…" I wiped my nose on my sleeve. "I've lived most of my life living in fear, thinking, believing I couldn't trust anyone. But I trusted you."

"Meg–"

"Jack, if you keep interrupting me, I won't be able to finish." I wasn't sure I could finish even if he didn't keep interrupting me.

He nodded.

John stood up. "We're going to give you some privacy." He waved everyone out.

"Thanks," Jack said as his father reached the door.

I turned back to Jack after the door closed. "If you're going to help me, you need to know the truth, all of it. No more secrets." I sounded braver than I felt. Even though he knew, I felt it was important for him to hear it from me.

I squeezed my bottle of water as I collected my thoughts. "My father's a drunk and a coward. He turned state's witness against Sullivan for a lighter sentence. They didn't consider him a threat. But Sullivan," I held back a sob. "He knows I was the one who called 9-1-1 because I called from his client's phone. He'll want revenge. After I testified against him, the FBI gave me a new name and arranged for me to get help at a women's shelter in Indiana. They gave me a chance at a normal life."

I looked at Jack. "That's how I knew you discovered my past. Megan's parents didn't go to jail, but Margaret's did."

He nodded. I gave a sad laugh and shook my head. "My mom got arrested at my father's trial. She was stoned out of her mind and thought she could prove her innocence by screaming at my father. The judge had her arrested. It was the only time that bitch stood up for me."

My hands trembled as I remembered the scene in the courtroom. I spilled water over my chin when I tried to take a sip, so I gave up and put the bottle down.

"My grandmother gave me this locket." My hand drifted to my throat and touched the pendant. "She believed my eyes were a blessing from God." Tears ran down my cheeks, but my voice was rough with hatred. "Sullivan destroyed that for me, my last good memory of my grandmother. He told me my eyes would make him a fortune," I made air quotes, "the innocent young beauty with the magic eyes." My nails bit into my hands as I balled my fists. I could still see his fat face leering over me, could still smell the stale cigar on his breath, as he held my face in his sausage fingers, turning it left and right.

I shook my head to clear the memory as I sucked in much needed air. Jack handed me a box of tissues across his desk. *I didn't notice him get up.*

He'd listened quietly as I explained. It had taken me forever to build up the nerve to tell someone and once I started; the words rushed from me like floodwaters. "I haven't talked to my father since his trial. The only contact I have with my mother is through email. When she remembers I exist." I blew my nose. "I left Indiana when I saw the news about Sullivan's release. He couldn't come after me without the police knowing because of his ankle monitor, but I needed to move. I wanted to be further away. My father sold me to that bastard to settle his debts, so not only did I help send Sullivan to jail, but he lost a lot of money, too." I sighed. My thoughts were all over the place.

I could hear a pin drop. I looked up to see Jack staring at me with tears in his eyes, a stark contradiction to the anger rolling off his body in waves.

"Meg." Jack's voice was raspy.

I stared into his eyes. There was sadness, anger, and… shock?

Shock? "I thought you knew…"

Jack shook his head slowly back and forth, his back teeth clamped together. "I didn't."

"Oh." I stared at my lap and asked softly, "What about your dad and the others?"

"Dad and Jamie knew more than I did, but I'm not sure how much more. They know what's in the court records, and what Agent Jones shared."

My head snapped up. "You talked to Agent Jones?" Would the hits ever stop?

"Jamie did. He said Jones didn't share much, he's very protective of you." He quickly added, "And AJ or Doug only know you might be in danger."

"Oh." I wrinkled my brow as my shoulders relaxed a little. "Why'd he tell you anything?" Agent Jones knew every ugly detail of my history. I didn't want to believe he'd share my information with just anyone.

"Jamie told him what we knew, and why we wanted to help. Once Jones verified our credentials, he was willing to talk to him."

"You really didn't know?" He'd told me more than once he didn't know, but I hadn't believed him.

I could see Jack struggling. So many emotions fought for dominance in his eyes. Shock, anger, sadness. And pride? He quickly wiped the tears off his cheeks. "No."

"But if you didn't know, why'd you want to help me? Why give me all those non-lessons? Was it out of pity?"

"Pity?" He stood up and rushed around the desk. He spun his chair until I faced him. He kneeled down, his arms caging me in. "I never pitied you. And I didn't want to help you because it's my job to protect people. I did it because I fell for you, hard. I fell for you before I did a single keystroke of research. That's why I kept offering you lessons."

My eyes almost jumped out of my head as my jaw fell open. I hadn't expected an emotional outburst. *He fell for me?* I couldn't process it all yet, so I latched on to the one thing I understood.

"I told you so."

He laughed without humor. "We both knew they were lessons, but I wanted to see you so I lied and said they weren't because you would have said no and… dammit Meg, I wanted to see you. I let you buy me coffee after because it made you feel better, and because I got to spend more time with you." This time there was humor in his laughter. "My point is, it wasn't about protecting you, not at first. I wanted to spend time with you…" Jack cupped my face gently and used his thumbs to wipe away the tears rolling down my cheeks. "But now it's both. I'll destroy anyone who tries to hurt you. Not because it's my job or out of pity. I'll give my life to protect you, because I'm in love with you."

Chapter 43

Jack

Dad sent Doug and AJ home, but he and Jamie waited for me. I quickly gave them the details I thought they needed.

Dad seethed after hearing Meg's father sold her to cover his debts. "That wasn't in the trial transcript. It's not bad enough he raped her-"

"WHAT?" I cut him off. As if everything I learned today wasn't enough of a mind fuck. *Christ, no wonder she doesn't trust anyone. She's been through so much.*

"Fuck," Jamie said softly from behind his desk.

"I'll kill the bastard myself."

"Calm down Jack. You can't help her if you keep losing your temper." Dad walked around his desk and put his hand on my shoulder. "We'll figure this out together. I won't let another son lose the woman he loves."

"Thanks dad." I sighed. He'd known I was in love with her all along. How was I the only one who hadn't realized it? It didn't matter. Now that I'd taken my head out of my ass and owned my feelings, I was going to do whatever it took to win her back and protect her. Meg thought Sullivan had to leave Boston to get his revenge, but we knew better. He had a gang of associates ready, willing, and able to grab her and drag her back to him, and that terrified me. We didn't know if he had Meg's new name or location yet, but we had to assume he was doing his research.

"Jackson." Dad must have called me at least twice to sound so annoyed.

"Yeah, sorry. Just thinking, we don't know how much Sullivan knows."

"Unfortunately, no." He paused. "I know she's been through a lot already, but we have a few more questions." The sympathy on his and Jamie's faces mirrored my own. It felt cruel to pick at open wounds. The downside to being an investigator, sometimes you had to ask hard questions to help someone. "But do you think she'll talk to us for a few minutes?"

"I'll ask." I put on a brave face as I walked back to my office. Meg had enough to deal with, she didn't need me adding my fears to hers.

Chapter 44

Meg

"**B**ecause I'm in love you." He was in love with me? How? Why? *Oh God. I can't believe I just told him everything.* I only felt brave enough because I thought he already knew.

I tried to process it all while he talked to his dad and brother, but my mind was spinning out of control. After a few minutes, he came back in, kneeled in front of me, and carefully placed his hands on the armrests. It was like he was trying to embrace me without actually touching me. His soft smile didn't hide the pain or fear in the depths of his eyes.

"All I want to do right now is hold you in my arms and chase away your pain."

All I wanted was to let him. I nodded. He opened his arms, and I leaned into him.

The flood of emotions that erupted when he held me against his chest and placed a soft kiss on the top of my head was more than I could handle. I broke down and sobbed as he held me, my tears flowing like a river onto his shirt. After a few seconds, I wrapped my arms around him. Out of habit, I told myself I couldn't trust him. *But I can.* Because for the first time in my life, I felt safe.

Jack relaxed his hold when he felt me pull away. I plucked a few tissues from the box and blew my nose. When I finally opened my eyes, I noticed the wet spot on Jack's shirt. "I'm sorry, I got your shirt all wet." I wiped at it with a fresh tissue.

Jack grabbed my hand and held it until I made eye contact. "I don't care about my shirt." He gave me a soft grin.

I nodded and smiled back. I grabbed my water bottle and finished it, needing to focus on anything but Jack. It was too much to handle right now. *I need to regroup.* The loud growl from my stomach interrupted my thoughts, reminding me I'd been too nervous to eat most of the day.

"I don't suppose you'll let me buy you dinner?" I shook my head no. All I wanted was a hot shower and a nap. He didn't give up. "Can I at least get you something to eat? I'm sure I have a protein bar or something floating around."

I nodded, not fully trusting myself to speak. What was I going to do? My head was a mess, my emotions were all over the place. Fuck. What was I thinking, asking SSI for help? I was leaving in a week, though I still didn't know where I was going. I needed my savings for the move, but I could do it on less if I had to. And Mary could give them my last paycheck. I'd have to make payments for the balance. Though I didn't know how I'd manage without a job. Fucking hell, If I move and don't tell them where I am, how can they help me? My shallow breaths came faster and faster; I felt like I couldn't get enough air as panic set in. God, what was I thinking? I just told Jack my darkest secrets and gave him permission to share them. *What have I done?*

I took a few deep breaths. A part of me felt relieved knowing I wasn't alone anymore, but it was also terrifying to think about them knowing my history, judging me, pitying me. How am I ever going to face any of them again? Fresh tears flowed down my cheeks. I was too overwhelmed, too exhausted to hold them back.

Jack kneeled down in front of me, a protein bar and a fresh bottle of water in his hands. "Want to talk about it?" He tucked my hair behind my ear to expose my face.

My head said no, but my mouth said yes. "I'm overwhelmed. I should run away, not get you more involved. Your mom, everyone at Grannie's, is at risk because of me. If anything happens, I'll never forgive myself. I have to leave here, but I don't know where I'm going and now I have to pay your dad because I messed up everything, all because I was stupid and let my guard down." My breaths were coming too fast, my head started spinning.

"Hey, hey, shhh, just breathe. Take a deep breath. Good. Let it out. Good. Once more." I followed Jack's lead through a couple more deep breaths and my heart slowed down to almost normal.

"Sorry."

Jack opened his mouth, then changed his mind and nodded instead. I didn't have the energy to ask what he was going to say.

"My dad has a few questions. I know you're tired, but do you think you're up for answering them? It's okay if you're not. I can take you home and we can do it another time."

Better to do it now. I'd lose my courage if I put it off. "No, I'll answer them. Can I have a few minutes, though?"

"Yeah, of course."

I scarfed down the granola bar to the sound of my sniffles. The last thing I wanted was for my stomach to grumble while I answered John's questions. I drank half the fresh bottle of water in one gulp, the cool liquid soothing my throat. I gave myself an internal pep-talk, then told Jack I was ready. He led me to the office John and Jamie shared. It was almost identical to Jack and AJ's, except it was bigger and had more filing cabinets.

I held my water bottle with a death grip and avoided making eye contact as I sat down.

"Thanks for doing this. I know none of this has been easy, but it'll help us help you if we have a little more information."

"Okay." I nodded. I shifted awkwardly in my seat the entire time, stuttering and pausing more than normal, as I struggled to answer their questions openly and honestly.

"Thank you. It's helpful knowing no one outside the FBI, and now SSI, knows your previous identity. It'll be harder for Sullivan to connect them, which buys us time."

"Thank you." I was getting ready to leave when I remembered to ask, "How do I pay you?"

"We'll figure it out later." He waved his hand as if to wipe the idea away. "You've got enough to deal with today. Why don't you let Jack take you home?"

"I have my car. Thanks." I didn't think I could handle being alone with Jack yet.

"Alright, goodnight, Megan. And thanks again."

Jack walked me to my SUV. "Is there a chance, any at all, you'll give me a second chance?" His voice trembled.

"I don't know. Part of me wants to say yes, but part of me wants to run away and avoid the risk." I shrugged. "Besides, I'm moving, so it doesn't make sense."

"You don't have to."

"Yes, I do. My last day at Grannie's is Friday and I don't…" I hesitated. "I don't think I can stay here. Too many people here know. I feel exposed, embarrassed. I, I need to start over."

"No one is judging you, I swear. Please. Give me a couple of weeks to show you that you can build your life here." He paused. When I didn't answer, he continued, "Ma told me she hasn't found your replacement yet, so you could stay on at Grannie's. Stay a little longer, please." Jack's voice cracked.

Two thoughts took up battle in my head: stay here with Jack against run away. It was giving me a headache. "I don't know. How do I face your mom everyday knowing I put her in danger? How do I handle seeing her everyday knowing I'm the reason you don't come in anymore? Do you really think she'd let me stay on after all the trouble I've caused?"

"My mom doesn't know anything, and it's up to you if you want to tell her. And believe me, she doesn't blame you for our breakup." He smiled. "And I know she'll let you stay because she likes you. All you have to do is ask."

I thought about what it'd be like to stay in Weatherford, at Grannie's, if I wasn't with Jack and I didn't like it. No way could I stay here if things didn't work out with him. Jack was standing close enough that if I leaned forward, I could rest my head on his chest. If I did, he'd wrap his arms around me and I'd feel safe. To be here with Jack, safe in his arms, was the only future I wanted. Staying here won the battle today. I saw the hope in his eyes when I met his gaze.

"If Mary says I can delay my notice, then I'll stay for a couple more weeks. But, you can't say anything. This has to be her choice."

Jack's sigh lifted my hair. He drew an X over his heart. "Cross my heart."

"And Jack. No more lies or secrets. We have to be honest with each other." It'd be harder for me than for him—my whole life was a secret.

"I promise." He smiled, but it didn't quite reach his eyes. "Full disclosure. Ma hasn't started looking for your replacement. She told me to fix this so she wouldn't lose you." Jack raised his hands in surrender when I raised an eyebrow. "Okay, fine. She knows how I feel about you, and she doesn't want me to lose you." He grabbed one of my hands. "I don't want to lose you."

I nodded, not sure what to say. After everything that happened, I couldn't believe he still wanted an 'us'. How could he possibly love me knowing everything he now knows?

"Can we meet for lunch tomorrow, after you're done with work?"

"Um," I paused, debating. Jack waited patiently while I twisted my purse strap in my hand. The words came out before I could stop them. "Yeah, I'll need time to run home and clean up. Where do you want to meet?" *Please don't let me regret this.*

I talked to Mary the next morning. She was happy to extend my notice, indefinitely if I wanted, just like Jack said she would.

Later, Jack and I met for a late lunch at a local deli. It went well, all things considered. Our conversation was stilted and a little awkward at first.

I noticed I was still censoring myself and admitted, "I don't know how to talk to someone I don't have to hide from. I keep analyzing every thought. But I don't have to anymore, not with you." I couldn't hold back my nervous laugh.

"No, you don't. Not now. Not ever." Jack reached over and laid his strong hand over my trembling one.

After lunch, Jack walked me to my car and asked if we could meet for lunch again on Thursday. I agreed. I could do lunch. Lunch felt safe.

Our lunch date on Thursday went better. We were more relaxed than we'd been on Tuesday. I even shared a few of my rare, happy family memories. Jack listened, asked a few questions, and shared some of his memories. Before we left, he asked me if he could take me on a date Friday night.

I hesitated. *Do I really want to do this? Should I be rekindling my relationship with Jack instead of searching for a new place to live?* Yes, I do and I should.

Jack waited patiently for my reply. To a casual observer, he might seem relaxed, but his clenched jaw and rigid back gave him away. His nervousness was the final straw to my camel's back of reluctance. I said yes. And I meant it.

I'd figure the rest out later. *I should have left Weatherford when I had the chance.* But it was too late now. I couldn't deny my feelings for Jack. But my presence was putting them all in danger, so the best thing for me to do was leave.

Jack handed me a gorgeous bouquet of pink roses when I answered the door on Friday. I should have known he'd bring flowers. I hugged him before taking the fragrant flowers to the kitchen.

The date was going well until Jack asked me if I wanted to get in some training over the weekend. I was about to say yes when I remembered the raffle table.

"There was only one SIG on the raffle table. And it was a different color than the one I won."

"Right." Jack had the good sense to look ashamed. "I donated the second gun when you didn't win."

At least he was honest. "So you bought me a gun? After I said I didn't want yours?"

"No." He shook his head. "I didn't buy it. I won it at a conference. It's the same one I suggested lending to you. I wanted you to win so you could train with your own gun. But you didn't," He picked up his beer but didn't take a sip, "So, I donated the second SIG and asked ma to say it was an anonymous donation made at the last minute."

"She helped you?"

"Please don't blame her. I harassed her until she agreed."

"I don't blame her." I left the rest unsaid. "What would you have done with the gun if you hadn't donated it?"

"Convince you to let me sell it to you. Guns depreciate, kind of like cars. The minute it's out of the store, it goes down in value, so I could sell you a new one at a used price."

"And if I ask someone if that's true…" I didn't know why I was being so ungrateful.

"They'll say yes. Dammit, I wanted to do something nice for you." Jack asked, "Is that a crime?"

"No." It was my turn to look ashamed. I picked up my water glass, smiled, and said, "Thank you," before taking a sip.

He reached over and held my free hand. "You're welcome."

On the ride home, Jack told me he wanted to teach me how to draw from a holster this weekend. It sounded like a lot to learn in one lesson, but Jack assured me it wasn't half as hard as it sounded.

He walked me to my door and gave me a long, tight hug. His strong arms always made me feel protected, loved. I felt a kiss on the top of my head before he released me, and adjusted us so he was blocking the line of sight of the camera. He brushed an errant hair behind my ear and trailed his hand down my chin, giving me goose bumps. "Can I kiss you?" His voice sounded deeper than normal.

I stared into his eyes, and after what felt like an eternity, nodded. *I really want him to kiss me.* "Yes."

Jack leaned down and placed a soft, lingering kiss on my lips. A perfectly respectable goodnight kiss. Tender. Brief. I sighed. He was respecting my wishes, taking it slow. It was what I wanted. Right? Right.

Jack interrupted my thoughts when he lifted my chin. I opened my eyes and smiled. "Good night." He kissed my forehead. "I'll pick you up Sunday at ten."

"Yeah, um, okay. Thank you. I had a nice evening." I tried to sound casual, to not give away my excitement, and was one hundred percent sure I had failed.

"You're welcome." He didn't walk away. I knew he wouldn't until he heard my door locks click.

Chapter 45

Meg

On Sunday, Jack taught me the basics of drawing from a holster. He said I could use one of his until I found one I liked, then he laughed and said I'd probably need a couple, because most women did. When I asked why, he said it was because women didn't wear the same things day in and day out, so one holster rarely served all our needs.

I asked Jack if he wanted to grab lunch after our range date. It was about time I told him how I felt. I didn't want to do it in public, so we ordered burgers and fries and went back to my apartment. I made small talk while we ate, not willing to bare my soul with a mouth full of cheeseburger and fries.

I sat back down after cleaning up and stared at my clasped hands. I wasn't sure where to start. Jack waited patiently. The only sign of his nervousness was the soft tapping of his foot.

Just do it. "I've thought a lot about what happened and while you weren't totally honest with me, I wasn't totally honest with you, either. I've already forgiven you, and I hope you can forgive me." My words ran together.

Jack opened his mouth to speak, but leaned back when I held up a hand to stop him. "I don't want to leave anymore, but how can I stay knowing I'm putting your family in danger just by being here?" I tried to hold back the tears, but failed. At least I wasn't sobbing this time.

Jack stood up and walked around the table. "I don't want you to leave either." He pulled me up into a hug. "Come here."

Jack walked me to the couch and pulled me onto his lap as he sat down. "There's nothing for me to forgive. I understand why you kept your secrets. You had to."

"But I put your family in danger," I said into his chest.

"No, you didn't. You took every precaution. The only person I, we, blame is Sullivan. And we're keeping tabs on him, his known associates, and your parents. They won't be able to make a move without us knowing about it. When, if, they do, we'll be ready for them. You're not alone anymore. We'll face this together."

I nodded into his chest. "Sorry, I'm blubbering like a fool." At least this time I wasn't crying because I was sad. I'd never felt so loved or supported. "How sad is it I don't know how to handle people being nice to me?"

"Very." Jack placed a finger under my chin and lifted until my eyes met his. "But you should get used to it, because I'm never going to stop being nice to you." He wiped the tears from my cheek with his thumb before kissing me.

I closed my eyes and let the emotion flowing through his kiss wash over me. He pulled me into a hug when the kiss ended. We stayed there for a couple of minutes, Jack's arms wrapped around me and my head tucked under his chin. I sighed into his chest. *Is this what happiness feels like?*

"I got your shirt all wet again."

Jack chuckled. "I'm not worried about it."

"Can you stay a while longer?" I felt silly asking, but didn't want him to leave yet.

"Yeah, I'm yours for as long as you want."

I smiled against his chest. "I'm going to go wash my face. There's some beer in the fridge, if you want one."

Jack handed me a pumpkin ale when I got back. I sat on the couch facing him, my knees bent. We drank our beers while we talked, sharing different parts of our pasts, the good and the bad.

For the first time in my life, I could talk to someone openly. It was a little scary, but also refreshing not having to censor every word. Though I was struggling to break the habit.

"It's weird talking to someone and not being worried I might slip."

"A good weird, I hope." Jack squeezed my knee.

"Yeah." I stretched my legs out over Jack's lap and scooted closer. I heard Jack suck in a breath. "Should I move?"

"No, you're fine. Well, since we're being honest," he grinned, "I think you're still too far away." He laughed and pulled me onto his lap.

I wrapped my arm around his neck and gave him a quick peck on the cheek. I hadn't planned on kissing him. Or wanting more. I hovered close, smelling the pumpkin ale on his breath. I wasn't sure if I should kiss him again or wait until he kissed me.

Jack grinned but didn't move, letting me know I was in the driver's seat. It was up to me to make the first move. Not ready to be that bold, yet, I laid my head on his shoulder and sighed.

The tension drained from my body as he held me. I fell asleep sitting in his lap, his strong protective arms wrapped around me.

I made dinner for Jack on Tuesday. Our relationship wasn't the same and probably never would be, but that was okay. This time, we were being completely honest, and it was taking some getting used to. I'd always had something to hide and never been able to be completely honest with anyone. It felt good, and a little scary, to be so open.

I apologized a lot because I'd still change the subject anytime Jack brought up something I could never talk about before. Like when he finally asked me about my parents. At first, I tried to change the subject.

"Meg, it's okay if you don't want to talk about something. But say it, no more deflecting," Jack said as he poured himself a glass of water. "Please."

"I'd rather not talk about that right now," I said to the pan of noodles I was stirring.

"Hey, look at me." He waited until I met his gaze. "Thank you." He relaxed against the counter. "Anything I can do to help?"

"Nah, all I have left is to mix and bake."

During dinner, Jack got a text. "I'm sorry, I need to call Jamie."

"Of course." My pulse quickened. Jack rarely ever did more than glance at his phone when we were together. *I hope everyone is okay.* I expected Jack to get up and seek some privacy, but he didn't.

"What's going on?" Jack asked. After a few seconds, he met my gaze, his eyes full of concern. *Shit. It's about me.* "Okay, thanks, I'll let her know."

"What?" My voice cracked.

"I'm sorry I have to tell you this, but Agent Jones called Jamie a few minutes ago. Your mom died earlier this week." I stared at my plate, but didn't react. "They're ruling it an accidental overdose." He stood and walked around the small table to kneel beside of me. "I'm sorry, Meg."

I stared at him. I should feel something. Shock, sadness, regret for cutting her out of my life. Any of those would be a normal reaction to losing a parent, but I felt nothing. "I should probably feel sad, but I don't. Am I a bad person for not feeling sad?"

Jack hugged me. "No."

He pulled back. "I'm sorry, but there's more." *More?* The way he said gave me chills. "Your father missed his parole check in this morning."

"Do they think he's dead, too?" It wouldn't be the worst news. I might not react to my mother's death, but I would celebrate his.

"They aren't speculating. They sent an officer to the apartment when he didn't show up. That's when they found your mom." *Given his history, he'll probably turn up drunk on a street somewhere.* "They've issued a warrant for his arrest. Jones said he'll keep us informed." Jack rubbed the back of my trembling hands with his thumbs.

"I shouldn't worry, right? I mean, he doesn't know my new name, or where I live, and he's a drunken loser. He won't be able to find me." My voice trembled. "Right?" I really needed him to reassure me.

"Probably not, but I'm not taking any chances," Jack said. "You should stay with me for a while."

"I, uh, I don't think..." I didn't know what I wanted to say, but I didn't want to stay with Jack. "Is it really necessary?"

"Yes, it is. If you don't want to stay with me, I can stay here. Until we know for sure what's going on with your father, we're considering him a threat."

He was only on the phone for a few seconds. How'd he plan all this? I pulled my hands free. My mind raced with panic and anger. I couldn't deal with the threat right now, so I latched on to my anger. "What the fuck Jack? You can't just tell me you're moving in."

Shock crossed his face when I pushed him away. He sounded tired when he said, "I wouldn't be moving in. This is a temporary solution."

I was over-reacting, but I still wasn't ready to let go of my anger. Or face my fear. I didn't know what to say, so I stared at the floor.

Jack put his hands on my knees. "Please look at me. I know you don't want to hear this, and I don't want to say it, but if we could connect your past to your present, others can, too. And that scares me."

"I know." Tears filled my eyes as my emotions overwhelmed me. It scared me to be alone, but I didn't think I could handle him spending the night.

"I'd feel a lot better if you weren't here alone." He paused. "If it makes you more comfortable, I can sleep on the couch."

"You can't." *Damn it.* My voice sounded a lot less confident than I wanted it to. I didn't want him to see me blinking back my tears, so I stared at my hands. Maybe someday I wouldn't cry over everything.

"Can't do what? Sleep on the couch? Stay over?"

"Announce that you're staying here without asking me."

Jack's eyes rounded. "Oh man, I'm sorry. You're right, I should have asked." He leaned back on his heels and looked genuinely ashamed.

"Yes, you should have. I'm not ready for you to stay here."

"Meg, if—"

"Please don't make this a bigger deal than it is. If there's proof he's on his way here, then I'll let you stay with me. Okay?" The likelihood of my father wanting to find me was slim, the likelihood of him having the ability to find me was slimmer. He probably passed out behind some bar or was hiding because he owed someone money again.

Jack clenched and unclenched his jaw a few times before answering. "I'll hold you to it. I mean it." He held my eyes for a second before leaning in and kissing me on my forehead. "Let's finish dinner."

We finished dinner in relative silence and Jack left shortly after. I'd expected nightmares to haunt me all night, but they didn't.

Wednesday was mostly normal, except my nerves were on edge. Jack had spooked me last night, though I'd never admit it. I didn't believe for a second my father could find me without a lot of help, and he couldn't afford to pay for the help he'd need. I kept telling myself not to worry. *So why am I so jumpy?*

After work, I went home to shower and change before driving to Beth's. Chase was a great kid, and I loved babysitting him. We played a couple of games of tag in the backyard. Every time he tagged me, he'd screech "You're it" at the top of his lungs.

After a tasty dinner of Chase's favorite meal, dinosaur shaped mac and cheese, we sat down and colored. Chase picked a Pterodactyl for me and a T-Rex for himself. I laughed when he called me 'a silly girl' for giving my dinosaur purple wings.

I texted Jack after reading Chase his favorite bed-time story.

Thank God Chase is finally asleep.

Did he wear you out?

Yeah. We colored after dinner. I colored my dino's wings purple.

Purple? Really?

Yup!

LOL What did Chase have to say about that?

He called me a silly girl.

I saw lights in the driveway.

Beth's home, gotta go.

Text me when you get home.

Please. xoxo

thumbs up

Chapter 46

Meg

I had plenty of time before Jack picked me up for our range date on Thursday, so I picked up my book and leaned back on my bed.

I jumped when I heard a loud knock at the door. *Did I lose track the time?* It wouldn't be the first time it happened when I was reading. I looked at the clock. *Nope.* It was too early for Jack, besides it didn't sound like Jack's normal knock. *And he always announces himself.*

Knock. Knock. Knock.

I put my book down and walked to the living room. Whoever was knocking at my door was really impatient. I was stretching up on my toes to look through the peephole when I heard: "Maggie, it's your dad. Open up."

The only thing moving was my heart as it beat out of my chest. *It can't be. How the hell did he find me?*

My breaths were too fast, too shallow. I forced myself to slow down.

I peered through the peephole. He looked older, thinner, sicker; but I'd know his face anywhere. It still haunted me.

I backed away. *He's probably not alone.* I walked backwards towards the couch, where my range bag was sitting on the floor, praying for Jack to come early.

KNOCK KNOCK KNOCK. "Come on Maggie, let me in. I've missed you." *He's got to be fucking kidding me!*

I shook with fear and anger as I pulled my SIG out of the bag and loaded a few rounds into a mag, ignoring the ones that fell from my shaking hands, before slapping it into the gun.

The sound of the wood cracking as my door shattered rattled my bones. I jumped up and raised my gun. *That's not my father.* I aimed my pistol at the tall guy in a black suit. "Get out!" My squeaking voice wasn't fooling anyone as I tried to yell.

My father walked in behind the black suit guy. When I turned towards him, my gun moved with me and was now pointing at my father instead of the real threat. That was a mistake.

"You won't shoot us, will you, Maggie?" The black suit guy taunted me as he closed the distance between us. "I can see you shaking. You're too scared to pull the—"

I whipped around to face him and pulled the trigger. CRACK! The sound echoed through the apartment, making my ears ring.

Black suit guy grabbed his side. "You bitch! You shot me." He closed the distance with two quick steps and knocked the gun out of my trembling hands before punching me in the face. My hands flew to my face as I fell to my knees, my eyes watering from the pain.

I tried to crawl towards my gun, but he grabbed my hair and yanked me up. He pushed me towards another guy in a black suit, who was waiting at the door. He was shorter than the one I shot, but no less menacing.

I bit the shorter guy when he put his hand over my mouth. He yelped before slapping me on the side of my head, making my eyes water again. He wrapped an arm around my neck, cutting off my air so I couldn't scream, and dragged me outside. Panicking, I fought against his arm, trying to remember what I should do. There wasn't much time for them to get me in the black van—even in Texas, a gunshot would attract attention. *Fight back and delay them!* I could see blood on the tall guy's arm as he put duct tape over my mouth. I stumbled forward when the short guy released me and bent over, hands clutching my bruised throat, as I tried to fill my lungs with oxygen.

Short guy yanked me back up by my hair. The duct tape muffled my scream. I head-butted him when he tried to tape my hands behind my back. *Damn that —*

Everything went dark.

Chapter 47

Jack

Beth called me to tell me some guy had come in earlier asking about Meg. He told Lisa he was Meg's father, and he wanted to surprise her but lost the slip of paper with her address. Lisa didn't know not to say anything, so she told him where Meg was staying.

"When? What did he look like?" I jumped up and ran to Jamie's office. AJ followed on my heels. I put my hand over the speaker, "Jamie, pull up the feed at Meg's."

"He came in a little over an hour ago. She said he's tall and skinny with short brown and grey hair."

"Okay, thanks for letting us know." I hung up just as Jamie said, "Fuck." He turned to dad, "Get Doug."

I was grateful today was one of those rare occasions when all of us were in the office. I had a feeling we'd need all hands on deck.

I ran around his desk and stared at the monitor. My knees almost gave out as I watched an unmarked black van speeding out of the parking lot.

Jamie reversed the feed until we saw the van pulling in. A man, fitting the description Beth had given me, got out of the van, looked around, then nodded before knocking on her door. He looked jumpy, and his impatience grew the longer he waited for Meg to answer.

"He told Lisa he's Meg's father," I said.

"I'll verify with facial recognition," Doug volunteered.

"Good. Janerek, run the plate," Dad ordered.

We watched as the man pounded on her door again. He turned toward the van and shrugged. *I wish we had audio.* Another man, dressed in a black suit, approached the door and pushed her father out of the way. He shattered the door with one well-placed kick. They went inside, out of view, while a third stood in the doorway.

"Come on, Meg, please tell me your gun was loaded. You can do this. Drop these guys." I didn't realize I was praying out loud until I felt my father's hand on my shoulder.

My heart stopped when we saw a muzzle flash. I didn't need words to know the depth of my father's support; he said it all with a squeeze of my shoulder. His strength was the only thing between me and full-blown panic. The third guy, who'd been guarding the door, rushed in.

"Fuck. We need to go." I started toward the door.

My dad grabbed me and held me by the shoulders. "We will, but first we need more information. They were leaving when we turned on the feed, so rushing in won't help her.

We don't know who they are or where they're going. Take a deep breath. Once we have more information, we'll make a plan and go."

"What if she's dead in the apartment and we can't see her?"

"She's not. They put her in the van. She fought like hell, kicking and screaming, and it looks like she shot the dude who kicked the door in. She head-butted the third guy before he knocked her out. They took her father with them." Jamie quickly filled us in, looking as worried as I felt. We all knew a person's chance of surviving an attack plummeted if they were taken to a second location.

AJ came in. "It's stolen." Not surprising.

Dad issued orders. "Janerek, text the plate number to everyone. Sharpe trace Meg's phone. Jamie, call WPD and get a BOLO on the plates. Janerek, Sharpe, you're with Jamie." He looked at me. "You're with me. We'll meet at the motel."

Weatherford PD was on sight when we arrived. They'd set a perimeter with yellow crime scene tape and were questioning witnesses. Luckily, dad knew the officer in charge and convinced him to let me inside.

I put on rubber gloves and plastic booties to preserve the integrity of the crime scene. I swallowed down bile as the smell of blood hit me. *We'll find you, Meg, keep fighting.*

My chest tightened in panic when I saw the blood on the floor. I took a deep breath and reminded myself it wasn't Meg's. She wasn't bleeding when they put her in the van.

I searched for Meg's phone. Doug hadn't been able to get a lock on it on the short drive over, not that it would matter if it was here. Meg's purse was on the coffee table. To my relief, her phone wasn't in it. My heart sank when I walked into her bedroom and saw her phone on her bed.

Her phone was evidence, so I couldn't take it, but I convinced the officer to let me review at her call history. "I'm her boyfriend, and might see something odd that could help."

The officer agreed, but told me I had to do it in front of him. He watched me closely as I pulled up Meg's incoming call history. I knew it was a long shot since her father shouldn't have had her number, but if he'd somehow gotten it and called her before coming over, then maybe we could find her by tracing his phone. There were several calls from the same unknown number, the most recent about thirty minutes before Meg's father knocked on her door. She hadn't answered them. I memorized the number and gave the phone to the officer. It might not be her father's phone number, but it was the only lead we had.

I went straight to Doug after leaving Meg's apartment and gave him the number so he could find out who it belonged to and trace it. I drummed my fingers on the roof of the truck as he searched. Unfortunately, the phone was off, so he couldn't trace it.

"I'll keep trying. The phone number belongs to Anthony Ramos." Doug asked, "Mean anything to you?"

I said no at the same time Jamie said, "He's one of Sullivan's men."

"Fuck." We'd suspected they were Sullivan's men, but having it confirmed still felt like a dagger to my heart. There was no way of knowing what horrors he'd subject her to, or how long before he killed her. An icy chill ran through my body. *I have to find her, fast.*

Dad finished talking to WPD and joined us. He told Jamie to turn over the footage from the camera to WPD. "Start when the van appears and cut it when it disappears out of the frame."

"On it." Jamie was already typing as he answered.

"Let's get back to the office and gear up. It's going to be a long night."

"Yes, sir," we all answered in unison.

On the drive back to the office, Dad warned me. "Jack, I know you're worried, but you can't let it get in the way."

I nodded. *Easier said than done.* "I know, Dad. I'll keep my shit together."

"Good, because Meg needs you."

I swallowed the lump in my throat. *I just hope we find her in time.*

"We'll find her." He paused when my phone vibrated, then added quickly, "She'll be okay. Meg's a fighter."

"Thanks dad." I hit the accept button and told Doug, "You're on speaker."

"Sullivan's MIA. Jamie just got the call. He's been off the radar for at least two days."

"Dammit." I hissed.

"Why didn't we hear about this two days ago?" Dad growled as he asked.

"There was a glitch in the system, causing his ankle monitor to be offline for sixty minutes. Enough time for him to take it off and put it on his dead parole officer." Doug filled us in.

"Given the circumstances, I think we need to assume he's coming here," Dad said. "Is there any way to track his movements using his known associates? We know at least one is already here."

"Janerek and I are working on it now. The FBI issued a nationwide BOLO. If he's on the move, he'll have to be cautious." Good. Cautious meant slow.

"Keep working on it. We'll help once we're back in the office," Dad said.

"This is bad." My voice cracked. "He could already be here."

"I know. We'll do everything in our power to bring her home. I won't let another son lose the woman he loves to a maniac."

Jamie ran home to get his sniper rifle and gear while the rest of us stayed at the office and searched traffic cams for the plate. He jumped on his computer to help search as soon as he got back. Doug's tech skills, and Air Force contacts, came in handy as he helped us gain access to video feeds we might not otherwise have.

Around eight, mom brought us pizza, coffee, and snacks. There wasn't much she could do to help other than feed us and offer moral support. She gave me a long mama bear hug before leaving, taking a second to re-assure me and address my unspoken fear. "You'll find her, Jack, and you'll save her." She pulled back and looked me in the eye before saying, "I have faith in you, in all my boys." I needed to hear that more than she could possibly know. She gave me a kiss on the cheek before breaking the hug and saying the rest of her goodbyes.

It was just after ten when we got our first hit on the license plate from a gas station camera west of Dallas. The time stamp read eight-eleven. Now that we had a general direction, we could refine the search parameters. Doug was checking the phone number every fifteen minutes, but they hadn't turned it back on.

Hold on Meg, keep fighting, we'll find you. Praying gave me something to focus on and helped keep my fear from overwhelming me. I remembered the scene in Ever After when the prince showed up after Cinderella had saved herself. I wouldn't be the least bit disappointed if that was how this story ended.

I was leaning back in my chair when I heard Doug say, "Gotcha." I jumped up and ran over to see what he'd found.

"They turned the phone on. I'm tracing it now."

I looked at my watch: four-thirty. *Please God, don't let us be too late.*

"The phone is less than an hour north of here, near Aurora. I'm zeroing in on the exact location now."

"Get ready to roll. I want everyone in a vest." Dad asked, "Can you track from the road?"

"Yeah, let me get a lock first, then I'm good to go."

"Sharpe, Janerek, you're with Jamie. Call us with the location once you've got a lock on it. Jack and I are heading in that direction now."

"Let's go." I said, already striding towards the door, pulling my black long-sleeve t-shirt over my vest as I walked. I wasn't willing to wait those precious minutes while Doug got the location.

Dad and I were only on the road for a few minutes when Doug called and gave us the coordinates. Meg was in a cabin in a wooded area outside Aurora.

Dad reminded me to hold it together. We'd need to assess the situation when we got on site, then make a plan. "We're not running in half cocked. I won't risk anyone getting killed."

"Yes, sir." I drummed my fingers on my thighs, willing him to drive faster.

Chapter 48

Meg

I woke up and blinked away the fog in my mind. *Where am I?* I tried sitting up, but everything hurt, and my wrists and ankles were bound. A quick look verified they'd duct taped me while I was unconscious.

I panicked as everything came rushing back. The duct tape covering my mouth was pulling at my lips as I tried to breathe through my mouth. My chest burned from a lack of air, and my eyes watered. I forced myself to take a few deep breaths through my nose as I tried to remember what I'd learned in the self defense class. Keep breathing so you don't hyperventilate and pass out.

First, I needed to get my hands in front of me. I wiggled my hands down the back of my legs, contorting so I could bring my feet through my arms.

Second, I needed to stand up and break the duct tape wrapped tightly around my wrists. I wiggled to the side of the bed. My head spun when I stood up too fast and I fell back down on the bed. I waited for my head to clear before trying again, slower this time. *So far, so good.* I raised my hands above my head and swung them down, pulling them apart like Jamie had showed us.

It didn't work. I tried again. It still didn't work.

Panic forced the air out of my lungs. *What do I do? What do I do?*

I searched frantically for something I could use to cut the duct tape.

Idiot. I ripped the tape off my mouth and choked back a scream. *So much worse than ripping off a bandaid!* I used my teeth to tear the duct tape on my wrists, then sat down and removed the tape from my ankles. I wiggled my hands and feet to get the blood flowing again.

I could hear the muffled sounds of people talking outside the door, so I tiptoed over to hear better.

Guy 1: Sullivan is gonna be pissed you bruised her face.

Guy 2: Bitch shot me. She deserved it.

Guy 2 was obviously the tall guy I shot, and he sounded really angry.

Guy 1: He won't care. You should have punched her in the gut or something.

Guy 2: You didn't hold back when she bit you. You're in as much trouble as me.

Guy 1: I slapped her. It won't leave nearly as much of a mark as punching her.

Guy 2: Whatever. I hope he gets here soon. I want first go at her when he's finished, so I can teach that bitch a lesson.

I put my hand over my mouth to muffle my cry as I backed away from the door. *Sullivan's on his way here.*

I searched the room for a weapon, scanning past the window as I looked for something I could use on the dresser below it. Nothing.

A window! The dresser was one of those solid, old-fashioned ones and I was confident it would support me.

I lifted myself onto it, opened the window, careful not to make a sound, then turned around and got on my belly. I pushed my feet through, then my knees, inching myself out so I'd be closer to the ground before jumping.

I landed with a thud, then checked to make sure I was alone.

Where the fuck am I? Which way do I go?

It didn't matter. I needed to run. *Now.* I ran towards an overgrown path to my left, hoping it'd take me to a road where I could flag down help. I really didn't want to get lost in the dark.

I didn't get far before I heard shouts and footsteps behind me. Someone was closing in, fast. I didn't dare look back, so I didn't realize how close he was until he tackled me. We fell forward, and I heard a snap as red hot pain shot through my left wrist. I screamed and kicked my legs, trying to get him off me.

He yanked me to my feet by my hair and held my head still so the tall guy could put more duct tape over my mouth. Fresh tears flowed down my cheeks as I held my throbbing left wrist in my right hand while they shoved me back to the cabin.

After we were back inside, they forced me into a chair across the table from my father and tied me up. They re-taped my wrists, not bothering to be careful of my now swollen and discolored wrist. I looked at my father's bruised, bloody face. They'd beaten him so badly he was barely recognizable. I hadn't heard him screaming because they gagged him.

I should probably feel sympathy for him, but I couldn't muster anything except loathing and anger. *It's his fault I'm here.* I could see the front door and the living room from where I was sitting, but it was too dark to see anything beyond the patio door behind us.

It felt like an eternity as I sat there with my wrist throbbing and tears running down my face and over the tape. I tried, and failed, to tune out the two guys as they took turns taunting me with all the horrible, painful things they wanted to do to me to make me pay for all the trouble I'd caused. It lasted late into the night. I dozed off from sheer exhaustion after they finally stopped.

The sound of a phone ringing jerked me awake. Immediately, I noticed how much my face hurt, but it was nothing compared to my throbbing wrist. I had no idea what time it was, but the sun wasn't up yet, so it had to be early.

"Boss is ten minutes out. We should clean her up." He sneered at me like it was my fault I was a bloody mess.

Sullivan. The thought was enough to make my whole body tremble.

The shorter guy got a rag from the kitchen and soaked it in water. I clenched my teeth to keep from screaming as he violently wiped at the blood on my face.

He stopped and stepped back when the door opened. Sullivan strutted in, looking the same as he did before going to jail. Fat, balding, arrogant. Two more guys in black suits followed him in, making the two guys who grabbed me look like jokes. They were wearing similar suits, but these guys were bigger and a lot meaner.

I flinched as he barked orders at his men, his eyes holding mine hostage. It took all my strength to break his paralyzing stare and turn away.

I felt his fat fingers on my chin as he forced me to turn my head. "Look at me."

I opened my tear-filled right eye and stared my worst fear in the face. Sullivan had me in his possession again, and this time I couldn't escape. *I won't survive this.*

"I'm sorry he hit you, Margaret. I gave them strict instructions not to hurt you." He shot daggers at the two guys who grabbed me. "It's a shame. I've been waiting a long time to see those magical eyes of yours again." The taste of bile choked me.

Sullivan leaned in as he spoke; his breath reeked of stale cigar smoke, causing me to gag. I tried to turn my head, but he tightened his grip, causing me to wince in pain.

"Untie her!" He barked.

Fresh pain tore through my wrist when they ripped off the tape. I cradled it in my trembling right hand.

Sullivan stared at my swollen wrist, his eyes growing darker by the second.

"What the fuck did you do to her?" If looks could kill, they'd be dead. "Who broke her arm?"

"I was an accident. She tried to run away, and I tripped when I grabbed her. We fell." He sounded scared.

Sullivan's flat voice was scarier than his bark when gave the order for one of the new guys to break his arm.

The ruthless brutality of the guy following Sullivan's orders terrified and sickened me. The duct tape pulled at my lips when I leaned over and dry heaved.

"Get her some ice and water." Sullivan ordered one of the new guys. Then to me, "You see what I'm willing to do to protect you," he caressed my face, "like I always said I would?"

It was a rhetorical question, so it didn't matter that I couldn't answer.

Sullivan handed me the ice pack and told me to ice my arm, then ripped the duct tape off my mouth.

I bit my cheek to keep from crying out. The pain of the tape being ripped off was nothing compared to my fear. All I could think about was how Sullivan planned on getting his revenge against me.

I heard a phone ring, followed by a muffled voice. One of the new guys said, "I'll tell him." He put his phone back in his pocket. "Boss, we got company." Based on his expression, they weren't expecting anyone.

Sullivan pointed at my father. "Shoot him. I don't need him anymore."

The guy I shot strode towards my father, who was shaking his head back and forth, pleading with his eyes. Sullivan's man didn't care—he shot my father in the temple. No hesitation. No guilt.

I closed my eyes in time to avoid seeing his blood splatter on the wall. The warm metallic smell assaulted my nose, causing my stomach to heave, but there was nothing left to vomit. *Will he tell one of them to shoot me? Or will my fate be worse?*

I opened my eyes when I heard Sullivan say, "He was never good enough for you, Margaret." His voice disgusted me. How could he be sweet talking to me mere seconds after ordering the execution of my father?

"You two," he pointed at two of his guys, "help secure the perimeter."

My whole body trembled. I was alone with Sullivan and his biggest guy.

Sullivan paced back and forth. *Should I be worried or relieved that he's nervous?* Maybe someone heard the gunshot and came to help. No, the call had come before the gunshot. It didn't matter, he'd kill anyone who came to-

The crack of multiple gunshots cut off my train of thought.

Sullivan sent the last guy outside to find out what was going on.

More gunshots followed by eerie silence. None of Sullivan's men came back.

Please God, let it be Jack. I'd barely finished the thought before all hell broke loose.

Sullivan yanked me out of the chair and grabbed me around the neck in a choke hold. He held his gun to my head as he moved us away from the table. His fat, sweaty arm was cutting off my air. Using me as a shield, he turned us towards the door when it shattered.

Jack and AJ rushed in, guns up. They stopped short when they saw us.

My legs buckled. It might have been from fear or relief, or both. All I knew was the only thing keeping me upright was Sullivan's arm around my neck. Sullivan yanked me up, forcing me to stand on my toes. "Put your guns down or I'll put a hole in her head."

Jack and AJ complied slowly as they moved further into the room, forcing Sullivan to turn, so he could keep using me as a human shield. Our backs were now to the patio doors near the table.

Jack and AJ held their guns down by their sides.

"Look at me, sweetheart, and only me. No matter what. Can you do that?"

I was afraid to answer, and couldn't nod, so I held eye contact until Sullivan grabbed my chin, forcing me to tilt my head back.

"Sweetheart? How cute." His voice was thick with venom when he spat out, "You get to watch your lover die too." He released my chin and wrapped his arm around my neck again.

I could barely see Jack through my tear-filled eyes. Knowing Sullivan would kill him too, I prayed. *Don't let him kill Jack, he can have me. Please don't let Jack die.*

I watched in slow-motion as Jack whipped his gun up and pointed it at Sullivan.

I felt the pressure of Sullivan's gun leave my temple a second before I saw it pointed at Jack. The flash in front of my face when he pulled the trigger made me flinch. The loud crack next to my head made my ears ring. The sound of glass shattering behind us cut through the ringing in my ears.

Sullivan's head snapped back, and his arm tightened on my throat as he dragged me down to the floor with him. On the way down, I saw Jack fall. His head slammed against the floor, knocking him unconscious. My screams had nothing to do with my landing on my wrist.

AJ shouted something about Sarah and drella, but it was hard to understand him with the ringing in my ears.

John rushed through the door, gun up, and scanned the room before dropping to his knees beside Jack.

As I fought to free myself from Sullivan's grasp, I turned and saw a pool of blood growing under his head. *Did someone shoot him? I didn't hear another gun go off.* My stomach retched as I jerked back in revulsion. Someone tried to grab me. I fought them off, forgetting the pain in my wrist in my desperation.

"DON'T TOUCH ME!" I slapped at the hands as I turned back to Jack.

I couldn't take my eyes off his motionless body. I crawled to him on my knees and good hand, screaming and crying. "JACK! Jack, you can't die! Please don't be dead, Jack. Please?"

I flung myself on Jack when I finally reached him, begging, "Please don't die Jack, I love you. You can't die. Don't be dead. Please."

I felt a hand on my shoulder and looked up.

It was John. He was kneeling next to Jack, applying pressure to Jack's right arm with his other hand.

"WHY AREN'T YOU HELPING HIM?" I yelled as I stared at Jack's blood on the floor.

"Sweetheart."

"Help him." My voice shook as I pleaded.

"Meg." I looked down. Jack's eyes were open.

Relief washed over me. *He's alive.* "Jack!" I threw myself on his chest and tried to hug him, causing him to groan. And me to wince as I landed on my left wrist.

Jack grimaced when he inhaled before saying, "Say it again," through gritted teeth.

"What?" I'd tell him anything if it'd make him better.

"Tell me you love me." He grinned.

"I love you." I hugged him as I whispered the words into his neck between sobs and sniffles.

"I love you too."

"Megan honey, let AJ help you up so I can help Jack." John put a hand on my shoulder.

When I looked up, I noticed Jamie and Doug standing behind John. I was so worried about Jack I hadn't seen or heard them come in. I felt a fresh wave of panic when I looked at the blood under Jack's arm. *He got shot! Wait, shouldn't there be more blood?* I turned to check Jack's chest.

"You got shot." I was certain I'd seen him get hit in the chest. Jack moaned when I put my hand on his ribs. "How are you alive?"

Jack tapped on his armor, making himself moan again. "Armor. Remember?" He pointed to the place my hand had been. I could see metal through the hole in his shirt.

"Megan honey. We need to get out you of here. The paramedics are on their way. You and Jack both need help." He repeated, "Let AJ help you up. Please."

I glanced at AJ. He was bleeding from scratches on his face. *How'd he get those?* I looked back at Jack.

"It's okay. I'm not going anywhere without you. I promise. Let AJ help you."

AJ helped me stand, carefully avoiding my left arm. My wrist was bent at a nasty angle, swollen, and a frightening shade of purple that extended halfway to my elbow. He tried to walk me out, but I refused to budge, not without Jack. I couldn't take my eyes off of him as John and Doug helped him stand. Not even for a second—I was too afraid of losing him.

Jack must have seen the fear on my face because he held out his left arm, inviting me into a hug. Without hesitation, I stepped into his one armed embrace. He held me loosely and kissed the top of my head. "It's over. He can't hurt you anymore."

"Is he really dead?" I turned to look at Sullivan's body to confirm for myself, but AJ stepped into my line of sight. My head started spinning when I saw the pool of blood on the floor.

"He is." Jamie answered as he slung a long rifle over his shoulder. He reached out a hand to support me as my knees buckled at the news. Sullivan was dead. My nightmare was finally over.

"Should have done it a few seconds sooner and spared me the pain." Jack said through gritted teeth. *Jamie shot Sullivan? When? How?*

"Wasn't a clean shot." He shrugged as he looked from Jack to me and back to Jack.

The paramedics arrived as we walked out.

And the sun was peeking over the horizon just like it did every day, not caring one bit about the hell I'd suffered over the last twelve hours.

Chapter 49

Jack

I rode in the ambulance with Meg. They tried to tell me no, but Dad stepped in when he saw me arguing with the paramedic. Whatever he said was enough to convince them. Not caring if I annoyed the doctor and nurses, I kept my promise to Meg and refused to leave her side when they transferred her from the ambulance to the emergency room.

I stood near the door, ignoring my injuries and pain, and argued with a nurse, "Listen, I'm her fiancé. She's having a panic attack and won't cooperate if I'm not in the room." I kept my voice as calm as I could, more for Meg's benefit than for the nurse's. "So I'm staying."

She sighed and backed down. "Fine." She huffed out. "Just don't get in my way." I nodded.

Meg whimpered through clenched teeth as the nurse gently cleaned her cuts and bruises. There was nothing I could do or say to stop the slow, steady stream of tears spilling down her cheeks, and it was killing me. Meg choked back a sob when the nurse said they needed an x-ray of her wrist. My heart swelled with pride as I watched her trying to be brave while drowning in fear. *She is so much stronger than she realizes.* I gave her unhurt hand a gentle squeeze to remind her I was still here with her. "It'll be okay."

After another battle with the nurse, she allowed me to accompany Meg as far as the radiology door.

Dad and Jamie were waiting outside Meg's room when we got back and followed me inside so we could talk. I stood near the door, angled towards Meg so I could see her, and more importantly, so she could see me. Dad looked at my arm, then my chest, worry etched all over his face. But I couldn't leave, not until I was sure she would be okay.

We whispered as the nurse wrapped Meg's arm in an ice wrap and elevated it on a soft block. I held her gaze as I listened to the nurse explain what she was doing each step of the way. I flinched when I heard Meg wince.

"How is she?" Dad asked.

It was taking a Herculean effort to keep myself from running to her. "She's scared. I don't think it's sunk in yet." I whispered, running a hand through my hair.

He nodded. "You haven't you seen a doctor yet." It wasn't a question.

"Not yet. I can't leave her, Dad."

Jamie came to my rescue. "I get it. Why don't you talk to the nurse? We'll say hi to Meg and remind her she's safe."

They talked to Meg while I asked the nurse about the x-ray results. Relief washed over me as I hurried over to tell Meg the good news. "Good news Meg, you won't need surgery. The doctor can set and cast your wrist after the swelling goes down." I didn't want to imagine how hard it would have been for her to hear she needed surgery.

She released a shaky sigh of relief as I stood at the edge of her bed, caressing the back of her hand with my thumb, offering what little comfort I could. I desperately wanted to hold her and chase away her pain and fear, but couldn't think of a way to do it without causing us both a lot of pain. It was a small price to pay to hold her, but it'd upset Meg if she thought I was in pain. *What a fucking mess.*

She leaned back and stared at the ceiling. "Thank you."

For the next few minutes, the only sound in the room was Meg's sniffles.

She startled us when she bolted upright, eyes wide in panic, "Oh my God, how the hell am I going to pay for all this? I can't work with a cast. Which means I won't be able to pay for it or the ambulance or the x-rays. I'm going to lose my job and if I lose my job, I'll get kicked out of my apartment." Her chest rose and fell in rapid succession as fresh tears ran down her cheeks.

We stared as Meg went from zero to sixty in no seconds flat, freaking herself out about a lot of things. It was probably a good idea for her to release some of her pent up fear, so I put a hand up to signal to them to let her ramble. She had yet to mention the bloody carpet, her dead father, or shooting someone.

"Those assholes broke down my door." I saw it in her eyes the second she remembered. "OH MY GOD I SHOT

SOMEONE! I'm going to jail!" Meg's voice went up several octaves.

That was enough. I didn't mind letting her ramble, but I couldn't let her worry about going to jail.

"Meg." I gently wiped the tears off her face with the back of my hand, being extra careful of the bruises on her left side. "Shhh, you won't go to jail, sweetheart. It was self-defense." I didn't mention her other fears. We could address them later.

I watched Meg's eyes for a sign she understood me. She took a deep breath, reminding me I needed to breathe too. My lungs were begging for air; I'd been holding my breath while I waited for her to answer me. I winced at the added pressure on my cracked ribs when I finally inhaled.

"I need you to listen to me, okay? Everything's going to be alright." I gave her a kiss on her temple. "I promise."

She was hyperventilating so I reminded her to take slow breaths in and out. I was going to do it with her, but it hurt too much, so I talked her through it instead.

"How will I pay for all this?" Her voice sounded so small.

My dad answered, "Megan, honey, the hospital will set up a payment plan for you." Meg looked at him but didn't say anything. "And I'll put in a good word with your boss. I'm sure she'll listen to me." He paused for effect. "I think she might have a crush on me." I couldn't hold back my smile when he winked, like they now shared a secret.

Thankfully, his wink had the desired effect. Some of the tension left Meg's shoulders as she leaned back and chuckled. Watching her relax had the same effect on me. The pressure on my chest subsided as my tension drained away. She was going to be okay.

I was sitting on the edge of the bed while Meg rested. When she heard the doctor come in, she opened her eyes and sat up. Panic written all over her face.

"Hi Meg, I'm Doctor Ainsley. You can call me Doc A, if you'd like." He gave her a big toothy smile, the kind you'd give a child. His voice was low and soothing. "I hear your wrist needs a cast."

She nodded. I placed a hand on her knee to offer what little comfort I could. It was killing me not being able to do more. I'd happily take on her pain if it meant she didn't have to feel it.

"Alright then, your fiancé can stay with you if you'd like, but everyone else has to leave."

"My what?" Meg's eyes bulged and her jaw dropped as she turned towards me. I'd completely forgotten about the little white lie I'd told so I could stay with her.

The doctor raised an eyebrow.

"Hey doc, can you, ah, give us a sec?" I asked.

"Sure." He reviewed Meg's x-rays as he waited on the other side of the room.

I squeezed her hand as I quickly and quietly explained. "I had to tell them we're engaged or they wouldn't let me stay with you."

"Oh, um. Okay." Her voice was flat. I thought I detected a hint of anger, but I couldn't be sure, and now wasn't the time to ask. I waved the doctor back over.

"It's going to hurt when I set your arm. It'll be easier for both of us if you're asleep." Doctor Ainsley said as he approached with a needle. "This is a mild sedativ-"

Meg shook her head back and forth, her breath coming in short ragged spurts as panic set in. "What if he comes back?"

The doctor asked, "Who?" at the same time I reassured her, "He won't, he can't. I promise."

She stared at me with wide eyes as I waved my dad over from the doorway.

"My dad's going to sit with you while I see if the doctor has something that won't knock you out, okay?" She nodded before looking at my dad. She was still nervous around my dad, but I knew he'd take care of her. I took the doctor aside.

Out of the corner of my eye, I saw my dad gently push Meg back onto the pillow when she tried to sit up. She cried out in pain when she bumped her arm. He signaled me to stay back, then held Meg's good hand in both of his.

I listened while he talked to her like a patient father. "The doctor doesn't want to hurt you when he sets and casts your arm. You don't want your arm to hurt anymore, do you?" His voice was gentle.

She shook her head. I barely heard her whisper, "I'm afraid."

"I know you are, but you've been so brave today. Can you be brave for a little while longer?" He brushed a lock of hair off her face. "It's almost over."

"What if he comes back?" The fear in her voice tore at my heart.

"He can't come back. He can never hurt you again. I promise."

Meg asked, "Is he really truly dead?"

He nodded. "He is, Jamie shot him." I hadn't expected my father to be so blunt, but it worked and Meg's shoulders relaxed a little. "Now, will you let the doctor give you a shot so it doesn't hurt anymore?"

"But, what if–"

"Megan, please look at me." I could tell by his tone his tactic had changed. "I'm going to be straight with you, okay? Jack really needs to see a doctor. Do you see his arm? How it's bleeding through the bandage?" She nodded. "And you can't see it, but the impact of getting shot at close range most likely cracked a few ribs. He needs to get fixed up, too." *Clever. But why did he think she'd respond better to me needing help than she would for herself?*

Meg sucked in a gulp of air, her eyes moving back and forth between me and my dad. She shook her head. "I, he, he said it was just a scratch."

"I know, honey, but he lied." He held up a finger to stop her from speaking. "You can yell at him for it later. Right now, every breath is excruciating, and he's refusing to get help because he's afraid to leave you."

I stood rigid beside the doctor as Meg stared at me. She'd be able to see the pain and fear etched all over my face because, despite my best effort, I could no longer hide it.

"I'm so sorry. Why didn't you tell me?"

I walked over and stood next to the bed. "I'll need a few stitches and some rest, that's all. Promise."

"But your dad said it's bad."

How the hell do I answer that? If I told her it was bad, she'd feel guilty. If I told her it wasn't bad, she'd think my dad lied. *Damned if I do, damned if I don't.*

Dad saved me from having to answer by changing the subject. "Meg, if you let the doc here give you the shot, you'll fall asleep and when you wake up, you'll both be patched up." She looked back and forth between us. "He'll be back before you wake up."

Meg grabbed my hand. I could see the fear in her eyes and feel it in her vise-like grip. "Mr. Sheppard, will you stay with me until Jack comes back?"

"Happy to." Dad stood up and turned to the doctor. "That won't be an issue, will it Doc." It wasn't a question. Dad was good at phrasing a command like a question. I'd rarely seen anyone challenge him. *I have so much to learn from him.*

"Not at all." The doctor wasn't nearly as concerned about breaking hospital protocol as the nurse had been earlier.

"Thanks, Dad," I said as I sat down beside Meg.

"Is it true? Does it hurt to breathe?"

"A little yeah," I admitted. "But it'll be better soon. I'll stay until you fall asleep, okay?"

"Okay. Then you'll get fixed up too?"

"I will, I promise." I kissed her forehead. "Now sit back."

I stayed until I felt her hand relax in mine.

Chapter 50

Meg

I heard voices as I woke up. After a second, I recognized them as Jack and John. I listened for a minute before opening my eyes.

Jack asked, "How'd you know she'd be okay with the sedative if you told her I needed help?"

"I remembered how fierce she was after you were shot. You didn't see her fighting off Sullivan to get to you. I don't think she realized he was dead. Then she fought off AJ when he tried to help her stand. She crawled to you on her knees and a broken wrist. Then she yelled at me for not helping you."

There was a pause before he continued, "Don't give me that look son. I verified your vest stopped the bullet and applied pressure to your arm."

"Good to know." Jack chuckled.

"She was worried about you, and a hell of a lot braver than she thinks. All I did was remind her."

Hearing John tell Jack about what happened after he got shot stirred a memory. I croaked out, "Jack, who's Sarah?" My throat felt like sandpaper.

"You're awake." Jack walked over, sat down, and held my good hand. "Are you in any pain?"

His right arm was in a sling. "No." I felt a little loopy, but felt no pain. "Is your arm okay?"

"Yeah, just a few stitches." Jack grabbed a cup with a straw in it. "Here, take a sip."

"Thanks." The cold water soothed my scratchy throat. "You need a sling for a few stitches?"

"The bullet nicked my muscle, so Doc said I shouldn't use the arm for a few days." He grinned and lifted his arm. "We'll have matching slings."

I stared at him for a few seconds. He was being cute, but I was too tired to laugh. "And your ribs?"

"A few cracks on the right side, no breaks. I'll have a bruise the size of Texas on my chest for a while. Luckily, it's all wrapped up because it's won't be pretty." He laughed, then moaned.

"Does it hurt?"

"A little." He must have seen how worried I was because he added, "But only until the pain meds kick in."

"So who's Sarah? I think that's what AJ was yelling after you got shot, that and," I searched my memory. "Drella or something..."

Jack and his dad both laughed. It was John who finally answered me. "I think you mean Sierra and Cinderella. Jack's call sign is Sierra Three, and we gave you Cinderella as your call sign."

"Oh." I yawned, too tired to ask why I needed a call sign. Then I remembered something John said and fought off my sleepiness. "Did I really hit AJ? Did I hurt him? Is he mad at me?"

John chuckled. "Yes, no, and no, he's not mad at you. He knows you didn't mean it."

I sighed. Thank God I didn't hurt him. I felt Jack squeeze my hand. I looked back at him and asked, "Are you really okay?"

"I am." He smiled. "Can I get you anything?"

I opened my mouth to answer, but yawned instead. "Sorry." I closed my eyes, too tired to stay awake for another second.

Chapter 51

Jack

I was talking to my dad and Jamie when Meg called my name.

"I'm right here." I reached out and brushed the hair off her face. "How are you feeling?"

"I want to go home." Her voice was thick with sleep.

I didn't answer right away, instead I begged my dad and Jamie for support with my eyes. She must have forgotten her apartment was a crime scene, and I didn't want to freak her out by reminding her while she was half asleep.

She looked between me, my dad, and Jamie, then closed her eyes. She covered her face with her hands, wincing when she hit her bruised face with her cast. "I can't, can I?" She sniffled. "I don't have anywhere to live."

I pulled her hands away from her face. "Meg." She wouldn't look at me, but I continued anyway. "It'll be okay." I brushed the tears off her cheek with the back of my hand, careful not to irritate her bruises. "You're coming home with me."

"What? No. I can't." She was shaking her head back and forth so violently I was afraid she'd hurt herself. "You live with Jamie and he doesn't want me living there."

"Meg–"

"No. You can't tell me what to do," she yelled. "We agreed. Or was that another lie?"

Damn it. I didn't know what I'd done to piss her off, and I was losing my patience. It'd been a long night, and all I wanted to do was go home and sleep for a week, with Meg safely by my side. I calmed myself down while collected my thoughts.

Reminding myself Meg was struggling with the events of the last two days and not thinking clearly, I took a deep breath and calmly answered. "You don't have a lot of options right now. Your apartment is a crime scene." Had she forgotten? "I didn't think you'd object." I gave her a second to think about it before asking, "And what other lies?"

"You lied about being badly hurt and in pain." Her quiet voice didn't mask her anger, or her fear. "You lied about being my fiancé. About–"

I rubbed a hand over my face, stopping to apply pressure to my temples. I was too emotionally drained, too physically exhausted to deal with this right now, so I cut her off. "Stop. Please, just stop. You're right, the thought of leaving you while you were having a panic attack and refusing treatment scared me fucking senseless, so I lied to the hospital staff, but not to you, about being your fiancé." I winced as I stood up.

She didn't deserve my anger, and I knew I'd regret yelling at her, but I couldn't hold back my frustration.

"Do you want to know what else I lied about? You paying your hospital bills on a stupid fucking payment plan. I put everything in my name." She shook her head and opened her mouth, but I didn't want to hear it, so I held my hand up to stop her. "Because there is no way in hell I'm letting the woman I want to marry, the future mother of my children, work herself to death to pay off a fucking hospital bill!" I put a hand over my ribs and held back a grimace. Yelling wasn't doing my cracked ribs any favors.

She noticed. "You said it doesn't hurt," her voice trembled, "another lie."

Oh good lord, she's challenging my patient and my sanity. I scraped together what control I had left before continuing through clenched teeth. "Of course it hurts. Can you honestly say you would've felt better knowing it hurt to move, to talk, to breathe?"

Meg's eyes rounded before she shook her head. "No."

"And I'm sorry if it sounds like I'm telling you what to do, but you're staying with me because I need you with me. To hold and comfort you, to know you're safe. The only thing I'm sorry for is not doing more to protect you." My voice was rough with fear and pain, and louder than I would have liked. I hated myself for losing control and yelling.

Meg stared at me with wide eyes and her mouth hanging open. She looked at my dad, and then at Jamie. I didn't have to see them to know they were almost as shocked as she was at my outburst.

"Please let me help you, Meg." I closed my eyes. "I'm begging you."

"Jack?" Her voice was barely above a whisper.

Please don't argue with me. I opened my eyes.

"Thank you." She said it softly, but to me it sounded like she'd shouted it through a megaphone. I had to sit down before I collapsed as the tension drained from my body. My rant had taken a lot out of me, and my ribs throbbed.

"Was that so hard?" I laughed to diffuse the tension between us.

"Jackson, don't be rude." Dad scolded me as I leaned down and kissed her forehead.

Ignoring him, I focused on what was important. "I love you Meg."

"Jackson." Meg's chuckle as she repeated my father's use of my full name was music to my ears. I didn't want to go another day with hearing the sweet sound of her laughter, and I'd do anything to make sure I never had to.

"Jamie, are you sure you don't mind me staying with you?" Meg asked softly.

"It was my idea. Jack will be insufferable if you're anywhere else. Honestly, you'd be doing me a favor. You might have noticed he can be a bit pig-headed, so I could use your help keeping him home while he recovers." He was only half-joking.

I'd never loved my brother more than I did at that moment and dipped my head to him in gratitude. He and my dad knew exactly what to say to convince Meg to listen and agree. *I have so much to learn from both of them.*

"Thank you, Jamie. Thank you all. For everything."

"You're welcome," we answered together.

Then I added, because I really needed to hear it again, "Now, tell me you love me."

Her eyes sparkled as she said, "I love you, Jackson."

She flinched when I kissed her lips. I pulled back and was about to apologize when Meg put her good hand on my arm. "Can we go home?"

"Yeah, sweetheart, we can." I hugged her. When she squeezed me back, pressing her cast into my ribcage, I groaned. "Gently."

Chapter 52

Jack

My mom had been at the hospital most of the day, lending her quiet support. She wanted to come with us, but I convinced her to wait a day, swearing we'd follow the doctor's orders and thanking her for being there to support us. Then hinted I wouldn't mind a pan of lasagna for dinner tomorrow. I bit back a groan when she hugged me goodbye so she wouldn't insist on coming home and taking care of me, of us.

Jamie drove us home after the hospital discharged us, and because we were all starving, he stopped at a driver-thru for burgers on the way.

Meg picked at her fries and ate two small bites of her burger before giving up. She was so exhausted, she almost face planted on the table more than once. Thankfully, Jamie encouraged her to eat a few more bites so she could take her pain pills before going to bed. If I had tried, she would have accused me of telling her what to do and I didn't have the physical or emotional strength to argue with her anymore tonight.

I walked Meg to my bedroom. "You can wear one of my t-shirts tonight. We can pick your stuff up tomorrow if you're feeling up for it." She nodded as she sank down on the bed.

"Thanks."

She hesitated when I offered to help her change, glancing at her cast, then up at me. I could see her struggling to decide.

"I promise not to peek." I almost winked to lighten the mood, but thought better of it. Winking might make me seem like a creeper.

"Okay. Thanks."

I helped her stand and turned her around so I was behind her, then lifted off her shirt, careful not to bump her newly cast wrist or the deep purple bruises on her face. My t-shirt slipped over her head easily as I helped her put it on. After getting her settled, I went to the hall bathroom. Getting cleaned up wasn't easy or painless.

Meg woke up when I came back in. I kissed her goodnight, then grabbed a pillow and walked towards the door, thinking she'd be more comfortable if I slept in the living room. Plus, I didn't think she'd want me in the bed with her.

"Where are you going?"

"The couch, so you can rest comfortably."

She looked at my arm, then my chest. "Oh." The word barely reached me.

I walked back and sat on the edge of the bed. After a long, uncomfortable pause, I asked. "Meg?" I waited for her to make eye contact. "Would you like me to stay with you?"

She nodded and asked, "Do you mind?"

I didn't. In fact, I preferred it. I eased myself onto my back. "Come here." I motioned for her to snuggle up to my left side and wrapped my good arm around her. The stress of the day melted away as I felt her head getting heavier on my shoulder as she fell asleep.

"I love you." I whispered as I closed my eyes. Thank God she wanted me to stay, because nothing had ever felt as right as holding her while she drifted off to sleep.

The next morning, I woke up surprisingly late. Not wanting to disturb Meg, who was still curled up against my side, I reached for my phone. My arm and ribs screamed in protest. I tried to hold back my "oomph" but failed and woke Meg up.

She panicked and bolted up to a sitting position, pushing off my bruised chest. "OW!" I yelped as her cast crushed my bruised ribs. Ignoring the pain the best I could, I sat up and tilted her face up so she met my eyes. "It's okay. Shhhh, you're okay. You're here with me. Take a deep breath." I struggled to keep my voice even. My ribs were throbbing, and it hurt to breathe. "Sweetheart, do you know where you are?" I waited as the seconds ticked by. Meg took a few quick breaths and looked around the room.

"Jack? I'm so sorry. I didn't know where I was. And then," she sniffled, "then it all came rushing back." A few tears escaped.

"Shhh." I brushed the hair away from her face and pulled her into a hug. "It's okay. You're safe now. I promise."

When her stomach growled, I suggested we get up and grab breakfast.

Jamie made scrambled eggs and sausage and insisted on serving us. "Enjoy it while you can," he said, laughing.

"Thanks Jamie." Meg said as he poured her a cup of steaming hot coffee. "For everything."

"You're welcome. Now eat up. You need to take your pain meds–"

I opened my mouth, but Jamie shut me up with his hand. "Both of you. I'll be here all day, and Mom and Dad will be here later. Ma insists on feeding you."

Jamie addressed my unspoken fear—I couldn't help Meg if I was asleep or dopey from pain pills. I nodded my gratitude, knowing I could relax because Meg wouldn't be alone, or unprotected, if the pills knocked me out. I knew Sullivan and his goonies were dead, but I couldn't stop seeing her in his clutches, knowing one twitch of his finger was all that had stood between life and death. The memory sent shivers down my spine.

"Thanks." I raised my coffee in salute. "Breakfast smells great."

Jamie told us Dad had assigned some SSI guys to watch her apartment. "The crime scene techs have finished, so we can go pick up your stuff when you're ready. Your gun and phone are evidence, so you won't get those back for a while. We can get you a new phone later."

She shrugged. "Everyone who might call me will know to call Jack." She chewed on a bite of greasy sausage. "Mmmm. Thanks Jamie, I was starving." We ate quietly for another minute.

"Well, everyone except my apartment manager. Oh God, I bet he's so pissed. Do you think he'll sue me for the damages?" I could hear her anxiety building.

"He can't. I'll talk to him to make sure he doesn't try something shady." I said, before taking a big bite of my cheesy scrambled eggs.

"Already done. Dad talked to him yesterday after we left the hospital," Jamie said. "And our guys have strict instructions that no one, not even the manager, goes in without your permission."

"Thanks." She groaned. "My apartment is a crime scene. God, this feels like a bad dream…"

"You don't have to go. We'd be happy to pack up all your stuff and bring it here." I reached over and rubbed her arm.

"No, I need to go. For one, I have cash locked in the safe. Two, I would rather not have someone from SSI packing up my… personal items."

"Not a snowball's chance in hell." I chuckled. "I'll be the only one helping you pack your personal items. If you want help, that is."

Meg looked terrified when Jamie reminded us we needed to give our statements to the Sherriff's Dept, and volunteered to drive us. She probably still thought she'd get arrested for defending herself. Jamie calmed her. "It's just a formality.

You're not in trouble. The rest of us gave our statements at the scene yesterday."

I loved my family every day, but today I was reminded of how extraordinarily lucky I was to have them in my life.

Chapter 53

Meg

I woke up to the rich smell of tomato sauce filling my nose and making my mouth water. There were worse ways to wake up from a nap.

Jack mumbled, "Mmm, mom's famous lasagna, my favorite."

Mary gave me a big, but gentle, hug when we joined everyone in the kitchen. "I'm so glad you're home safe."

I wiped away my tears as I pulled away. "Thank you."

"Hi Mr. Sheppard."

"Hi Megan, how're you feeling?"

"Okay, thanks." I didn't want to admit I was sore and tired, though it was probably obvious. I felt awkward around him after everything that had happened at the hospital. *He probably thinks I'm a weak fool.*

"Can I help with anything?" I asked, knowing I wouldn't be much help but needing to offer.

"Sure, you can keep me company while I finish making the lasagna. It'll give us a chance to catch up." She turned to John and her sons. "You boys go watch TV or something."

"Yes, ma'am," they answered in unison. Jack gave me a quick kiss on the cheek before leaving.

John must have told her I was worried, because Mary wasted no time reminding me I still had my job at Grannie's. I thanked her and apologized for causing her and her family so much trouble. I didn't want to cry anymore, but I couldn't stop a few stray tears from falling when Mary reassured me that none of this was my fault. *How can she be so supportive after all the trouble I've caused?*

She changed the subject and told me how happy she was Jack and I had worked things out. "You two are good for each other."

By the time dinner was ready, I was ravenous enough to eat two small helpings of lasagna and three slices of homemade garlic bread. I would have felt guilty about eating so much, but Jack polished off twice as much and then asked his mom if she'd made dessert. He was thrilled when Jamie and John came back with a pan of brownies and a tub of vanilla ice cream after clearing the table.

While we were eating dessert, Mary invited me to Christmas dinner.

With so much going on, I couldn't think about it yet, so I stared down at my plate and avoided making eye contact with anyone. I didn't want to seem ungrateful or rude by saying no after they'd done so much for me. *So much? They literally saved my life.* I scratched my hand at the edge of my cast. Jack's love and support were clear in his eyes when he reached over and placed his hand on mine.

So much had happened so fast and I wasn't sure I could handle a family holiday so soon. Not to mention, I was still worried John was only being nice out of sympathy and wouldn't want me there. *Not that I blame him, I put his family in danger and got his son shot.* The uncomfortable silence stretched out. Unable to take it anymore, I excused myself and ran to Jack's room.

Jack followed me. "Meg, what's wrong?"

"I don't know if I can do this." I was sitting on his bed, crying.

"Do what?" he asked, his voice filled with worry.

"Have Christmas dinner with your family. It'll be weird with presents and traditions, not to mention I don't think your dad likes me. After all this, who could blame him?" I swept my good arm wide.

Jack exhaled. *Great, he's probably mad at me.* "We don't have to go if you don't want to. Or we could go for dinner only. Or we could stop by, say hi and," he waved his hand, "Merry Christmas, then leave. We'll do whatever you want. Whatever you're comfortable with."

Too many things were circling around in my head and I couldn't think straight.

Jack rubbed my back in small circles. "Why do you think my dad doesn't like you?"

"He always seems upset when he looks at me, and he's the only person who calls me Megan, and he doesn't want you to go out with me." I started crying again. "Oh Jack, I can't make you choose between me and your family. I'll stay-"

Jack put a finger over my lips. "There's no choice. It's you. Always." He kissed me on the forehead. "And my dad likes you. It was the circumstances he didn't like. Haven't you noticed he's been calling you Megan honey? And maybe he hasn't said it to you yet, but he respects you."

He respects me? Why? "He does?" I thought back, his dad had called me that a few times at the hospital. Maybe I could do this. "I don't know. Maybe we can go for a little while." I hugged him. I could always change my mind later.

We walked back to the kitchen table and sat down. I was going to apologize, but Mary beat me to it.

"I'm sorry I put you on-the-spot Meg. I already consider you family, and, well, I didn't think about it being awkward for you."

I felt the sting of tears in my eyes yet again. At least they weren't tears of sadness or pain. I blinked them away and thanked Mary. I added my apology for over-reacting and accepted her invitation. Jack held my hand the entire time.

The conversation returned to normal, but then Mary interrupted. "Meg."

I didn't understand why she whispered my name as if she was hearing it for the first time. "What?" I asked with some hesitation.

Mary had a wicked gleam in her eyes. "It just now occurred to me you fit in with our naming system." She laughed as if she'd told a joke. "The boys have J names and the girls have M names. It's almost like it was meant to be."

Jack laughed and raised his glass. Everyone raised theirs and clinked before taking a sip.

Dare I dream? If things with Jack worked out, I'd finally have the family I'd always wanted.

We were sitting in the living room after dinner, when I remembered something I wanted to ask John.

"Mr. Sheppard?"

"Please Megan, call me John."

"Um, okay." I wasn't sure I could call him by his first name. "Can I ask you a question?"

"Of course."

"How come when you told us about head-butting people, you didn't mention we might pass out? I mean, you said it would hurt, and it did. But I didn't expect to pass out."

Everyone except Mary looked at me with raised eyebrows while they held back their laughs. "What?" I had no idea what I'd said to amuse them.

John finally answered me. "You didn't pass out from head-butting that asshole. He hit you in the head with the grip of his gun."

"Really?" I was sure I sounded like a maniac when I chuckled. This was all too crazy. I started rambling. "And here I thought I did that wrong, too. I couldn't get the tape on my wrists to break doing it the way you taught us. Of course, Jack didn't wrap it as tight, or wrap my ankles, and he didn't punch me, but still. I tried it and it didn't work and I panicked. Then I figured out if I took the stupid tape off my mouth, I could bite the tape off. I felt so stupid for not thinking of it sooner." I was staring down at my lap, rubbing my arm, not wanting to see their expressions as I confessed my failures.

I apologized. "Sorry, I'm babbling." When I looked up, they were all staring at me.

"No need to apologize. And we're glad you figured it out," Jamie said.

John nodded before asking, "How'd you break your wrist?"

A weird question, since he knew. "I jumped out of the window and tried to run away, but the guys chased me down and one of them tackled me."

"My brave girl," Jack said with a smile before kissing my cheek.

"Brave? No, I'm a coward. I was terrified. I've spent my entire adult life running and hiding, and I was so scared of what Sullivan would do to me, all I could do was cry."

"Megan, honey, you are one of the bravest individuals I have ever met. You're not just a survivor, you're a warrior."

"I am?" There was no way that could be true.

"Meg, you've done so many brave things. The most recent was yelling at me for not helping Jack." He paused, then chuckled.

I should have felt flattered, but I was too nervous. He still intimidated me, and I really didn't want to piss him off. "I didn't, did I? Did I really yell at you? I didn't mean to." My eyes felt like they were about to pop out of my head. "You scare the shit out of me." *Shit!* I hadn't meant to say that out loud. Mary, who'd been sitting quietly, listening the whole time, busted out laughing.

"I'm so sorry, Mr Sheppard."

"It's John, and it's okay. I've been told I can be intimidating." He and Mary shared a look. "Despite me 'scaring the shit out of you', you didn't hesitate to accuse me of not helping my son. You have balls of steel, Meg, and any doubts I might've had about you being the right girl for Jack disappeared at that moment. He needs someone like you, someone who's not afraid to call him out on his bullshit, and you've got what it takes."

"Thank you." I croaked out as tears threatened to spill over again. Never in a million years did I expect to get a stamp of approval from Jack's dad. *John, he wants me to call him John. And he called me Meg.*

Chapter 54

Meg

Jack and I adjusted to living together as we healed. I'd always had to be responsible for myself, and I didn't know how to let others take care of me, so I struggled with Jamie was doing so much and never letting me help. After a week of accepting his help without arguing. *Well, not too much anyway.* I decided I'd had enough.

"Jamie, why won't you let me do anything to help?"

"Because you need to rest and recover."

"You're already helping me so much by letting me stay here. The least I can do is earn my keep." I paused and pointed at Jack. "You're letting Jack do stuff."

"Because my injuries aren't as bad as yours. I'm almost completely healed." I stared daggers at him because he should've been on my side.

"It's not like I'm crippled or laid up in bed. It's a cast." I lifted my arm to show them. "A cast doesn't prevent me from taking care of myself." My voice was barely above a whisper. "I can, you know, take care of myself."

"I know you can, but you don't have to. Not anymore." Jack begged, "Let us spoil you a little while longer, please?"

"Can I at least help cook? I don't like feeling useless, and sitting around doing nothing makes me anxious."

Jack and Jamie looked at each other. I couldn't tell exactly what messages they were sending each other, but I felt like I was close to getting my way. "Please?" I begged, my hands in prayer position. "I promise I won't overdo it."

"I'll make you a deal. I'll let you help cook, but you can't complain anymore. If, at your next checkup, the doctor says you're healing and there aren't any issues with your arm, then maybe we can let you help out a little more. Agreed?" Jamie asked.

"Yes! Thank you. Thank you. Thank you." I gave Jamie a big hug. He was treating me like a kid sister, and I loved every minute of it.

"Where's mine?" Jack feigned jealousy.

Christmas morning, I gave Jack the only gift he asked for and threw away my contacts. After breakfast, we went to John and Mary's. Our original plan was to leave after lunch, but I felt so comfortable we ended up staying the whole day. The best part of the day was the hug John gave me as a greeting, and finally meeting Jamie's twin, Madi, and their youngest brother, Jaden, even if it was via video chat.

Jack went back to work, on light duty, per his father's orders, the week after Christmas. SSI had a backlog of paperwork, which no one enjoyed doing, and his dad figured it was the perfect job for Jack while he recovered. He asked me if I wanted to tag along.

"What will I do?"

"You can read, keep me company, watch a movie on my laptop."

"If I say no, will you still go in?"

"Nope." I knew it. He tried to play it off like a joke, but he meant it.

"You know I'll be okay here by myself for a few hours, right?"

"Yup, but the answer is still no. I'm not ready to let you out of my sight yet." He flashed me his famous grin and wink combination, turning me to putty in his hands. I could never say no to that, and he knew it.

"Fine." I was learning to accept his occasionally over-bearing protective side without arguing, much. "I'll bring a book." I smiled and gave him a hug. "Thanks for asking."

"You're welcome."

I tried to read in Jack's office but ended up helping him file the back log of client folders instead. It felt good to be doing something, to feel useful. I wasn't going back to work at Grannie's until after the new year, so I went with him to the office every day that week and helped in any way I could. While I was there, I got to know AJ and Doug better.

On New Year's Eve, AJ and Doug came over and the guys had a gaming session instead of a party. They ordered pizza and wings, and we had plenty of beer and snacks on hand. Per their request, I made Mexican brownies and bacon chocolate chip cookies. I heard Jack ask if anyone needed anything over the sound of the music playing softly in the kitchen while I cleaned up. I didn't realize he was watching me sing and dance until I spun around. Jack stood frozen in place, gawking at me as I sang into my invisible microphone. I opened my eyes as wide as I could and wiggled my eyebrows, laughing.

"Marry me." Jack blurted out, his voice huskier than usual.

My eyes almost bulged out of my face. I opened my mouth, but my brain was empty.

"Don't move." Jack ordered before running down the hall.

I looked at the surprised faces staring at me from the living room. "Did he just, um, propose and run away?"

"I believe he did." AJ shook his head and laughed. "Idiot."

Jack ran back to me. "I know I told you I'd wait," He grabbed my uncast hand, "but since I just blurted it out…" He got down on one knee. "Megan Hayes, I want to spend every day of the rest of my life loving you. Will you make me the happiest man on Earth and marry me?"

Jack opened the red velvet jewelry box. Inside was a gorgeous round diamond framed by two emerald hearts.

I covered my gasp with my hands as happy tears formed in my eyes. Then I leaned over, wrapped my arms around his neck, and kissed him. For once, I didn't mind my tears.

Jack pulled back and stared into my contact-free eyes. "I'm gonna need an answer, sweetheart."

"Yes. Yes, I'll marry you." I wiped away my stupid, happy tears and kissed him again.

He placed the ring on my right ring finger. It fit perfectly. He pulled me onto his knee and kissed me. A kiss so full of love, I completely forgot about the three men in the living room, until I heard them clapping and cheering.

"This calls for a celebration! Let's pop the champagne early!" Jamie called out.

They took turns shaking Jack's hand and hugging me.

"Welcome to the family," Jamie said as he hugged me.

"I'm so happy for you." AJ picked me up in a big brother hug.

"Congratulations. Jack's a lucky guy." Doug gave me a quick hug.

Jack asked me to move in with him officially a few days after proposing. I thought it might be weird, but Jamie reminded me we'd been living together for a while and nothing needed to change.

We learned the art of compromise as we balanced my need to be independent with his need to take care of me.

"Have I told you how much I love your fierce independence?" Jack asked as he wrapped his arms around me, pulling my back to his chest.

"Even if it occasionally makes you crazy?"

Jack kissed my neck. "Yes."

"Have I told you how much I love your fierce protectiveness?" I asked, enjoying the feel of his warm lips against my skin.

"Even if it occasionally makes you crazy?" He teased.

"Yes." I turned in his arms and kissed him.

Six months later...

The June sun reflected off the tinted windows as John gave his speech at the ribbon cutting ceremony for the new Sheppard & Sons Investigations office.

I was wearing a navy blue polo, like all the other employees of SSI. Back in February, John had offered me a job as an administrative assistant. The company was growing fast, so they needed the help, and it made perfect sense to offer me the job since I was already helping around the office. He even got Mary's blessing first. At first, I hadn't wanted to admit my excitement about working at SSI because I was afraid of upsetting Mary. But she was happy for me.

At first I argued. I was helping around the office to pay off my debt to SSI, but John ended my argument when he said, "Family doesn't pay." It was the first time he used his argument ending tone with me, and I secretly loved it.

"Thank you." *I have a family.*

I shook my head to clear the memory.

Life is good. I clapped along with the small crowd as John cut the big gold ribbon Jack and Jamie were holding across the front door.

The FBI reward for taking down Sullivan, and the influx of new client contracts, helped fund the new office and training building. The training facility was still under construction, but the large two story office building was complete. Mary and I had helped John, Jamie and Jack design the space, so it was both functional and welcoming.

My fingers fluttered over my grandmother's heart pendant as I stared absentmindedly at Jack. He was talking to Jamie and Chris, Jamie's best friend. *I think you'd like Jack, Grandma.* Jack excused himself when he caught me staring and made his way through the crowd, grabbing two glasses of champagne on his way.

He handed me one. "Penny for your thoughts."

"I was thinking about my grandmother."

"She'd be proud of you." Jack brushed a loose strand of hair off my face. "And she'd be glad you're happy."

"I am happy, Jack. Very."

"So am I." Jack held his glass out and waited for me to tap his. "Cheers." He drained his champagne in one long gulp before sweeping me into his arms and kissing me.

The sound of the crowd faded away as I lost myself in the love of his kiss and the safety of his arms.

Also by

Sheppard & Sons Investigations:

TAKEN: Jack and Meg's story
BEATEN: Jamie and Emily's story
MISSING: Doug and Beth's story
BETRAYED: AJ and Blake's story
CAGED: Jaden and Catelyn's story
TRAPPED: Ashley & Nathan's story
The Storm Outside is Frightful: The Sheppards
BURNED: Madi & Matt's story
HUNTED: Nina & Austin's story
ABDUCTED: John & Mary's

WebPage

Acknowledgements

Thank you, Reader, for choosing to spend some time in my world. I hope you enjoyed it.

I want to thank my Proof Readers: Nina, Paige and Jocelyn. And my editor: Maria Secoy. Your feedback was invaluable in helping me polish my story. A big thanks to Maria Secoy, and the mentor team at All Write Well–this book wouldn't be in your hands if I hadn't found them!

I also want to thank my friends, who have surrounded me with love and support while listening to me chatter on endlessly about my characters and plot lines over many glasses of wine.

Thank you all!

About the Author

 Eveline's promise to you: every small town romantic suspense novel will include a protective male hero who will save the woman he loves, not because she needs him to, but because she's important. The HEA is guaranteed, but it won't be easy.

Eveline Rose is an award-winning author who fell in love with storytelling in a high school creative writing class. She currently lives in the Chicago area with her cat, HRH, the Prince of Destruction, where she pours her heart and soul into her characters for your reading pleasure. She spends her free time volunteering in her community, hanging out with her friends, and of course reading. Random fun fact, she can chat about for hours Tudor history.

Eveline is a member of Chicago North Romance Writers Group.

You can purchase signed copies of her protector romance books at www.EvelineRoseAuthor.com